FOR MALCOLM & SHEILA

Published by Gin & Tonic Press
Los Angeles, California
First Edition

PREFACE

Like many of my books, this one began many years ago, specifically in 2006. Unsure I was happy with it, I then treated it like a wine not yet ready to be drunk, and stuck it in the (metaphorical) cellar. My father did this with many a bottle of (non-metaphorical) wine. He would grow too attached to them, so that no night was special enough to open one to drink. As a result, he became the regretful owner of some very expensive vinegar. "No wine in its time!" we jokingly said was his motto. He would bring one of these bottles up from the basement, blow the dust off, and declare, "At one point, this was some very good wine." Then, he would open it, hoping the cork hadn't dried out, and pour. Sometimes, he would go "yech!" and toss it out (after first offering a sip to anyone who wished to confirm its awfulness). Other times he would declare it still worth drinking. An ignominious end to what had once been a very fine bottle. Very occasionally, he would take a sip and find that, despite his loving neglect—it was still excellent. It was with a similar amount of trepidation that I pulled out this old story, dusted it off, and took a sip. Much to my surprise, I found it quite enjoyable and thought others might as well. So, I poured it into a glass of a book, let it breathe with a few edits, and offer it to you here. It's mostly an adventure story, and perhaps a little bit more. I suggest pairing it with a glass of actual wine, preferably one that is *au point*.

Enjoy.
CJR

The Orcs of New York

PROLOGUE

"Blood is the water that nourishes that roots of dynasty."
– Lord Darkoth

Tributaries of tourists, students, and a few locals joined to form the river of visitors who were dammed at the chapel doors. A trio of Norwegians in their twenties took turns feigning stepping on the grass. Stepping on the grass was a violation of college rules. Only 'fellows' were permitted to do so. Balancing on one foot, the three blonde men waved their soles above the blades repeatedly. This went on until one lost his balance and landed flat. He jumped back as if electrified. The others laughed. The young men glanced about to see if anyone had noticed. No one had. Other visitors, American, French, Chinese, were too busy chatting among themselves, or taking selfies below the chapel's twin spires. They were excited. This was Kings College, arguably the most famous of the colleges of Cambridge University. Its cloister walls separated it from the bustle of the cobblestone college town outside. Its ornate stone work instilled respect in visitors and served to remind them of the college's rich history and tradition. The tourists were all waiting to go inside for evensong. Christians, Jews, Muslims and non-believers were here to hear the most famous choir in the world, and to post about it on Facebook later.

The doors opened. The visitors filed in.

Several minutes later, the sweet tenors of young boys' voices swelled and somehow managed to fill the voluminous interior of the chapel. The tourists, now packed into pews, were enthralled. Even the Norwegians briefly forgot to point, snicker and wonder what to have for supper afterwards.

And did those Feet in ancient time
Walk upon England's mountains green?
And was the holy Lamb of God
In England's pleasant pastures seen?
And did the Countenance Divine Shine
down upon those clouded hills;
And was Jerusalem builded here
Among those dark Satanic mills?

"Oh, it's that song from Chariots of Fire," whispered an old American man to his wife. His fellow tour group members nodded in agreement. The smattering of college students and faculty in attendance had been here many times before. Still, the angelic voices of the boys choir never truly lost their power to impress. All listened raptly. All, that is, save for an older man dressed in black college academic gowns at the end of the back row. Professor Gilles Pinchent couldn't hear the choir, or anything else for that matter. His head, with its tousled mess of wispy white hair, was bent.

His face was scrunched in dour concentration. He was fiddling with his hearing aid, *again*. "God damn it!" he shouted as the choir suddenly blared in his ear. The audience were briefly drawn out of their reverie to stare in surprise at the old man. The professor didn't notice. He yanked the offending white plug out of his ear canal and glared at it accusingly. Standing beside him, also dressed in academic gowns, was his dear friend and colleague, Professor Deepak Raman. Deepak chuckled with amusement, but also sympathy. The audience turned back to the soaring voices of the choir. A pair of other visitors—late arrivals—did not. They were neither college members, nor typical tourists. One was a tall, reed-like man with sharp features and a widow's peak of slicked black hair. He was dressed in an Armani suit and tie. The other was shorter, with a powerful, wrestler's frame stuffed into a suit, a shaved head, and a grimace to match. They were not interested in the boys' choir or even the splendid chapel walls around them. Their eyes remained fixed on Professor Pinchent. The predominantly deaf college professor continued to mutter and futz. The tall observer turned to his companion for confirmation. The stocky man glanced at the black and white picture of Professor Pinchent on his phone and nodded.

Minutes later, the disparate audience members exited the great college chapel. The tourists babbled with excitement and began taking new rounds of selfies in front of the doors and in the quad. Professors Pinchent and Raman followed. The old academic continued to be distracted by his hearing-aid troubles. He paused to glower at it the tiny white plug. "That's the problem with the mail-order things—they're simply not reliable!"

"You need to get a real hearing aid, Gilles," said Deepak with a smirk.

"What?"

"I said, you need–"

"Hold on," said the old man, his finger raised. He paused to turn the dial on the side of the device. He then nodded with satisfaction and reinserted it back into his ear. "There, that should do it."

"You can hear me now?"

"Go on, say something," said Gilles, looking at his friend expectantly.

"I just did," said Deepak.

"Damnation!" Gilles yanked the hearing aid from his ear and made ready to hurl it across the lawn. He then hesitated. "You know, I think the battery must be dead." Behind the faculty members, under the shadow of the chapel entrance, the two strangers exited. The stocky man gestured towards the professors. They approached. "I mean, I'm always telling my wife that, but this time it may actually be true..."

Professor Raman waved his hand in front of his old friend's face to get his attention. Gilles looked up. "You're talking very LOUDLY," said Deepak.

Gilles stared at his old friend, then shouted with annoyance. "Speak up! I don't read lips, you know. Latin, Greek, a smattering of Persian, but not lips."

Deepak shook his head.

"Professor Pinchent? Professor Gilles Pinchent?"

Deepak looked up to see, for the first time, the two strangers. It was the tall, thin man who had spoken. His sullen companion hung back. The tall man walked forward wearing a broad effusive smile, his hand extended in greeting. Gilles, oblivious, was now peering into the microphone hole in the hearing aid, looking for any possible obstruction. Feeling snubbed, the tall man's smile vanished. "Nothing," muttered Gilles. "Five easy payments of nine pounds, ninety-nine p. I haven't even paid the last instalment!"

"He can't hear you," explained Professor Raman.

The tall man's chagrin dissipated. "I see."

"Oh hello!" said Gilles, noticing the visitor for the first time. "You shouldn't sneak up on people like that! Anyway, I can't hear a damn thing.

My hearing-aid's on the fritz."

The man smiled and proffered his card. "I'm sorry to hear that, Professor Pinchent. My name's Roland Griff, perhaps you've heard of me?"

Gilles accepted the business card and peered at it. Although the name meant nothing to him, he nodded politely.

"I have," said Professor Raman. "There was a bit about you in *The Economist*. Something like 'tomorrow's tycoons'?"

"An old article."

Professor Pinchent, unable to follow the conversation, began one of his own. "I really have to get a proper hearing aid. They're so damned expensive though, and it may surprise you to know that a Cambridge professor's salary isn't exactly entrée into aristocratic circles."

Griff snapped his fingers in the air. "Antoine, pen and paper."

The bald man stepped forward, producing a small note pad and a gold Cross pen from his inside coat pocket. He handed both to his employer who jotted quickly.

"Oh sure, 'university professor' sounds sexy," Gilles continued, "but you'd be surprised at —"

Roland Griff tapped the old academic on his shoulder. He handed him the note he'd written. "Will this help?"

Professor Pinchent stared at the paper. He then looked in disbelief at Griff. The tall man nodded. Professor Pinchent looked back at the note. "Oh my, oh my...."

"I believe that will cover the cost of a new hearing aid."

Abruptly, his hearing aid cut back in and Gilles was able to hear this last sentence. He nodded "Yes, yes, I expect it will." He numbly handed the note to Deepak, who looked at it and gasped.

1

"You can't eat gold." – Dwarf proverb

The fawn fennec fox perked up its oversized ears. It froze. Its bright black pupils gazed blankly. It was seeing with sound. It was seeing if it could hear again the distinctive *scritch-scratch* of mouse paws on stone. The hot African sun baked its tawny fur. Still, the fox did not move. It was used to the heat. It was evolved for it. The fox's large radar dish ears twitched. *There it was again!* The mouse was moving, looking for food. The fox sniffed. *But where?* The close cropping of rocks served both to visually and sonically conceal its intended prey. *Movement!* A shadow of displaced sand. The fox honed in with all of its acute senses. There, just beyond a rounded rock, a sprig of dry grass bent the wrong way. Motion was death in this near desert land. Death or dinner, that is, depending upon one's perspective. The fox leapt over the rock and landed on... *a snake!* The saw-scaled viper spasmed and recoiled under the impact. The mouse both predators had been stalking, vanished between two stone slabs. Realizing its mortal danger, the fox turned to flee. In a single motion, the snake righted itself and reared up with fangs ready. The viper rubbed its coils, sending a sizzling warning the fox knew to fear. The fox's next move would determine its fate. Too slow and the snake's venom would flood its small body, causing instant internal hemorrhage that would bleed the fox to death from the inside out.

The mouse scurried along a seam between two shelves of sedimentary stone. It stopped. No fox. No snake. Continuing to run could bring new dangers. Besides, there were seeds here. The tiny rodent picked one up and began to gnaw busily on its shell. This was not the mouse's first brush with death. It had lost the skin off its back days earlier to a pygmy falcon. That injury was almost healed. Spiny mice are unique among mammals. They alone have the ability to regenerate flesh. As it ate, the mouse watched the plains below. To humans, this land was called 'Libya'. To the mouse, it was simply 'the world'. It could imagine no other. It was a world of dry grasses, rugged terrain, and near desert conditions. Nearby, spanned the edge of the Sahara—that endless ocean of hot yellow-white sand whose burning swells swallowed life entirely. There was one point of interest amid the brush far below, though the mouse cared not. It was a small compound. A chain-link fence cut a square border around three flimsy make-shift buildings. One of the buildings was an outhouse. One was a storage shed to house equipment. The third was an office, with shuttered windows and a rattling air conditioning unit straining in the heat. A dirt road led past a gate where a sign read '*Epoch Oil Exploration, Inc. — EOE*'.

"Oh, I am on fire, I'm like... LeBron!"

The office was as spartan inside as out. Particle board tables and desks served as the only furniture. The walls were covered with maps of drilling sites, surveying charts, topographical models, and blown-up geological satellite photos. Field equipment, mostly in stacked cardboard boxes, some strewn loose, took up half the room. Its only occupants were two men and one woman. The men, Marc Aaron and Donald Roscow, were sitting back in their desk chairs, taking turns lobbing chocolates wrapped in pink paper into a grey metal trash can.

"Cuz he's the only Basketball player you can name?" said Don. As he said this, he lined up his own nougat filled bonbon.

"I can name Shaq," said Marc.

Don put down his chocolate to shake his head at his colleague. "You're such a friggin' Canadian."

"Hey, *respect*—we invented the game."

"*A* Canadian did, while living the US. And then y'all washed your hands of it!"

"What about the Raptors? They're champions!"

"With a bunch of American players, you mean? Seriously, stick to hockey, and whatever that broom-sport is." Don and Marc had worked together for years. It was a professional relationship that had evolved into genuine friendship. They had been together at companies big and small, but none nearly as small as this. Marc was the 'talent'. He was a man with a particular gift. A self-described geek, he was forty-seven, medium height and build, with walnut-brown hair cut in bangs. His normally pale complexion was now deeply tanned from months in the Libyan sun. Don was the business acumen and common sense—the CFO. He was a big black man with a shaved head and generous smile. He had the build of a football player and had lost count of the number of times people assumed he'd gone to Harvard on a sports scholarship. The truth was, he only liked to watch sports and run the numbers for his fantasy league. Despite his bulk, he too was a self-described geek, albeit in a different way. On paper, Marc was the President, but he knew nothing about business. His job was to sniff out the oil, then get out of the way. If they found anything, their CEO, Gilbert Wong, would start operations for real. For now, they were nothing more than a 'flyer' for the Hong Kong-based parent company—a small negligible spin-off that would be readily written off if it failed to deliver. "What the Hell, why not?" Gilbert had said as he agreed to the ten million dollar start-up cost. No one else thought there was oil in this so-called 'armpit of Africa'. To be sure, Libya has oil, lots of it—just not *there,* they said. Marc insisted it was, and it was his track-record for being right that got them funded. Of course, it came with strings—a loss of equity and a requirement they accept 'adult supervision' from China. The third person in the room was the only other full-time employee of Epoch, Amita Kuna. Amita, originally from Kenya, had been hired locally as their office administrator. After all, they couldn't have the President or CFO answering the phone. Not if they wanted anyone to take them seriously, anyway. Besides that, she also spoke the language better than Marc, who spoke a little, and Don, who spoke none.

"Actually, I just pretend the wastebasket's a hockey net, instead of a basket," said Marc.

"Uh-huh." Don lined up his shot once more. "Like you were any good at hockey either."

"He shoots, and..."

Don's chocolate flew in a long arc. Too high for its intended target. The chocolate rebounded off the back wall and landed on the floor. "...doesn't score. What a shame!" said Marc.

Amita, who had been watching with arms crossed, shook her head disapprovingly. "How do think Mrs. Aaron would feel if she knew you two were playing games with her present?"

"Amita, if my wife knew how stale these chocolates were by the time they got here, she would understand. She sent these last Christmas!"

"Well, all I know is, I am not going to be the one to clean up that mess."

Marc grinned. "Nah, that's gonna be Don's job, unless he sinks the next three in a row."

As he said this the gate buzzer sounded. Amita looked at the monitor. It was a feed from the security camera at the front gate. As usual, the image was partially obscured by dust on the lens. "Fed Ex," said Amita. Marc and Don sat up with interest. Amita pressed the button to open the gate.

A moment later, the door opened. Don, having conceded defeat, scooped the sweets into the trash. "Hello. Just one today," said the uniformed driver with a nod. He started to hand Amita the white envelope. Both Marc and Don jumped to their feet. "We'll take that," said Marc. The driver shrugged and handed him the package. "Signature required."

Marc signed eagerly and handed the tablet back to the deliveryman, who then turned and left.

"Is it...?" asked Don. The big man clenched his hands in anticipation, like a child at Christmas.

Marc looked at the label. He nodded.

"The lab analysis?" asked Amita. She too was now anxious.

Marc tore open the envelope. He pulled out the papers inside and began to scan them. The room brimmed with nervous anticipation. This was the moment that would make or break their little company. "Yes!" Marc shouted.

Don grinned broadly. "We got oil?"

"The kid from Alberta, who said there was some, when others said none. Score!"

"We got oil! We got oil!" Don shouted and began to dance.

"We got oil!" Marc joined in. The men locked arms and began to swing about in a happy jig.

"Boo-yeah. Duff-man says we got oil!" shouted Don.

"We got oil," said Marc to Amita. Their assistant watched them with amusement. Marc grabbed her by the shoulders and gave her a kiss on the cheek. "We got oil!"

"We are *so* gonna celebrate," said Don. "Bonuses here we come!

You too, Amita!"

The two men began to sing *"Ce-le-brate, good times, come on!"*

At that moment, the black phone on Amita's desk *rang*. She picked it up, covering one ear to hear above Marc and Don's signing. "Epoch Oil, how may I direct your call?" The tall African woman pressed the hold button. "Marc, it's for you." The two men continued to cavort. "Marc," shouted Amita, waving at him, "It's for you!"

"I'm sorry... what?" Marc stopped dancing. Don continued to shimmy.

"It's for you," Amita repeated, covering the receiver.

"Do I have to take it?"

"I think so."

"Oh." Marc felt something under his foot. He looked down to see a smashed gooey bonbon stuck to the bottom of his shoe. "Dang."

The long shadows of the parked cars stretched across the parking lot of the Kimshawa Inn. The sun was low in the sky and would soon set. Already, the air was beginning to cool. On the hood of a pink and white Range Rover, three guards played cards. The game was crazy-eights, but they played it for money. Their AK-47s were also laid across the car hood. It was their job to protect the foreign hotel guests. Dead or kidnapped guests were bad for business. Of course, once a guest left the small hotel, they were on their own.

Marc watched the guards from between the slats of his room blinds. He wasn't interested in what they were doing. They did it every night, and he had been living here for months. He held his phone to his ear. Finally, he seized his moment to speak. "Honey, listen, fine, one day I will get a job that allows me to work at home, but you knew when you married me that I traveled. You used to like it too..." he said. He listened while nodding pointlessly. "Okay, yes... yes, I know that was before the kids, but that's exactly my point. This won't be the middle-of-nowhere, this is New York we're talking. Heck, it's a one hour flight from Toronto!" Marc understood his wife's confusion. The idea had left him feeling spun and disoriented himself. After the lab results, he knew his major work here was done, but he'd still planned to stay and help direct the set-up of operations. He'd expected to remain in Libya for months more, a year even. He'd go home, of course, to visit. Maybe he'd even bring the family here for while. That had been the plan, provided they found oil. The phone call earlier had changed all of that. Marc sighed and held the receiver away from his ear. She was shouting again. *Silence.* "I don't know. An exact figure wasn't given, but if a billionaire like Roland Griff sends his word that it'll be 'worth your while', you listen. Right? This is for all of us. ... Okay. Honey, but... Honey, just..." Marc bit his tongue. He was beginning to get impatient. This was how it always started. "Honey, listen! Get the tickets and take the kids out of school for the week. At the very least it'll be a week long family vacation in the Big Apple, all expenses paid." He pulled the phone away from his ear, far enough that her voice was reduced to Charlie Brown's teacher gibberish. Remain calm, Marc told himself, don't fight back. After a brief pause, he spoke again, "It'll be an education for them! ... Whatever. ... Fine. I'll see you there on Tuesday." Finally, calm. Resolution, peace, or perhaps just resignation? Whichever it was, she'd stopped shouting. "I'm talking on the company cell right now," he said, "you can reach me on that... Okay, goodbye. Oh, and I love..." The line had gone dead. Marc rolled his eyes. "...it when you hang up on me."

Marc closed the old-style flip phone and shoved it into his pocket. He exhaled and stared about the small dilapidated hotel room dejectedly. He should celebrating. *They'd found oil!* That meant significant bonuses, plus their shares would skyrocket. If all went well, they would be rich. His reputation as an oil diviner was now beyond doubt. He could write his own ticket. And now, before this venture was even done, he was looking at... at what? A lucrative consulting job? That, he wasn't sure of. It was certainly intriguing. But what was it exactly? He walked to the bed where he'd left his laptop open. The hotel's internet was half the speed of dial-up. Still, it was the only accommodations anywhere near the drill site that didn't involve a tent. On the laptop screen the webpage had finally loaded. On it was the Wikipedia article on Roland Griff and his company Griff International. What he had been waiting to load, with painful slowness, was a YouTube video. Marc crouched down beside the bed and pressed play. The video was of Roland Griff at a conference a year earlier. He was being interviewed on stage with soft ball questions from an MC. Griff sat back in the leather chair, at ease. The lanky billionaire ran his fingers through his black widow's peak of hair. Despite the interview format, he turned and addressed his remarks directly to the camera. "People say that the last frontiers have all been conquered, or that the only frontier left is space. I say, they haven't looked hard enough. When others only saw the edge of the world, a precipice leading to disaster, Columbus saw a new frontier. I say there are more such frontiers, right there in front of us, larger than life, and waiting to be discovered. At Griff International, we embrace the 'unknown' as simply an unknown *opportunity*. And, let me assure you, opportunity *is* knocking. Don't be scared to open the door and let it in."

Three days later, Marc and Don stood on a windblown airfield south of Tazirbu. Marc watched as the small twin engine propeller plane taxied slowly around. He covered his eyes and squinted between fingers to minimize the beige dust flying into his eyes and sticking to his lashes. Suitcases lay at his feet.

"Gonna miss you," said Don, affectionately.

"Ha! You'll be too busy to miss me," said Marc.

"I just mean, gonna miss you doin' some of the work."

The two men exchanged grins. The plane completed its long slow arc to roll to a stop a few feet away. Its white wings trembled in the strong wind. Abruptly, its engine stalled.

"I got it, I got it!" shouted the pilot in a thick Australian accent. He wore a plaid shirt, a mess of red tousled hair, and a bushy mountain-man moustache. They knew him. His name was Dave. Dave tried to restart the engine. It burbled, but failed to turn over. He tried again. It gasped and sputtered to life.

"Well, that's reassuring," said Don.

"Better here than at thirty-thousand feet," said Marc.

"Not really an *either-or*," said Don, shaking his head. "You sure you want to go?"

Marc glanced about at the barren, desiccated land and nodded. Despite its harshness, it had been good to them both. "I'm sure." Marc picked up two of his bags. Don picked up the other two.

"You know, the more bags you take, the more there are to lose."

Marc shrugged. "It's a number's game. I figure at least one of them should make it there."

"Mmm-hmm." The two men loaded the bags into the plane. They then stopped to gaze at one another with bittersweet smiles. "Well, we did it," said Don.

"We did."

"You really don't want to stay for all the fun?"

Marc shook his head. "I'd just get in the way. It's all business now. You've got it from here."

Don nodded. "Well, you know, if you get sick of all those Manhattan restaurants and theatres and galleries and crap, you know you're always welcome back here in Shangri-La."

Marc laughed. "Thanks Don. It's good to know there's always a home for me in the roasting ovens of Africa."

"There are worse parts."

"And we've been in all of them."

"And found oil in most."

The two men embraced warmly, slapping each other on the back.

Marc stepped up into the small plane. He sat in his seat and buckled his seat belt.

"Take care," said Don.

"In New York?" Marc laughed.

"At least here you can tell the killers by sight."

Marc paused at the earnest look in his friend's eyes. He nodded, and closed the door.

Dave glanced back and shouted over the engine. "Ready, mate?"

"This thing's not going to stall once we're in the air is it?"

Dave considered this for a moment, then said, "Prob'ly not. She usually only gives out once a day, so... should be fine."

"Oh good."

The plane rolled forward with a jolt. Marc gave a last wave to Don, who responded with a thumbs-up. Moments later, the rickety aircraft left the Earth and soared high into the limitless blue.

2

"Home is the place you miss." – Elii Ver

Snowflakes danced and twirled on the comparatively warm updrafts from the city below. They pirouetted past the naked dome of the Empire State Building. They twirled in arabesques across the shining spire of the Chrysler Building. Finally, an entire dance company of snowflakes rode across the rooftops until finally coming down, six blocks away, on the awning above the entrance of the Waldorf Astoria Hotel. A taxi cab rolled to a stop in front of the triumvirate of doors. Two doormen in wool long coats stepped forward. The first, a young man with red cheeks and a practiced smile, opened the door. "Welcome the Waldorf Astoria Hotel," he said, as he offered a white gloved hand.

Diane Aaron ignored him while she waited for her credit card to process. *Approved.* She stood up, and gazed at the grand hotel. Despite being only five pm, the sky was winter dark. In contrast, the lamps of the hotel and surrounding buildings fostered an aura light that surrounded them. Diane was tired. She brushed away a wisp of black hair from her face. She could feel the shadows under her eyes like time stamps. It had been a long day. Most of her days were long. The kids were good, for the most part, but constantly shepherding them about was still work.

Jack, age seven, shuffled out of the car behind her. He was bundled up against the cold in a navy blue winter coat and red mittens. He immediately took ahold of his mother's coat sleeve with one hand. In the other, he clutched his blanket. He wanted to suck his thumb, but he only had two hands. He gazed in wonder up at the illuminated awning. Here, it was as bright as day. The second doorman, an avuncular older man with a bushy white moustache, stepped forward. He crouched down and, with a warm smile, addressed Jack directly. "Welcome to the Waldorf Astoria, young fella." Jack tried to hide behind his mother.

"He's not used to men," Diane explained.

The doorman nodded sympathetically. "Reminds me of my grandson. He's a shy one too. Help with your bags?"

"Please."

The two doormen headed to the back of the taxi where the driver was unloading the last of three suitcases.

Thirteen-year-old Naomi climbed out of the cab and closed the door behind her. She had her mother's dark hair, but tied into braids. The scowl she had been wearing all day briefly vanished at the sight of the splendid facade. "Well, it doesn't totally suck."

Moments later, inside the warm confines of the grand hotel lobby, Jack and Naomi continued to gawk. Naomi had raced ahead up the great marble steps. Diane trudged wearily behind. Jack refused to let go of his mother's sleeve, but craned his neck to gaze about from the safety of her side. The cavernous luxury interior was busy with guests and hotel staff. It was made more wondrous by the presence of several lit Christmas trees, each nearly tall enough to touch the high ceiling. As tired as Diane was, she was happy to have the travel behind her. The flight from Toronto had been on time. They hadn't lost their luggage. Jack hadn't been carsick in the cab. All this considered, it had gone as smoothly as possible. She stepped up to the open clerk she spotted at the check-in desk. "Welcome to the –"

"Waldorf Astoria Hotel, got it." Diane stopped herself. "Sorry, that was uncalled for."

The attendant merely smiled, "Name?"

"Aaron, Diane Aaron."

The desk attendant looked down at his terminal and typed. "Here we are, Mrs. Aaron. Everything has been pre-arranged, let me just check you in.

A short distance away, Marc Aaron was somewhat surprised to find himself standing in the lobby of the Waldorf Astoria Hotel. It had taken three flights over seventeen hours to get here, but it still seemed unexpected. He drummed his fingers playfully on surface of the check-in desk. He studied the decorated border on the ceiling. He gazed at the Christmas trees. The front desk attendant nodded as she read the results on her screen. "Yes sir, Mr. Aaron, it is on a non-smoking floor. Is there anything else I can do for you?"

"Can you tell me if my wife has checked in yet?"

"Certainly sir," she said and looked down once more. A look a mild surprise crossed her face. "That's odd, I..." She glanced to one side and laughed. "Oh, I see!"

"What? Is there a problem?" asked Marc. A problem with his reservation was the last thing he needed. He was exhausted from jet-lag and travel. Worse, he could only imagine how Diane would react if there was a mistake.

"She's right beside you, sir," said the attendant with a smile.

Marc turned to see his wife and two children standing at the next terminal. It was the first time he'd see them in almost a year. Diane looked tired. "Diane!" Diane awoke from the momentary daze she'd entered into while waiting for her keys. She turned to see her husband just a few feet away. He was wearing a dark blue duffel coat, baseball cap, and three days growth of beard. He was smiling. For a moment, her brain failed to process this as reality. "It's me," he said.

"Oh... Oh, yes. Hi," she said.

For moment, no one moved. Naomi simply stared at her father. Jack clutched his mother's coat and eyed him suspiciously. Marc stepped forward with open arms. They embraced. It was a hug made awkward, in part, by the heavy winter coats. Diane and Marc looked into each other's eyes. Each were searching for something. They kissed tentatively. "Good to see you," said Marc.

"Yeah," said Diane. "Good to see you too."

Marc let go and turned his attention to his daughter. Naomi hung back. She eyed him now with suspicion. "Hey."

"Can I get hug?" he asked, opening his arms.

"Maybe later," she said. "So, how's the greenhouse-gas biz going?"

"The what...?" For a moment Marc was confused. "You mean my work?"

"Yup."

"The work that pays for you to have a comfortable childhood?"

"It's not my childhood I'm worried about."

"Okay, then..." said Marc, taken aback. He frowned, then looked at Jack. The seven-year-old was now gazing once more at the Christmas tree. Marc knelt down on the polished marble floor and looked directly into his young son's eyes. "Jack? Remember your old Dad?"

Jack looked up from under knitted brows. Suddenly, his eyes went wide and a bright smile exploded on his small face. "Daddy!" he shouted and leapt into his father's arms.

Marc swept his little boy up into the air with a fierce hug. "You were the one I was worried most might forget me," he said. Whatever else was wrong, he thought, *this* was right. He tousled Jack's honey brow curls and cradled his small head on his shoulder. As he did, he caught sight of Diane's face as she watched. He could see the complex swirl of emotions at play there. She was happy to see Jack happy. That mattered, Marc decided. Whatever else, *that* mattered. She looked at her husband with a sombreness that belied her words. "Welcome back," she said flatly.

The interior of the hotel room was cozy and warm. It was also distant and cold. Diane matter-of-factly unpacked her suitcase and began hanging items in the closet. Marc had less to unpack. Despite his several bags, only one contained clothes and gear suited to winter in New York. He felt decidedly like a fish-out-of-water. "Spend too much time in a warm climate, your blood will thin and you won't want to go back," Don liked to say. Of course, Don's own marriage had ended years ago. He had nothing to go back to. Still, Marc thought, Don was right about his blood thinning. He was surprised at how frigid he felt. Despite having not seen each other in months, husband and wife unpacked in silence. The only sound was that of the TV in the adjoining room. Jack and Naomi were watching cartoons.

"So...," Marc began tentatively. "What's with the blanket? He's a little old for that isn't he?"

Diane answered without looking at him. "Jack's blanket? I don't know. He takes it everywhere. The other kids have started calling him

'Linus'."

"I see," said Marc. His son had had the blanket since he was a baby. He'd always slept with it, but he hadn't used to cart it around.

"He's been doing great in French immersion," said Diane. "He's also picked up some Spanish from Carmen. His teachers say he has a real knack for languages."

Diane smoothed out a dress on the bed, then lifted it up to hang. "So...," she said as if discussing the weather. "what's with the ring?"

Marc was momentarily puzzled, then understood. He looked down at his bare ring finger. There was no longer even a tan line there. "I was going to tell you about that," he said. "It fell off. It's at the bottom of a barrel of oil, I think."

Diane stopped. "I see."

Marc studied her expression. He used to be able to read her thoughts simply by the looking at her. Now, all he saw were foreign hieroglyphs from a forgotten tongue. "I want to get another."

"Another...?"

"Ring. You know, a replacement."

For a moment, husband and wife regarded one another in silence.

"Uh, Dad?"

Marc turned to see Naomi looking at him through the doorway.

"Yes, honey, what's up?"

"Jack wants to know if you'll watch TV with him."

Marc hesitated. He thought he should continue the conversation with his wife. "Um..." Diane turned and walked to the bathroom with her bag of toiletries.

"It's the best offer you're likely to get," said Naomi.

Marc stared at her in surprise. He wanted to ask her what she meant by that, but decided against it. She looked back it him squarely, her gaze defiant, piercing. She really does have her mother's eyes, he thought. "Right."

Naomi glanced at the bathroom to make sure her mother was still there, then lowered her voice. "She's really mad at you, you know."

Marc stared at his daughter for a moment in surprise. "I know." There was a knock on the hotel room door. Marc turned to answer it, then looked back at his daughter. "You were still a kid when I left."

"You've been gone a long time."

Marc nodded, then went to the door. He opened it to find a bellman waiting. "Message for you, sir," said the young man. He handed Marc a small white envelope.

"Um..." Marc fumbled for a tip. He realized he hadn't any cash.

"That's okay, sir," said the Bellman. He bowed curtly and departed.

Marc closed the door and turned to see that Jack had joined Naomi in the adjoining room doorway. Jack clutched his blue blanket and looked at his father expectantly. "I'll be with you kids in a few minutes, okay?"

Naomi and Jack both nodded and disappeared. Marc looked at the envelope. 'Mr. & Mrs. Marc Aaron' it read in raised script. Curious, he tore it open and extracted a crisp white card from inside.

"Who was it? At the door?" said Diane from inside the bathroom.

"It's an invitation," he said, turning the card over in his hand, "to a gala event. Tomorrow night!"

"Oh yes?" Diane stepped out, fiddling with an earring. She watched him as he read.

"Black tie!" he said.

"I don't have that kind of dress."

Marc read aloud in a mock snooty voice, "Provided if necessary."

Diane stepped forward and took the invitation from him to read for herself.

"Some sort of shindig to welcome new employees, I guess."

"You haven't even accepted an offer!"

Marc shrugged. "I don't even know the details of the job. I guess Mr. Griff is fairly confident I'll accept. I'm to meet him tomorrow morning."

Diane read the smaller print at the bottom of the card. Her eyebrow cocked. "'A car will arrive to take you.' I'm impressed... and a little suspicious. This all seems too good to be true."

Marc laughed. "I haven't signed anything yet!"

Diane frowned. "Well, just make sure if you do, it isn't in blood."

3

"Pillars are the cages of kings." – Kiri, Duchess of Sri

The bright gold battle axe gleamed in the morning sun. It was thirty feet high and at odds with the modern white Manhattan office facade it adorned. Beside it, also in gold, was the name of the tower's owner, Griff Corporation. The axe logo was stylized, modern and minimal, but unmistakable in both what it was and meant. Marc gazed up at the monolithic fifty-story structure from the plaza square below. There were no windows at all between the lobby and twenty-fifth floor. He tried to imagine working here. It was a different world from the places he'd worked before. There was a dull *roar*. Marc glanced down the side of the building. An automatic gate clattered up and an eighteen wheeler truck rumbled out, guided by a security guard with a baton. The massive tractor-trailer paused at the curb as a yellow taxi sped past. It then sighed, lurched forward, turned left, and rolled out. It was headed, Marc assumed, for the Brooklyn Bridge. As impressive as the office tower was, this truck was part of the true mystery of Griff Corp. After all, Manhattan was full of grandiose buildings. It was not, however, full of factories. Nor had it been for decades. *The Wall Street Journal* had dubbed it 'The Griff Enigma'. Every day, scores of trucks left Griff Plaza bearing goods to be sold at prices the local competition couldn't touch, and without the shipping costs from China. No one knew how it was done. Many a journalist had tried to gain access or find an employee who would talk. None had succeeded. As a privately held company, Griff had no obligation to divulge his company's secrets, and he clearly enjoyed confounding everyone. There had been calls for government investigations and environmental assessments, but those were stymied by lobbied politicians, or tied up in the courts. "Oompaloompas, of course!" the billionaire had joked during an interview on CNBC. Marc watched the massive truck roll away down the street. He blew on his frigid hands and glanced behind him. The private car that had picked him up was still at the curb. The driver watched him expectantly. "Oh, tip!" said Marc, reaching for his wallet.

"Please sir, no need. I was merely waiting to see if you required anything more."

"No, um... thanks. I'm fine."

"Very good, sir." Despite this, the driver remained.

Marc turned and trotted up the front steps of the plaza. At the top, he pushed through one of six sets of revolving doors and into the lobby of the main tower. The walls here were glass that stretched to the thirty foot ceiling. The floor was polished black marble. The space itself was immense and wrapped around a central tier that housed three banks of elevators broken out by floor. Numerous office workers in suits and ties passed to and fro. Marc approached the massive marble block that served as a security desk. Whatever manufacturing or other work supposedly went on inside here, there was no sign of it at lobby level. This, he thought, looks like any large corporate or banking headquarters—formidable, yet unremarkable for New York. The guard watched him approach. He wore a blue-grey uniform and perfunctory smile. "Um, hello, I–" Marc began.

"Executive floor, Mr. Aaron. Mr. Griff is looking forward to meeting you," said the guard.

"Okay... Do I need a pass?"

"No, sir."

"I thought this was a, you know, super-secure building and all?"

"Yes, sir."

Marc puzzled at this for a moment, then looked toward the banks of elevators.

"Last elevator in the last set of elevators."

"Oh, right. Thank-you."

Marc walked to the back corridor. All of the elevators had blank silver-steel doors. All, except the last. It had a gold door, and *no* buttons. As Marc approach, the doors chimed and opened. He paused to let anyone out. The car was empty. He stepped inside. The door closed behind him. "Executive floor. Welcome Mr. Aaron," said a woman's voice. Marc guessed it was a computer talking, but he wasn't sure. He decided not to ask.

Moments later, the doors opened on a large executive lobby. A woman sat opposite, behind a ridiculously wide black mahogany desk, with absolutely nothing on it. Just as the guard before, she waited for him expectantly. Marc, feeling somewhat uneasy, shuffled forward. As he did, he observed the floor-to-ceiling wall of glass to his right. All of New York was laid out below, with clear views of the Empire State Building and the Chrysler Building just blocks away. On the other side of the lobby, was a featureless grey wall, save for a single massive oil painting in the middle. It was a full length portrait of Roland Griff done in a style meant to evoke Jacques-Louis David's neoclassical portraits of Napoleon Bonaparte. It depicted the billionaire in a suit, resting one arm on a shelf. Also on the shelf was the decapitated head of a dragon. The dragon was startlingly realistic, with scaled reptilian skin and a half-open mouth girded with creosote-stained teeth. "That's quite some picture!" said Marc.

"It's Mr. Griff's favourite, Mr. Aaron," said the receptionist, with a smile.

"The dragon's head... some sort of metaphor, I suppose?"

"If you like, sir."

Double doors behind the desk swung open with a babble of loud debate. Roland Griff, flanked by a man and a woman in suits, barrelled into the room. Griff's commanding presence swept over everything like a wave. Marc, in spite of himself, was instantly impressed. A fourth person, a stocky bald man in a shark-skin suit, followed. Despite his expensive clothes, the man had more the bearing of a pit-bull than an office worker. While the three executives bantered, the pit-bull's fierce eyes instantly alighted upon the stranger in the room. Marc felt as though he were being assessed as friend or foe.

"Are those numbers accurate?" repeated the woman. She was Tania Greely, Roland Griff's Chief Marketing Officer. Her tone made it clear, she was going to keep asking until she got a clear answer.

"Of course, they are," said the man on the other side. He was John Boshain, the company CFO. His nose wrinkled in annoyance. He liked to leave wiggle-room where numbers were concerned. Tania did not. John knew better than to argue with her.

Griff chuckled. "Those numbers are conservative, Tania. Once Project Pretoria is complete, I expect margins to be considerably higher. You can—" The bald enforcer pointedly cleared his throat. The CEO looked up and spotted Marc standing awkwardly, several feet away. Griff smiled. "Ah, Mr. Aaron, wonderful!" He dismissed the two executives with a flutter of fingers and strode forward with hand outstretched.

"Oh, um, it's Marc, please. A pleasure to meet you, sir."

"Right. Well then, you must call me Mr. Griff," the billionaire said solemnly.

"Oh... okay, sure."

The raven-haired businessman grinned. "I kid, of course, call me 'Roland'."

"Yes, sir... Roland."

Griff spun about and pointed to his grim-face companion. "And this is my assistant, Antoine. Don't be alarmed, he doesn't bite. Not unless I tell him to, anyway."

"A pleasure to meet you as well," said Marc. He always abided by his father's advice to befriend assistants, 'It's the right thing to do and you never know, when they might save your neck.' Marc offered his hand.

Antoine shook it firmly. "The pleasure's mine."

"And now to the important question," said Roland Griff, ushering them towards an open hallway with a sweep of his hand, "how do you take your coffee?"

Roland Griff's office was enormous, taking up nearly a quarter of the entire floor. As with the rest of the building, the interior design was modern, with crisp lines, grey panels, and more floor-to-ceiling glass windows. The furniture too, was spartan, rectangular, and expensive. Griff's desk was an altar of ebony and glass. Unlike the prior rooms, there were decorations here—very striking ones, and not the least bit modern. The wall behind Griff's desk was a phalanx of shields. Their origin was a mystery to Marc. While no expert, he had studied enough history to feel he could recognize British or European Heraldry. These were neither. They didn't appear Eastern, Middle Eastern, or classical either. Their markings ranged from simple arrangements of circles, to what appeared to be claws and teeth. There was a savagery about them that was vaguely Viking, but not quite. There were also, he noted, what appeared to be gouge marks and scrapes, as if they had actually seen battle. His best guess was older European. Perhaps Goth, Celtic, or Pict Fir Bolg? "Interesting stuff, no?" said Roland Griff as he strode to his desk and retrieved a notebook from a drawer. He was evidently amused by his guest's bafflement. Antoine took up a position against the wall, more like a sentry than assistant.

"I'm never seen anything like them," said Marc. "Definitely marauders of some kind."

"Well, you're not wrong there."

Marc turned his attention to the wall on his right. On it hung a massive animal skin. What kind of animal, he couldn't hazard to guess. It was over thirty feet wide. Sewn together from several animals, he decided, albeit seamlessly. On the skin was a map drawn in black ink. The drawing was as primitive as the shield markings. Definitely from the Dark Ages, he thought. What the map was of was equally puzzling. There were rivers, mountains and towns he could not place, labeled in a strange script he could not recognize. If there was one thing Marc knew, aside from oil, it was maps. He'd spent his life studying them. This, was nowhere on Earth. It's not real, he thought. These are all just fakes. They must be! Movie props, perhaps? That would explain it. "Wait, are these all–" He stopped himself. Griff was holding out a folded piece of paper.

"My first and only offer," said the billionaire with a wry smile.

Marc opened the paper. He gawked. A rush of bewilderment and excitement took him. It was an eye-popping amount. More than he'd made in his entire career. He stared at his host. "Is this a joke?"

"Plus benefits, of course. Most of that is stock options, profit-sharing. We're only interested in a long term commitment."

"I have a company. Sort of."

"You have shares in a company. Perhaps we'll buy it. It looks like a good investment. Otherwise, non-exclusive arrangements are acceptable with the right legal silo-ing."

Marc, who was used to having to sell himself and extol his value, found himself instead questioning it. "Why? Why so much? Why me?"

Griff shrugged. "Your reputation is as the best young oil man out there. What was it they called you—the 'refiner diviner'? I want the best, and I usually get what I want. I need someone young and able, willing to work under possibly extreme conditions. You're all of those things."

Marc stared again at the note to make sure he hadn't misread it. He counted the zeros. "Um..."

"Think it over. Discuss it with your wife. Make sure it's a..."

"I'll take it!" Marc blurted. "I mean, this is very generous. I—I'll take it."

"Excellent." The billionaire toyed briefly with a strange looking gold figurine on his desk, before putting it down with '*clack!*' He then looked up and nodded with satisfaction. "Well, then if you're ready to sign some confidentiality what-not, I can show you what you'll be working on."

"Now?"

"Now," said Roland Griff. He then snapped his fingers at Antoine. His bullet-headed assistant promptly cracked open a black briefcase and withdrew a sheaf of papers for Marc to sign. Griff then added, with an almost mischievous grin, "Oh, and let me assure you, Marc, this is a company tour you'll not soon forget."

4

"Sight is unimaginable to those born blind."
– *The Obfuscation of Men*

Antoine's hand reached down past all of the elevator buttons, below even the parking levels, to an unmarked plate at the bottom. When pressed, it turned first yellow, then green. "Greetings Mr. Griff, Mr. Veros," said the elevator. "Facial scan identifies an additional unauthorized member in your party, Mr. Marc Aaron."

"Access authorized by me," said Griff. The elevator began its rapid descent to below street level. "As you can see, we use facial recognition to ensure no unwelcome visitors get past the elevator," said the billionaire, adjusting his cuff links. Marc noted they were adorned with over-sized opals. "We'll have you entered in the system in a few minutes, but I don't like to wait." Marc had signed and initialed the tome of legal documents in fifteen places while in Griff's office. His new employer had advised him to take his time and read all of it. "Run it by your lawyer if you like." Marc had been too excited to give it more than a cursory glance. It mostly looked like standard boilerplate NDA and Non-compete. The penalties were harsher and the restrictions tighter but that, he decided, went with the greater reward. There were also extensive non-indemnity clauses concerning personal risk, and potential loss of life in dangerous environs. Marc was used to these things. Half his career had been spent in backwater banana republics complete with corrupt governments and warring factions. Three times he'd been trapped in his hotel for weeks on end to avoid outright armed conflict in the streets. Twice he'd been shot at. He expected this to be more of the same. "The 'Arrivals Floor' requires top level security access," Griff continued. "Once that floor has been selected, no other floor may be stopped at to avoid unintended visitors."

Marc noted that the rest of the buttons were no longer illuminated. "The 'Arrivals Floor'? Isn't this a bit subterranean for 'arrivals'?"

Griff smirked. "Marc, you don't need to have done much research on our company to know that it is a source of speculation as to how exactly we are so competitive."

"Well..."

"After all, we deal in common enough trade, steel, gold, lumber and so on. We have some rare-earths, but mostly commodities available everywhere."

"And yet your profit margins routinely beat what anyone else has been able to bring those goods to market for. I did notice the truck rolling out as I arrived. It looked like it was shipping *out*."

"Mmm, yes, but Manhattan is a destination for goods, not a source of them, isn't it?" Griff smirked. He clearly delighted in the apparent paradox. The elevator doors opened. Marc followed Griff out into a large industrial lobby. The spacious interior was fashioned out of poured concrete, with flat grey floors and walls, and large round pillars. While impressively voluminous, it had none of the style of the floors above. This was a strictly utilitarian venue. A large bank of industrial elevators girded the wall to one side. From there, dozens of workers in orange jump suits walked through a line of chrome turnstiles, placing their palms on biometric plates as they passed. A few of the workers glanced up as the trio entered. They showed no interest in Marc. On seeing Griff, however, they reflexively straightened up and moved about more briskly. Marc glanced back. He saw Antoine watching him with a kind of studious suspicion Marc suspected he reserved for everyone. "Each individual who works on this floor and their families are under the same strict confidentiality agreements you have just signed," said Griff. "Agreements that, if broken, will ruin them until the day they die." He strode towards a separate plexiglass door. Marc hurried to follow. A guard pressed a button to admit them. Marc glanced about, noting the myriad guards, cameras, and other surveillance methods monitoring them from every angle. He could see over a half-dozen sentries in this room alone. The mirrored walls, he suspected, meant many more were watching. "Are you coming?" said Griff, now several feet ahead.

"Oh... oh, yes!" said Marc.

Marc hurried to catch up with his new employer. They proceeded down a broad corridor, made wide enough for utility vehicles. More workers in jumpsuits passed them, coming and going. It was another day at 'the office'. Some glanced over as they passed, nodding at Griff respectfully.

"On your left!" someone shouted. Marc turned in surprise. Antoine's unyielding hand gripped his shoulder and pulled him aside to allow a forklift to roll past, beeping its horn.

"Watch yourself, or get killed," said Antoine grimly.

"Um, yes, right. Thank-you," said Marc, slightly shaken. He looked ahead. Griff had continued on blithely toward a set of tall double-doors. Marc trotted after him.

"You see, Marc, what I am about to show you is our trade secret," said Griff, "Colonel Saunders had his eleven herbs and spices, Coca-Cola has its formula. We have, well..." As he spoke, the tall double doors opened.

Whatever Marc might have guessed laid beyond those doors, it wasn't this. The vast chamber was abuzz with activity. Workers, wagons, forklifts, and small cranes rushed about. All of it surrounded a raised circular dais in the center of the room. The dais was a concrete slab, reinforced with steel bands wrapped around and laid across it. It was clearly intended to support great weight. Presently, the platform was all but empty. A single worker in an orange jumpsuit cut across it in a hurry. In the center of the dais was a shiny stony sphere. The orb was about the size of a grapefruit and appeared to be made of obsidian or black marble. It was sunk partially into a hole designed to keep it from rolling away. Stranger still were the inscrutable runes and symbols carved into the outer rim of the dais. They appeared both foreign and ancient. More of the same decorated the walls as friezes at both floor and ceiling levels. On the walls, the markings gleamed gold. On the dais edges they were black as if burnt. Two ramps led from the floor up to the round platform, each wide enough to accommodate vehicles. Spotlights shone down upon it all. These reinforced the sense that this was a stage set for something spectacular that was about to happen. Lastly, Marc's eyes were drawn to the huge digital message board mounted on the wall above. Highlighter-yellow letters flashed 'KEEP DECK CLEAR! LOAD ARRIVAL 06150610050-S IN 00:01:05'. As he watched the last digits changed.

"They're counting down," said Marc.

Griff nodded, beaming with pleasure.

"To what?"

Griff smirked cryptically. "Wait."

"One minute to arrival," said a woman's voice over a loudspeaker. "All personnel, keep clear of the gate area." Yellow beacons began to the flash on either side of the message board while a warning alarm sounded, *Breeep! ... Breeep! ... Breeep! ...* A pair of workers who had been sitting on the edge of the dais sipping coffee, stood up and walked several feet away before turning back to watch. Two more workers continued to sweep detritus from the flat grey surface. In general, Marc noted, the people in the room were expectant, but not excited. Like dock workers waiting for a big ship to land, he thought. They're alert, but accustomed to it. "I don't understand," said Marc.

"You ever hear of the book *Flatland*, Marc?" asked Griff. He spoke without taking his eyes from the floor below. "It's a sort of mathematical fiction adventure where all of the main characters are two-dimensional shapes. They can't conceive of a third dimension because nothing in their experience, or their faculties, allows for it. That is what separates great men from the rest. They rise above lowly flat existence. They do so by the only 'sense' not limited by mere experience, the sense of imagination. You should put those on." Antoine was handing Marc a pair of wrap-around dark glasses. Griff donned a pair of his own. Antoine was already wearing his. Around the great chamber, Marc now saw the workers were doing likewise.

He hurriedly put on the proffered eyewear. It was so dark, it reminded him of glasses he'd once worn to witness a solar eclipse. He could now barely make out the room.

The seconds ticked past 00:00:30. The beacons changed to red. The alarm pace doubled, *Breeep! Breeep! Breeep!* The two workers who had been sweeping, brushed their piles into dust pans, then hopped down to the floor. The great round slab was now vacant, save for the orb and the strobe of red beacon lights that danced across its surface.

"Juncture in 10, 9, 8..." said the announcer.

"So... something is going to appear on that thing?" asked Marc, incredulous.

"...7,6,5,4..."

"Something or, more accurately, some*where.*"

"3,2,1..."

Marc wanted to ask what that could possibly mean but, at that same moment, the clock ticked to 00:00:00. The black orb in the center of the platform began to glow with a cool blue light. Like a ball of lightening, thought Marc. All at once, there was a flash of white light like a magnesium flare and a *WHOOMP!* The dark glasses protected his eyes, but he was still startled by the explosion and for a moment he saw only stars and after images of white phosphor. When could see again, he couldn't accept what he saw.

"Amazing, n'est pas?" said Griff, with a feline grin.

"Shipment 06150610050-S received on arrivals platform," said the Loudspeaker, "Teams, begin inventory! Packing teams on deck."

It had to be a trick, Marc decided. No other explanation made sense. The platform below was now covered in grass. Not cut grass, but growing grass, growing in rich black soil. On top of it were heaped great stacks of crates—hundreds of them. There were also carts, primitive looking with what appeared to be leather harnesses attached. The carts were stuffed with bars of iron, nickel, and what looked to be gold ore! The details, while odd, paled in the face of the real question—*how had several tonnes of materials appeared on a platform that, seconds earlier, had been empty?* The rational part of Marc's mind looked for a simple explanation. If magician David Copperfield could make the Statue of Liberty appear to disappear, surely this was possible too. The stage-like setting suggested sleight-of-hand. He had been briefly blinded by the light, after all. The rational part of his brain knew the platform must have been switched. The less rational part of his brain couldn't let go of the sense that he was seeing something truly astonishing.

Teams rushed the platform. They clutched clipboards and iPads and engaged in an efficient inventory of every crate and cart. Counts were estimated or scanned with handheld devices. Occasionally, lifters were used to move items to access the cargo behind. A whistle was blown three times. On queue, forklifts rolled forward up the ramps and began lifting loads onto trucks and wagons that rolled alongside.

"We open the gateway for 20 minutes to allow for the unloading of goods," said Griff, as if this explained everything. "This goes on all day, everyday. Cheaper than China, with no shipping costs, no tariffs, and no time-to-market."

"I don't understand," said Marc.

"What don't you understand?"

"Any of it."

Griff looked at him and chuckled. "No, of course you don't. No one ever does. I suppose you think it's some kind of trick, eh? Delicious. I always love watching different peoples reactions when they see this for the first time. I think it's very telling. Yours I like. Honest. You see something that makes no sense and you admit it to yourself and to me. Many aren't so honest. Admitting ignorance to yourself is always a good idea. Admitting it to others? Well, you might want to rethink that."

"So okay, fine, I'm honestly confused. What did I just witness?"

5

"Immortality is the quest of fools." – The Prophet of Da

Jack's skates wobbled on the rough ice. As he passed, he looked up at the great gold statue of the man flying above. He did not know that it was Prometheus, the ancient Greek figure who brought man the gift of fire stolen from the Gods. He only knew that it was beautiful. Distracted, he let his blanket trail on the ice before him. His skate blade caught the tip and he fell face down on the ice. "Ow!"

"Jack," said Naomi sharply, "that wouldn't happen if you'd let go of that stupid blanket for one second." She paused to see if he was really hurt. For a moment, Jack didn't move. He wanted to cry, but he fought down the urge. Instead he grimaced and picked himself up. He ignored Naomi's offer to help, glared at her with annoyance, and skated away. Despite being only seven, thanks to the rink at Lawrence Park in Toronto, he was already a capable skater when he paid attention. "Jack, I'm sorry! Forget it!" his sister called after him. Jack never looked back. There was no real escape. They were, after all, going in a circle.

The incident went unnoticed among the throng of other skaters circling the famous rink at Rockefeller Plaza. Novices wobbled uneasily, or gripped the boards, stopping for the occasional fall. Experienced ice skaters weaved between them, occasionally skating backwards to take selfies on their phones. Behind the ever-present gold statue was the towering Christmas tree. Ephemeral yet constant, its white lights shone brightly over the crowded ice-rink. On the terrace above, crowds of tourists gathered to gawk at the skaters, point at the tree, and take photos of everything. Among them were Marc and Diane. Wearing winter coats, they were squeezed in against the railing. Each held a cup of steaming Starbucks coffee as they watched their children circle below.

"I can't believe he knows how to skate!" said Marc.

Diane shook her head. "Yeah, well, there's a lot of things you don't know when you live away for two years." Diane was more than annoyed. She was furious over what Marc had told her moments earlier. The more she thought about it, the more her anger began to boil. She pressed her tongue against the inside of her cheek, like tapping a valve used to release steam. Finally, she slapped the cold metal railing with her hand. "I can't believe you took that job without even pretending to consult me." She paused, then added, "Or, maybe I can."

"Diane look, I mean, I know I should have asked you first, okay? I should have—but did you hear what I said it pays?" Marc couldn't help but think he'd forgotten how to navigate the waters of his wife's anger. In his work, the decisions were easier. Money, or the prospect of making more money, was always the winning argument.

"We're already plenty comfortable on what you can make wherever you work. Besides, your find in Africa is supposed to make us rich, right?"

"Yes, eventually... probably. But it's a year away at least, and in Africa anything can happen. This is here, in New York City! It's a salaried position. We can all live together, like a regular family. That is what you want, isn't it?" Marc looked at her expectantly, believing he'd found an angle she couldn't argue.

Instead of conceding, Diane glared at him with a look of renewed fury. It was the kind of look that told him he'd just tried to douse a fire with gasoline. "What *I* want? What *I* want is a husband who treats me like a full partner. This isn't about the money! I may not have seen much of you in the past year, but I still know you better than anyone, and I know that look in your eyes. You didn't say 'yes' because of the money, you said 'yes' because you were intrigued and excited. Just once I'd like what's best for your family to be the reason for your decisions—not a rationale cooked up after-the-fact."

Marc swallowed. He could sense nearby tourists turning their attention to the family drama in their midst. Marc hated making a scene. Diane, when she was angry enough, didn't care. Marc squirmed. He tamped down the air with his hands. "Diane, please..."

"Don't 'please' me."

"Everyone's watching."

"Good."

Marc realized anything he said now would only make matters worse. He bowed his head in acknowledgement of defeat. He turned to watch the kids skate past. Jack had accepted his sister's atonement. Once more, the two were gliding side-by-side.

Several minutes passed in silence.

"Naomi taught him how to skate," said Diane. "She wants to teach him to play hockey. She's terrified her little brother is turning into a geek."

"She still on the school team?" asked Marc, tentatively.

"Oh yes. She's the jock of the family. Jack's become quite the little reader..." Diane unzipped her purse and pulled out a worn paperback. She handed it to Marc. The cover showed a serpentine monster with large bat wings recoiled menacingly at the mouth of the gaping chasm. Above the image read, *The Dragon's Cave. Part IV of the Chronicles of Eirlost.* "It's all fantasy and science-fiction stuff. He's even started playing *Dungeons & Dragons.* I don't get any of it."

Marc chuckled, turning the book over to read the predictable blurb on the back. "Yup, a classic case of 'geek'. You know, this isn't scary. Kids who see their fathers every day get into this stuff too. It's good for the imagination, reading skills, it's—"

"It's an escape, Marc. It's not real."

Marc opened his mouth to argue. He knew his wife never liked these things, but weren't seven-year-olds supposed to be into fantasy? Certainly, there were worse things. The look in Diane's eyes told him that arguing was not a good course of action. Not now, anyway. He nodded with a look meant to convey he had heard her concern and would think more about it.

For a moment, both turned back to watch the packed rink below. Jack and Naomi were actually holding hands now. Naomi had convinced her little brother to wrap his towel around his neck like a scarf. Jack was smiling. Out of the corner of his eyes, he saw Diane's shoulders soften slightly. He hadn't noticed how hunched they were before. He now realized that they'd been like that from the moment he'd first see her in the hotel lobby. He hadn't told her what he'd seen in Griff's tower. He'd intended to. He'd been trying describe it when he'd let slip that he'd accepted the offer. After that, she wasn't interested in the 'amazing things' he'd seen there. "Don't try to deflect," she'd said. "This time is different," he'd pleaded. "That's what you always say," she'd countered. He'd conceded that was true, but it was also true that this time really was different. "It's unlike anything I—or anyone—has ever seen!" Diane said she wasn't interested in hyperbole, or excuses. She was trying to raise a family and had been doing so as a single mum for two years. Marc had realized then that he'd better stop talking. He wasn't sure she'd believe him anyway. He glanced down at the pulp fantasy in his hand. He wasn't sure he believed it, and he'd seen it with his own eyes. That, he decided, was the best course of action. Let her see it for herself. At last, Marc spoke in a hushed tone, unnecessarily discreet amid the hubbub of the crowd and piped-in notes of *Joy to the World*. "Honey, I'm very glad you're coming to the dinner with me tonight. I think, you'll be very pleasantly surprised—in more ways than one."

Marc watched Diane's reaction. She gazed obliquely ahead. The slow circle of skaters continued to rotate below—a kind of backdrop dance. Marc could sense now the strain in her face. It was like re-learning a language he'd not spoken in years. Her thoughts were braille, meant to be felt, not seen. There was turmoil below the surface. Without her turning, her expression coalesced into a look that said she had heard him, but conceded nothing. "Let's hope so."

6

"Just when you think it's over, it is." – Nirish Gamba

Floodlights turned night into day at the foot of Griff Tower. Red carpets cascaded like rivers of luxury down marble steps. Limousines lined up to drop off guests in black-tie and flowing designer gowns.

"It's like the Oscars!" said Naomi breathlessly as she and Jack peered through the tinted glass of their own limousine. "But without anyone you recognize."

"I think the idea is to make us feel like we're stars," said Diane. She was amused by her kids' wide-eyed excitement at the gala event. In spite of herself, she was excited too. It had been a long time since she'd been to anything like this.

Marc frowned as he fiddled with his bowtie in the backseat vanity. He'd spent fifteen minutes in the hotel room watching and rewatching a

YouTube video to learn how to tie it right. Clothes had been provided, but no clip-ons. It was the first time in their married life Diane had been ready before he was.

"They must really want you," said Naomi. "I guess it's good that someone does."

"Gee thanks, honey," said Marc. "Anyway, it's not all for me. There are several new hires, and besides, this event is also for investors and business partners. We're just here for the party."

"You guys are here for the party," said Naomi with an eye roll. "We're here for the babysitting."

"Look!" said Jack. He was pointing to the searchlights being shone skyward, projecting pillars of light into the sky, casting crisscrossing circles on the front of Griff Tower. "It's like the Bat-signal."

"Without the bat," Naomi muttered sulkily.

The limousine rolled forward.

"We're next," said Diane.

The limousine doors were opened by footmen. The Aaron family rose from the car to be greeted by a bearded, bald photographer who insisted on taking their picture. "I'm not a real paparazzi," he promised, "for memento purposes only." He shepherded them together. "Smile!" he shouted. Marc and Diane dutifully smiled, Naomi glowered and Jack looked surprised. "We'll email you the pictures!" said the photographer, before turning his attention to the next arriving guests.

Realizing they had to move or be underfoot, Marc and Diane herded their children up the carpeted steps to the top of Griff Plaza. There, previously arrived guests milled about, chatting or pausing to gawk before heading inside. Garlands of flowers decorated draped tables where attendees sat smiling with stacks of guest cards to distribute. A floral frame surrounded a life size photograph of Roland Griff, beaming beatifically. "Doesn't exactly suffer from lack of ego does he?" said Diane under her breath with a smirk.

"What's ego?" asked Jack.

"I'll explain later," said Marc. He felt a secret delight that Diane had made the comment to him in confidence. Sharing a secret joke is something normal couples do, he thought. He approached the table. A woman with horn-rimmed glasses looked up at him. "My name is—"

"Mr. Aaron," she said. "Of course." With a smile, she handed them the name cards she already had in hand. Marc wasn't sure if the Griff staff always recognizing him was flattering, or creepy.

"We were told there'd be childcare?" said Diane with her hands on Jack and Naomi's shoulders.

"Of course," said the greeter. She turned to call to a nearby woman with dark hair tied back in a bun. "Ms. Dolan?"

Ms. Dolan walked over with a bright, pleasant smile. "This must be Jack and Naomi!" she said in a bright Irish accent.

"Uh, yes," said Diane, "Jack's allergic to walnuts."

"That's fine. It's going to be a nut-free night," the woman said reassuringly, kneeling down to look Jack in the eye. "Unless you count me, of course!" she said, making a funny face at him. Jack giggled. Ms. Dolan looked back up at Diane and said earnestly, "We'll take magnificent care of 'em."

"Oh... good. Excellent." Diane leaned down to kiss Jack on the cheek. She then saw what she'd done and wiped the lipstick mark off with a tissue. She blew a kiss at Naomi who made a half-hearted feint to catch it.

Marc followed suit, kissing his son on the cheek. Jack hugged him back, eagerly. He only dared wave his fingers at Naomi, who rolled her eyes again. Jack's allergy to walnuts was news to Marc, but he didn't dare admit it.

Ms. Dolan led the children away.

"If you'll just sign here," said the greeter. She slid a document across the table to Diane and offered her a pen.

"What is this?" said Diane.

"It's an NDA. There will be some sensitive company information being discussed tonight. This just says you promise not to divulge it. Your husband already signed his."

Diane shot a glance at Marc. It hadn't occurred to him that spouses would be required to sign. "It's fine hon," he said. "Standard stuff."

"Okay," said Diane, skeptically. She then shrugged and signed her name. The ink was a festive bright red. "I suppose it's this or no party."

"Exactly. Just follow the signs inside to the ballroom," said the greeter. She then turned to the next arriving guests. "Mr. and Mrs. Chiang?"

"Shall we?" said Marc, placing his hand in the small of his wife's back. The gown she was wearing had a gap there, so his fingers met warm skin. The provided dress was white with silver brocade. Marc knew nothing about dresses, but he knew it was expensive as Hell—and sexy as Hell, too. Diane nodded, and began to walk towards the brightly lit lobby.

Naomi looked back at her parents. Despite the annoyance simmering inside her, she felt a certain undeniable joy at seeing them together, dressed to the nines. It was like catching a glimpse of an alternate reality—the one that should have been. She wondered what would happen, when her father learned the truth.

Several minutes later, Marc and Diane exited an elevator on the fourth floor, along with a half dozen other guests. The group buzzed with excitement like children at a circus. None knew exactly what to expect, but the titillation was intoxicating and contagious. This floor too was a contradiction of decor, at odds with the sleek office building in which it was housed. Here they found old New York grandiosity, reminiscent of a great hotel—a black and white checkerboard floor, white plaster crown molding, and dark wood wainscotting. Worlds within worlds, thought Marc. Velvet ropes and signs guided them to a pair of double doors with a bronze plaque that read 'Griff Ballroom'. There was a moment of congestion as the group filed through.

"Do they really have to put 'Griff' in front of everything?" said Diane with a smirk. "Smacks a bit of insecurity, don't you think?"

Marc put his finger to his lips and winked.

"What? You think they're listening to everything we say?" She then hesitated, glancing about. On the opposite wall, another oil painting of Griff, close-cropped in dramatic chiaroscuro darkness, seemed to stare back at them. "Actually, I could believe it."

"Mr. and Mrs. Marc Aaron of Toronto, Canada" declared a man in a footman's jacket.

Diane and Marc looked surprised. They had been too distracted to notice the couples in front of them being announced as they'd entered the room. Wide steps led down to the open floor of the palatial ballroom. It was two-thirds filled already. All of the guests were dressed in black tie or formal gowns. Some watched the new arrivals. Others were too busy chatting or sipping cocktails to notice. Waiters passed among them, adroitly ferrying platters of drinks and delicate canapés. "I've been subsumed," muttered

Diane under her breath.

"What do you mean?" said Marc, smiling and nodding to strangers as they descended the steps to the ballroom floor.

"Mr. and Mrs. Marc Aaron?"

"Oh that. Yes, he's a bit old-school, I guess."

"He's a bit medieval, you mean."

"Champagne?" said a waiter as they reached the bottom.

"Definitely," said Diane, lifting a slender flute and taking a gulp.

"Thank-you," said Marc.

For a moment, they stood surveying the great room. Heavy purple curtains hung from the rafters, framing a row of two-story lead paned windows. More oil paintings decorated the walls between. Most were Renaissance works from France and Italy. Diane, who had studied art history in college, recognized a large canvas by British naturalist John Constable. "Do you think they're real?" she gasped.

"I expect so," said Marc, taking a bite of seared foie gras on parmesan crisp between sips of champagne. "He may be shallow, but I don't think he does fake."

"It is like a sort of fantasy world," she said, "Except real. Sort of."

"You have to admit, it is fun."

"Mmm.... yes," Diane conceded, "it *is* fun." She continued to gaze about. The room had been roped into two halves. This was the reception area. Here, long white tables were laid with hors d'oeuvres and amuse-bouche of every description. There were both waiters and open bars to ensure no one waited for food or drink. The other half of the room was furnished for dining. Round tables with place settings were assembled before a stage with a speaker's podium.

"Pretty good huh?" said a voice with a Southern drawl. Marc and Diane turned in surprise. They saw a big man in a black tuxedo chuckling at them, while offering his large welcoming hand. "Bob Crosby," he said, "and this lovely lady is m'wife Beatrice." He nodded graciously towards a plump, middle-aged woman with strawberry blonde hair tied up. She was shorter than her husband, but almost as wide. Her smile was equally wide and warm.

"Call me Bea," she said, "We're from Texas."

"Marc and Diane Aaron," said Marc. Bob's hand engulfed his own.

"We're from Toronto," added Diane, shaking Bea's hand.

"But we know a lot of people from Texas," said Marc. "Dallas, mostly. I'm in the oil business."

"Construction," said Bob. He took Diane's hand and kissed it. "Charmed."

Diane's usual reaction to such outdated gallantry was stymied by the Texan's sincerity. "I'm sure," she said, with a smile.

Bob glanced about the opulent gathering and chuckled again. "Beats the pants offa the gettin'ta-know-ya shindig at my last job. Buncha Krispee Kremes and coffee at the construction site. Not that gettin' fresh doughnuts to Kooowait was a laughin' matter, but you know..."

"You were in Kuwait?"

"I was fur a wal. Greenland a'fore that. Buildin' facilities to help 'em dig fur rare earths. Make 'em less dependent on the Cha-nese. Like that'll ever happen."

Marc looked at the Texas businessman in surprise. Bob didn't look like a rough-terrain kind of guy. He looked like he'd be more at home in a strip mall than a strip mine. Still, years in the field had taught him not to judge anyone by appearances. He supposed none of them looked very rugged standing there in three-piece-suits and bow ties. "There's more than Texas in that accent," he said.

"'Ah, ya got me!" said Bob, slapping his chest with his palm as if shot. "We're originally from N'Orleans. But you know, gotta go where the money is."

"Yes," said Marc, snatching a fresh glass of champagne from a passing tray. "Absolutely."

7

"The children of men are precious, and succulent."
– Abath Fal

Ms. Dolan opened the heavy oak door of the fifth floor daycare centre and ushered the two children inside. Naomi stopped to see what they were getting into. Jack shuffled after, thumb in mouth and blanket under arm. Over two dozen children of varying ages played with toys, sat for story-time, or tapped iPads. Designed as a daycare for the company office workers, the room was large enough to hold many more. The carpet was blue and green. The walls were a giant wraparound undersea mural of smiling dolphins, laughing clown fish, and juggling octopuses. None of the children looked up as they entered. They were all having too much fun. Naomi scrunched up her nose. *Nope*, she thought. Jack took her hand. The grey-haired woman reading a picture book to a circle of rapt toddlers looked up and smiled. "Well hello! Who have we here?"

"This is Jack and this is Naomi," said Ms. Dolan.

"Oh yes, the Aaron children. You can call me Mrs. Clarke."

"Do you, like, memorize people's names or something?" asked Naomi.

"We just want you to know that we know who you are, and how welcome you are, my dear."

"Yeah? Well, it's freaky."

Mrs. Clarke just smiled. "Make yourselves at home, my dears." She then returned her attention to the book and circle of expectant three and four-year olds.

"Would you like some cookies and milk?" said Ms. Dolan.

Jack nodded solemnly. Naomi scowled.

Dinner was almost finished. After the reception, they had all been ushered into the other half of the ballroom for supper. They had been sat at a round table along with five other guests. Introductions had been made. Wine glasses had been filled. Appetizers had arrived. Marc had spent most of the meal chatting with his neighbours on his right, Joseph and Karen Takashi. Karen, a transportation engineer, was a new employee as well. Joe was a banker. He explained that most of the guests were investors and partners who were 'in on the deal'. "They seated the new VIP employees together so we could get to know each other," Karen said. "At least, that's my guess." That all diners at their table were also new employees leant credence to Joe's theory. Doug and Lucy Farland sat opposite. Doug, a big man with a walrus moustache, was in the coal industry. Sam Dooley, a bachelor seated on

Diane's left, was a diamond prospector. Sam spent most of the evening chatting with her. Normally, Marc wouldn't have minded, but Sam, a lean black South African man with neatly shaved hair, had the annoying traits of being both handsome and charming. He also had a habit of leaning in and saying things to Diane that Marc couldn't hear. It was distracting enough that Marc missed half of what Joe was saying.

The main course consisted of a choice of steak, swordfish, or vegan soufflé. This was followed by 'molecular' chocolate cake, apple tart, or cheese. By the time coffee was brought, Marc knew everything about Karen and Joe. He knew how they'd met at college, married in Cancun, and lived in Boston for three years before traveling to the Ukraine as part of Karen's Ph'D. Technically, she was Dr. Karen Takashi, but never introduced herself that way except at conferences. As Marc sipped his coffee, he stole a glance at Diane. Sam was still talking, but she looked bored. Good, Marc thought. A motion caught the corner of his eye. It was the big Texan, Bob Crosby, seated with his wife Bea at another table. He was waving at Marc, while wearing a cheery grin. Marc waved back. Bob lifted his wine glass in a silent cheers, then returned to the conversation at his own table. Marc stirred his coffee. There was no need. The coffee was black. He did it anyway. He stole a glance at Diane and caught her eye. He smiled. She smiled back. It was a muted smile.

"That was quite delicious," Doug announced from the other side of the table. "Apparently, we're all being treated like the most 'V' of V-I-Ps. And paid like kings!"

"And queens," said Karen.

"Quite right, m'lady," said Doug with deferential flourish and grin. "Well, if this what it's like to be a Griff employee—I say, count me in."

"Uh-huh. Well, I say there's no such thing as a free filet mignon," said Sam, helping himself to a florentine cookie from a plate in the center of the table.

"Ha! This all makes perfect sense. He wants to make sure we're in," said Doug. "After all, in order to work for Griff, he had to show us his company's secret."

Karen's eyes lit up. "So his secret portal... you all saw it?"

There was a moment of hushed silence and exchanged glances around the table. Marc nodded.

"I didn't," said Diane.

"It's okay," said Joe, "none of us spouses did."

"But you know what it is," said Diane, shooting a pointed glance at Marc. "I didn't even hear about it."

Marc shifted uncomfortably in his seat. He'd meant to tell her, but not in front of the kids. "I figured you'd find out about it tonight," he said, then added sheepishly, "It's really something you have to see to believe."

Karen frowned.

"Anyhoo," said Doug, "keeping the gateway secret is essential, so keeping employees loyal is essential. Thus the free filet and stuff."

"You can't keep something like that secret for long," said Sam.

"O'course not," said Doug. "But that don't mean you don't keep it secret for as long as possible."

"Apparently, he has for a few of years," said Alice.

"There were rumours," said Sam.

Doug snorted. "Yeah, but so fantastic, no one took them seriously. You go out and tell a Times reporter tonight that Griff's business is shipping cheap goods from another dimension and see what he says. You might as well try and sell him the Brooklyn Bridge while you're at it!"

Diane turned to Marc. Her stunned surprise had eclipsed her anger, at least for now. "Another dimension? Seriously, what's going on here?"

Before Marc could answer, Sam spoke. "What I want to know is, why *us?*" He glanced around the table, inviting answers. "I've spent too much time dealing with cartels in Pretoria to know that no one treats you like a prince, unless they think you can help crown them king."

Noddy ran across Toy Town. He had just found the clue that solved the mystery of the missing hat. Jack sat cross-legged on the floor with his thumb in his mouth, clutching his towel, watching the cartoon character race across the TV screen. Naomi, in turn, watched Jack. She was also watching Mrs. Clarke. Ms. Dolan had left shortly after dropping them off, but had returned three more times with more children. It had been over an hour now. Naomi guessed that was it. They were to wait here, playing, watching, or sleeping, until their parents returned. Naomi was waiting by the air hockey table. She wasn't planning to play. She had a plan.

Finally, *it* happened. Ms. Dolan returned. She escorted in a pizza delivery man. He was carrying a brown insulated bag filled with six boxes of pizza. Mrs. Clarke had said it was coming, and Naomi had been waiting for it. Immediately, the children rushed to a side table where Mrs. Clarke started to open boxes of mostly cheese pizza. Jack eagerly joined the throng, waiting his turn. Naomi stayed where she was. Jack picked up a slice of pepperoni. He looked about and spotted Naomi. She put her finger to her lips and motioned him over. Jack wandered towards her, trying to lift the limp slice into his mouth. Ms. Dolan went to escort the pizza delivery man out of the building. She paused to unlock the door with her passcard before exiting. It was this precise moment that Naomi had been anticipating. She placed the air hockey puck on the floor and kicked. The thin plastic disc skated across the wood tile and hit the door frame. As the door closed, the puck flipped up and lodged itself between, leaving the exit very slightly ajar. "Come on!" she said to Jack. She grabbed him by his free hand and led him toward the door. As she did, she stole a glance over to the table where children gathered around Mrs. Clarke, munching pizza slices while waiting for her to dole out cups of lemonade. As Naomi had hoped, she was far too distracted to notice them. Naomi pulled on the unlatched door and slipped out into the hallway beyond, dragging Jack after.

8

"Never confuse hope with truth." – The Book of Knives

Applause filled the ballroom as Roland Griff strode confidently across the stage to the lectern. He raised his hand in acknowledgement. The Griff battle-axe logo was projected behind him, animated with glints and gleams. Below it were the words 'Welcome to the *New* New World'. Griff reached the podium and raised both arms in triumph. The applause continued. Marc paused to sip his coffee. He noticed then, from his side-line position, that he could see Antoine standing off-stage, just visible behind a wall panel. He was mostly in shadow, save for the shine of spotlights on his bald head. Still, Marc could just make out his permanent scowl and his keen eyes scanning the room continuously, as if anticipating trouble. Griff lowered his hands, tamping down the applause, and stepped up to the mike. "Thank-you ladies and gentlemen—or I should say, partners, colleagues, team members... *friends*. I'm glad to see you've all found your way to the company lunch room." The audience chuckled and applauded. Griff smiled beatifically. "Of course, I can't promise you that every meal will be like this. Some will be even better!" Laughter erupted, as well as some cheers.

At a nearby table, Bob Crosby excused himself and rose from his seat. He needed to check his blood sugar. With muttered apologies, he made his way between chairs towards where he guessed the bathrooms to be.

"Welcome to the *New, New World*," said Griff, gesturing to the words on the wall behind him. "Thank-you to all of you investors and partners who believed, sometimes incredulously..." He paused to allow for more chuckles and light applause. "...in what we set out to do. We did it! We've made those who build mere rockets to space look middling by comparison. This journey would not have been possible with you and your leap of imagination." He now stopped to applaud them, and was joined by everyone in the room. "Next, I speak to the new employees who have most recently joined us. I've enjoyed meeting each and every one of you over the last several weeks. You have each been selected as the leaders in your fields. You each have proven track records for success. You each know how to do the amazing in seemingly impossible circumstances. You are the new nobility here at Griff Corporation." Griff paused again to clap, gazing appreciatively about the room. Marc saw now that Antoine's attention was divided. In between his scans of the room, he would steal surreptitious glances to his side. There, Marc could just make out, was another figure. This figure was entirely in shadow. Marc could see only that it was even bigger and burlier than Antoine. That alone made it notable. "By now you have all seen, or at least heard of our gateway," Griff continued. As he spoke, video of the gateway appeared behind him. The camera orbited the great circular dais Marc had seen the day before. Busy workers drove forklifts, rode golf carts, or simply walked dollies of goods and equipment to and fro. It looked like countless other industrial workplace corporate videos Marc had seen in his career, except this one centered around a portal to an alternate universe.

Bob Crosby reached the door he'd thought was a restroom, only to discover it was a service closet. "Gol darn it," he grumbled. He looked about for other possible options. Seeing a nearby corridor he began down it.

A security guard stepped forward to block his path. "I'm sorry sir, you can't come up here."

"Oh, I am sorry," said Bob. As he spoke, he caught a glimpse over the guard's shoulder and realized he'd stumbled into the stage side-entrance. The passageway disappeared into the shadow of the wings, followed by the bright-as-day lights of the stage beyond. Bob could see the video playing stretched across the back wall. Closer to him, just off stage, he recognize the bald-headed man who seemed to accompany Griff everywhere. He didn't know the man's name, but he reminded Bob of a lineman who used to play for the Saints football team. Bob was about to retreat, when another face turned to look at him from shadows. He could now make out the figure previously cloaked in darkness, standing a head taller than the angry bald man. The sight of the face made Bob's heart stop. Even in the dim off-stage light, Bob could see the face had a moss-green pallor. A trick of the light? Their eyes met. The face grimaced disapprovingly at Bob. It then snorted, nostrils flaring, before turning its attention back to the stage. As it did so, it leaned back, disappearing once more into shadow. The visage, however, remained indelibly imprinted on Bob's mind like the after-image of a lamp light looked at too long.

"Sir," said the guard insistently.

"Sorry, I was... I was looking for the restroom," said Bob, shaken.

"Back there, on your left."

"Thank-you." Bob turned away and began walking in a dazed state in the direction indicated. Surely, his eyes had been deceived! He tried to shake the hideous face from his mind. He could not. It hung like a nightmare mask in his mind—brutish, savage, and scornful. Its eyes were not the empty eyes of a mask. They were malevolent and cold, but clearly alive. What was it? A man in a costume? Why? Some sort of joke perhaps? Bob forgot the restroom and numbly made his way back to his table. He was unsure what to say, even to Bea. He thought if he described it to his table mates, they would think him mad. No, he thought, better to keep it to myself.

Marc took a sip of wine. Diane's hand was on the white table cloth inches from his own. He considered laying his hand on hers. He regretted not telling her about the gate. All the others had told their spouses. It was like he'd forgotten the first rule of marriage his father had told him at their wedding, 'Don't keep secrets'. He hadn't meant it as a secret. He simply hadn't told her. He become used to not telling her things. That, he realized, might be worse. She didn't look angry anymore. Not since seeing what the gate was. Has she forgiven me, or has her anger simply been displaced by surprise? Or, perhaps, indifference. He didn't know what to do. He wished he'd told her. Another thought occurred to him then—were there things she hadn't told him too?

"You are now all confidants of the great Griff Corporation secret," said Roland Griff, pacing the stage excitedly, "confidants and beneficiaries." Behind him, the screen showed a montage of clips from newspapers, websites, and magazines. *The Griff Revolution*, The New York Times called it. 'Roll Over Rockefeller, Roland Griff is here!' said a Time magazine cover featuring Griff standing with arms brashly crossed. He had been a runner-up for 'Person of the Year'. "Next time," said Griff with a chuckle as the slide appeared.

Marc noticed Bob Crosby making his way back to his seat. The stout Texan's usually cheery demeanour was gone. His face appeared pale and strained. Bob sat down shakily next to his wife. Bea leaned over to ask him what was wrong. "Nothing," Bob muttered "I'm fine." Bea knew her husband too well. "Is your blood sugar okay?" Marc saw, but could not hear the exchange. He wondered if something in the meal had disagreed with the big man.

More fawning headlines played out on screen until, finally, Griff raised his hands as if it were all too much. "Enough," he said. "You get the point." On cue, the screen went black. "Of course, I hardly achieved all of this alone. That's where you all come in. Investors who have had the foresight, insight, and yes, faith to back me, often with little understanding of what it was I wanted to do. And you, my new team, hand-picked to take us forward from here. You are all critical components of what is to come. For, if you thought act one was impressive, well, get ready for act two!"

Naomi and Jack huddled behind a potted rubber tree plant. Jack crouched low. Naomi poked her head just above the rim to watch the passing security guard. It wasn't a good hiding place, but it was the only one available in the long marbled corridor. They'd heard the guard come around the corner. Fortunately, the man's mind was elsewhere. He was bored and had no reason to expect anything of interest on his patrol. He made it eight times a night. Nothing untoward ever happened. It was after-hours on the fifth floor for Christ's sake! There were layers of security below. The guard paused to pull a pack of Trident wintergreen gum from his pocket. He unwrapped a stick and popped it into his mouth. Naomi didn't move. She had her hand on Jack's shoulder to ensure he didn't either. Movement catches people's eyes. It was something she'd read in a book. She wasn't sure why she'd felt compelled to escape the daycare. It's not like it was anything terrible. Lately, she'd been possessed by a desire to break rules and not do as she was told. It had led to more than one shouting match with her mum. She knew something was wrong, but did it anyway. Or, maybe *because* it was. This, however, was to a whole new level. This could really land her in hot water. Worse, she'd involved her baby brother. Still, there was no turning back now—literally. They'd slipped through a closing door behind a different guard, only to discover it wouldn't open without a pass-card. So now, here they were, trying to find a way out. Jack wanted to go back for more pizza. "Where—" Jack started to ask. Naomi clamped her hand over his mouth. The guard looked up in surprise. He glanced about, unsure what he'd heard. Naomi glared at her brother, mouthing a silent a *shhh!* Jack looked back with apologetic eyes. After an achingly long minute, the security guard shrugged and resumed his lazy stroll down the long hallway, before disappearing around the corner at the end.

Naomi crept from behind the rubber tree plant and peered around a different corner. It led to a bank of elevators. She considered taking one of the elevators downstairs to see if they could find their Mum and Dad. Of course, she didn't know exactly where they were. Worse, there had been a lot staff and security downstairs. They could walk right into a hornets' nest. She felt Jack's small hand slip into hers. She looked down at him to see if he was all right. Jack's attention was on what he saw at the other end of the corridor, past the elevators. It was a wide arched opening into what was clearly a large, high ceilinged room. Visible through the opening was a suit of medieval armour in a glass case. The armour was posed holding a sword and shield as if ready for battle. "Neat," said Naomi. Jack nodded eagerly.

They crept silently past the elevators towards the entrance. Naomi scanned for any sign of guards. The area appeared deserted. The room, however, was far from empty. Naomi and Jack gawked with eyes and mouths open wide. It was clearly a sort of museum. Jack and Naomi both loved museums. Their mother had taken them several times to the Royal Ontario Museum in Toronto. Like the ROM, this had grand two story ceilings with monumental marble walls and round pillars. The content most closely resembled a tour of medieval life and art they'd once seen. Manikins wore various kinds of armour and bore weapons of wood and steel. The walls were hung with tapestries and shields. Glass cases held well-worn books and ancient looking artifacts. Despite the similarities, there was something strikingly strange about it all.

"Wow," said Jack. "Cool."

Jack was entranced. He began to wander about, unsure where to look first. Naomi was also intrigued. The banners were decorated with foreign looking scripts. They didn't resemble any language or characters she'd seen. Most intriguing, were the fantastical images of the tapestries themselves. The largest stretched across the entire back wall, forty feet at least. On it, armies converged in battle. One side was clearly human, along with what appeared to be elves and dwarves. The other was humanoid, but clearly not human. These were monsters with fangs, pointed ears, and clawed finger tips clutching murderous blades, spiked clubs, and spears.

"It's like one of your books," Naomi said to Jack, with a gasp.

Jack wasn't listening. Utterly mesmerized by the amazing exhibit, he was walking past a long row of glass display cases that lined the walls. He stared at a gilded daggers, diamond topped vials, and tattered scrolls. Each looked authentic, ancient, and utterly alien.

"This is wicked!" said Naomi, gazing up at a suit of armour embossed with more of the strange letters. "It must be from a movie!" She noticed then a second tapestry on another wall. This too portrayed a hoard of similarly horrid creatures. Above them all was a looming figure in black. If the humanoids were man-sized, the figure must have been a hundred feet tall. Despite this, it was mostly featureless, save for the silhouette with ragged wings and eyes of green fire. "Bit scary, eh Jack?" After hearing no response, Naomi turned to look for him. "Jack?"

Jack was on the opposite side of the museum hall. His enchantment had drawn him to an illuminated display case there. Even from across the room, Naomi could see the glass contained a very large book. It was spread open for presentation purposes. The tome lay alone, suggesting it to be of singular importance. Jack stepped up on a stool to take a closer look. "What are you looking at Jack?" Naomi whisper-shouted, as she walked over to join him. Jack shrugged, but continued to study it. As she drew closer, Naomi could see the thick leather cover and antiquated pages—yellowed and brittle. These were decorated with more unfamiliar letters. Naomi could see the words were hand-written in raised ink or paint. The open spread showed a map. It was a map of nowhere Naomi had ever seen before. It depicted a land surrounded by water. This was then illuminated with decorations of serpents, ships, and monsters. Next to the tome, unprotected by glass, was a second, much smaller book. Naomi had not noticed it at first.

It was a modern spiral notebook, closed and held with a metal clasp. Naomi read the plaque below. "Private Journal of Dr. Gilles Pinchent. Professor of Literature, Cambridge, England." She looked at Jack. "Who's that?"

"Dum-num," said Jack, with thumb in mouth. This was his mouthful way of saying *'don't know'*.

Naomi turned her attention back to the map. "It must be from the dark ages. Back when people thought 'here there be giants' and stuff."

From the corner of her eye, Naomi saw Jack's curious hand reaching. "Jack!"

"What?" he said, lifting the book up to look at it. It was one of these astonishing acts of rebellion he was capable of from time to time. Usually, these were directed at their mother. Not this time. He smiled at her defiantly.

"Put that back!" she hissed.

Below the display case, unseen by either of them, a red LED light began to flash.

9

"Chance is the gardener of faith." – Ulmach Vandor III

An entire world swept past. It was comprised of vast plains, rolling hills and sumptuous green forests. The audience gasped at the sight. It was fully rendered in rich 3D computer graphics from what had previously been a flat map of a strange land. It was the very same map Naomi and Jack had been wondering at moments earlier in the museum, now brought to life on the projection screen. Wine glasses sat un-drunk, coffee cups sat un-sipped, as Roland Griff told a tale too impossible to believe. He revelled in the awe of his audience. Marc too, sat in stunned silence. Despite having seen the gate the day before, somewhat ironically, this animated presentation made the idea of another world seem more real. Griff reached for the rendered land behind him as if plucking fruit from a tree. "...ours for the taking," he said. "Instead of off-shoring, we're off-*worlding*. And we're the only ones who can. But, therein lies the challenge." Griff paused to look around the room, waiting for the audience's attention. The animation slowed to orbit smoothly above the strange terrain. Griff continued, "The challenge is this: the very thing which makes them so eager to trade with us for mere trinkets, their primitive barbarism, is also the thing that currently limits our growth. For, while the price is low, so too is their productivity. The creatures that live in 'The Fourth World', as we call it, haven't the science or engineering to exploit its true potential. That is where you all come in." Once again, the animation zoomed and panned across the continent, this time low enough to see individual trees, sparkling rivers, and herds of animals. Lumber yards, mines, and oil refineries sprung up as if by magic, populating the world with industry and infrastructure in seconds. Roads and railways flowed like rivers between meadows and mountains. These, in turn, were instantly crowded with trucks and trains. "Each of you are experts both in your field, and in *the* field. You have all worked in the dirt and dust to find gold, oil, diamonds, and more, where others saw only dirt and dust. So..." Griff paused for effect. "I am asking you to join me as we move forward with 'Phase Two'. Instead of merely trading with the inhabitants of The Fourth World, we will begin our forays into that world ourselves!" A ripple of surprise chatter began throughout the ballroom.

"You're going to go there?" asked Diane.

"I... I guess?" said Marc. He hadn't considered the idea of actually entering the gate himself. It was shocking, terrifying, and exciting all at the same time.

On stage, Antoine held his hand over his earpiece, listening. He then walked to Griff and leaned in to whisper in his ear. Griff nodded, then looked directly at Marc and Diane. He then waved his assistant away and turned again to the entire audience. The showman's grin reappeared on the billionaire's face. "Now, where were we? Ah yes, exploring a new universe."

"Did he just...?" asked Diane.

"I thought so too," said Marc, "but it seems fine now." Still, he couldn't help but feel unsettled by Griff's glance.

"Now, I know this is a bit of a surprise to you all," Griff continued. "Hopefully, an exciting and positive one."

Sam's hand shot up. Without waiting to be asked, he rose to his feet, still with his hand in the air. "I have a question," he shouted. The entire room turned its attention to their table.

Griff looked momentarily annoyed. He then smiled as if being interrupted in the middle of his speech was exactly what he wanted. "Yes, of course, Sam, by all means."

Sam cleared his throat. "Not to rain on anyone's parade but, is this all legal? I mean, shouldn't... I don't know... the government know about this inter-dimensional portal of ours?"

Griff looked down. His head bobbed thoughtfully for a moment. The motion, along with his widow's peak of raven-black hair, and curved nose, suddenly reminded Marc of a bird of prey. The tycoon then looked up and smiled beatifically at the diamond mine prospector. "Of course, they should, Sam." He then turned to address the room. "Our friend Sam here, raises a very valid concern. First, let me assure you, our legal counsel has examined this issue thoroughly and found... well, remarkably few statutes concerning the legalities of inter-dimensional travel." The audience laughed. Griff stifled the laughter with his hands, and continued. "Indeed, jurisdiction alone is a bit of a conundrum. In all seriousness, I hear what you're saying, Sam. I hear you and I agree with you. So, let me assure you that we will be bringing in the government... in the fullness of time. We want them to be involved, for the good of *all* mankind. Once, that is, we've had an opportunity to properly secure our investment. We have, after all, a responsibility to our investors first and foremost—many of whom are with us here tonight. And let us not forget, some of the greatest companies of today were built by leveraging new technologies before they could be legislated out of their advantage. We must be responsible, but we must also be pragmatic."

Griff appeared ready to move on to his next point. Sam was not. He stubbornly remained standing. His hand shot up once more. Again, he did not wait to be called. "But how can we just invade another world like this? Take advantage of a less developed society to steal their resources and labor? I mean, it sounds like Old World colonialism!"

There were murmurs around the room. Marc shifted uncomfortably in his seat. Diane, sitting right next to Sam, watched the exchange with fascination. On stage, Roland Griff grimaced, gathering his thoughts. Marc felt he could see the billionaire's face briefly flush with anger, his eyes smoulder. He then closed one hand in the air as if capturing that anger and quelling it. "Now, Sam," said the billionaire, "that is where you're wrong. You see, we are *not* invaders, or colonialists or whatever you called it. No, not at all. Not one bit. We are welcome guests. Equal partners, if anything. They need us. They want us." There were skeptical murmurs around the room. "But please, don't take my word for it. I think perhaps it's time for you all to meet one of the leading natives of The Fourth World. And, perhaps, Sam, you can ask him that question yourself!"

The crowd babbled with excitement. Marc threw a wide-eyed glance at Diane. He'd never thought to meet actual aliens from this other world. Not before dessert, anyway. Diane looked back, equally stunned. "What the...?" she mouthed.

On stage, the billionaire businessman beamed, bathing in the bonfire of excitement he'd just ignited. Ever the showman, Griff paused for a moment, allowing anticipation to mount. He then swept his hand back towards stage left and said, "Ladies and gentlemen, our liaison with the denizens of 'The Fourth World', and my personal friend, General Bragad'oc!"

For a moment, nothing happened—then the large shadowy figure Marc had glimpsed earlier strode boldly into the bright lights of the stage. The audience gasped.

"Oh come on, it's a man in make-up!" said Sam. He made as if to scoff, but his voice sounded hollow.

"Damn good make-up," said Diane.

Marc nodded his agreement.

All attempts had been made to make the guest appear less threatening. Its bulky frame had been stuffed into an expensive tuxedo. Still, whatever it was, it was clearly *not* human. Its skin was olive-green grey. Its facial features were pronounced, with a brow ridge that gave him a savage neanderthal scowl. Most disturbing were the points of fangs jutting up just above the lower lip line on either side of its dour mouth. Despite its monstrous features, even from here, Marc could see its black eyes sparkled with a keen intelligence as they surveyed the room. The monster then did something even more incongruous—it smiled.

Murmurs rippled the crowd like wind gusts across the surface of a pond. *What is it? Is this for real? Can it talk?*

This last question was answered promptly. The green-skinned visitor walked directly to the lectern, where it paused to shake Griff's hand. It then leaned into the microphone, and boomed, "Good evening!"

There were more gasps, then shocked silence stole the room. For a long, pained moment, the audience simply stared at the creature.

"Is this for real?" said Diane, under her breath.

"Either that or it's the best hoax I've ever seen. What is it?"

"I don't know. I mean, look at those teeth!"

"It? Should we say 'he'?"

The bizarre visitor looked slowly about the room, both observing and allowing himself to be observed. His heavy brow made for a permanent scowl, regardless his mood. He leaned forward into the microphone again. "Appearances can be frightening. Scary, in fact..." he said. His deep voice was so resonant it would have commanded attention, even if his appearance did not. "...but, let me assure you, I will not let your lack of green skin and fangs prejudice my opinion of you in any way!" The room erupted into laughter.

Marc remembered then what Griff had said, that the visitor was a general. Marc had held meetings with many generals over the course of his career, ranging from the corrupt commanders of the Russian Army to the belligerent warlords of Northern Africa. This general was certainly stranger than any of them but, Marc decided, could not be more savage than some he'd dealt with. With a sense of purpose, Marc rose to his feet, and began to clap. Almost immediately, others began to join in. More rose to their feet. Finally, the entire room began to applaud. With the tension broken, the General's shoulders dropped perceptively. He nodded about in acknowledgement as if accepting an award. Excited chatter buzzed again, but the tone was entirely different. *We should welcome them! They're just like us! The world will never be the same!*

General Bragad'oc looked over at Roland Griff. The billionaire met his gaze, and smiled back with satisfaction.

Marc felt a tap on his shoulder. He turned in surprise to see Antoine standing behind him.

Jack's feet dangled above the polished marble floor. This was despite his sitting on the very edge of the large armchair seat. Naomi's feet touched the tile, but only just barely. Jack stared straight ahead, as if studying a single particle of dust hanging in the air too small to be seen by anyone else. He clutched his ever-present baby blue blanket as if his life depended upon it. Naomi frowned at the floor. The two Griff Plaza security guards sat in stoney silence, as they had done since apprehending the two errant children and ordering them to wait.

"Look, it's been like hours. Can we go already?" said Naomi. When neither guard responded, she added, "Are you deaf? No parlé anglais?"

"Our orders are to keep you here until your parents come to get you. And it's only been fifty minutes," said one of the guards. It was the one Naomi had secretly named 'Dumb-Dumb'. She'd named the other 'Stupid.' It was infuriating to sit here for so long. It seemed liked longer. They were still seated in the strange private museum they'd stumbled upon earlier. The fascinating menagerie of objects and artifacts screamed out to be explored further. Instead, they had spent the entire time sitting in these, admittedly very comfortable, chairs. Jack, terrified at being caught, had retreated into a kind of semi-comatose state. He hadn't spoken a word, or even looked at his sister since being ordered to sit. Naomi hadn't been so docile. She had spent her time trying to study the exhibits from afar as best she could. She'd craned her neck, sat up to the point of almost standing, and squinted. Much of the room was blocked from view by a kind of boat. So, she had studied the boat in detail. It was a row boat, with three sets of oar locks, and wide enough for several passengers. It was mostly made of wood, the gunnels were carved into braids and what looked to be skulls, although clearly not human. The front of the boat was plated with copper, hammered into sheets, and nailed into the wood. Finally, a pointed spear stuck out from the bow, tipped with an iron point. Even with her limited historical knowledge, it seemed to Naomi like something that belonged in the dark ages of Europe. She could also see a sort of war helmet mounted on a pedestal display inside a glass case. There were several stone carvings, and painted vessels of clay, copper and what looked like gold. A myriad of weapons lined the walls wherever there wasn't a tapestry, battle axes, spears, swords, bows and arrows. Besides the two main entrances, there was also a closed door in the corner. Naomi had not noticed it for a long while. Now, she observed that it was made of steel, locked with an electronic dead bolt, as well as several chains and padlocks. It looked, she decided, far too secure to be a utility closet. "What's behind that door?" she asked.

"You ask too many questions, kid," said Stupid.

"So... you don't know," muttered Naomi. "Too low down the totem pole, I guess."

"I do so know!" said the Guard, and to prove it he waggled a keycard clipped to his belt. "We have access to all—"

"Jack! Naomi!"

At the sound of their mother's voice, the kids looked eagerly to the nearest of the two open entrances to the museum area. Diane rushed towards them with open arms. Marc followed. Roland Griff and Antoine hung back to watch from the square archway. After reassuring herself that they were both healthy, Diane stood up and raised her finger. Her expression had changed from relief to annoyance. "You two have some serious explaining to do," she scolded. Marc, behind her, tried to reinforce this with a stern look of his own. He was, however, having trouble focusing on the children. The astonishing artifacts of the museum compelled attention and wonder. His eyes darted from relic to relic. Naomi managed her best penitent look, while Jack steadfastly clung to his mother's leg. "Now, you both owe Mr. Griff an apology."

"Nonsense, Diane, I think it's great!" said Griff, slowly clapping as he finally entered the room. "They just have their father's urge to explore. I, of all people, can't fault them for that!" Antoine followed, pausing to dismiss the guards with a tilt of his head. Griff addressed the children directly. Jack refused to look up. Naomi, glared back defiantly. "And you really found something to explore, didn't you kids? What do you think?"

Naomi was disarmed by the billionaire's engaging grin. She managed a weak smile. "It's pretty awesome," she said. "It looks like stuff out of one of Jack's fantasy books or games. I kept expecting to see a real dragon!"

"You wouldn't like that," said a well-deep voice.

All turned to see General Bragad'oc standing under the entrance-way arch. Here, fluorescent museum lights gleamed on his algae-hued complexion. The children's mouths hung open in shock. Terrified, Jack gripped his mother's flesh through her evening gown. Diane winced, and patted his shoulder reassuringly. "It's okay kids. I know he looks scary, but he's a friend. Really!"

Naomi looked to her mother, then to her father. Marc nodded in agreement. Naomi looked back once more to the strange being standing before them. The General managed another of his awkward smiles. It was far from successful, as if requiring an unnatural contortion for his facial muscles. Still the effort was comically reassuring. Even Jack managed to peep one eye towards the strange visitor.

"A dragon would make quite a mess here," General Bragad'oc continued. "Trust me, I've seen one."

This was greeted with a moment of surprised silence. Neither the children, nor their parents could tell if the General was lying. It seemed entirely plausible he was telling the truth.

Roland Griff laughed. "Who knows Naomi? Maybe you'll get to see a dragon too some day! We've come to believe the sources of so many of our own stories and myths may be from other worlds that *really* exist. Worlds where elves, dwarves, and magic are a real as you and I. The General here is what you and I would call a 'goblin'—or an 'orc', as Tolkien had it."

"An orc?" said Naomi. She took a few steps closer to the General, as if approaching another museum artifact.

"I've read *The Lord of the Rings*," said Marc. "In it, aren't the orcs , um..."

Naomi, continued her slow approach, gazing up at the General all the while. General Bragad'oc looked down, as if amused by the cautious courage of the young girl. "Evil?" said the General. With another awkward smile as he knelt down to Naomi's level so she could see him more closely. "Do I look evil, child? Or just ugly, perhaps?"

"Marc, Marc, Marc..." said Griff, "reality is never so black and white. You know that as well as anyone. A bunch of fantasy stories written by humans from an age even more xenophobic than our own would have to be a one-sided perspective at best!"

"Propaganda and lies," said the General, without looking up. "Fake news."

"Anyway, we are long past such ancient quarrels," said Griff. "It's late and tomorrow is a big day. In the morning, we begin the inaugural expedition into The Fourth World. I do hope this has not all been too much, and that you will be joining us on this grand adventure, Marc? Your oil expertise is a crucial part of our plans."

"Oh." Marc and Diane exchanged shocked glances. Griff in his presentation had not mentioned an expedition into the gate was so imminent. It was amazing enough to imagine one day visiting the orc world, the idea of doing so the next day left Marc dumbfounded. "You want me to go through the gate?"

"No! No, not tomorrow. That will come later. This is just to see off the 'Away Team'. You'll be safely ensconced as spectators."

"Um... I..." Marc looked to Diane, who was equally flabbergasted by the prospect.

Griff, an expert negotiator, knew when a cast die was teetering on the edge. He didn't believe in letting chance decide which way it would fall. "Of course, seeing what young explorers your children are," he ventured, "I'd also like to invite them to watch tomorrow's initial foray. All from the safety and comfort of the viewing gallery of course! Would you like to see the gateway to the orc world, children?"

The excitement of such an adventure overwhelmed both children, washing away any fear they might have had. "Oh, can we Dad? Can we?" said Naomi, jumping up and down. Jack vigorously nodded his agreement.

Neither Diane nor Marc had seen Naomi this excited in years. Marc relented immediately. He looked to Diane. "It would be an extraordinary opportunity for them."

Diane was skeptical. Having not yet seen the gate with her own eyes, she had no idea how safe it was. She couldn't help feeling that, for all of the science and grandeur, they were meddling with forces none of them truly understood. Still, it was hard to argue that it wouldn't be a once in a lifetime experience.

"Please, please! It's educational!"

Diane looked to Roland Griff. "We've opened the portal literally tens of thousands of times," he said. "It's perfectly safe. Plus it's not like you'd be going inside yourselves. Merely bidding adieu to those that will."

Diane glanced down at Jack, who looked back with hopeful eyes. "Fine," she said.

"Yay!" shouted Naomi.

Moments later, the family rode the elevator down to the lobby. They were alone. There was no need for an escort as the lift required a passcard to visit any floor other than the lobby. Once inside, there was nowhere else they could go but down. Naomi and Jack were abuzz with excitement. Jack, for once, didn't grip his blanket close. Instead, he let it drag on the elevator floor. The kids made faces at one another, in imitation of General Bragad'oc.

"That guy, Sam, has a point you know," said Diane.

"Sam?" said Marc, who had been lost in the reverie of his own imagination. "You've got to be kidding! He's a loose-cannon."

"Why? Because he questioned the great Roland Griff's scheme?"

"Because he doesn't know what he's talking about."

"Do any of us?" said Diane, shooting her husband a challenging stare. They stood apart behind their children.

Marc sighed. "Honey, look I get it. You're concerned. And you should be. But this is not just some job offer. This is not even about money anymore. This is about making history. This is like going to the moon! Bigger even! We always knew the moon existed. This? Well, it's a chance to be a part of the future! It's important!"

Diane scowled. "You're right, Marc. It is important. Definitely more important than silly little issues like—we haven't seen each other in two years, and this..." She paused to glance down at the five foot gap between them. "...is as close as we want to get." Diane turned to stare fixedly ahead at the polished gold elevator doors. Marc opened his mouth to object. Before he could speak, the doors chimed open. Diane and the two children stepped out.

10

"The dead talk. The living don't listen."
– Elvin proverb.

The yellow morning sun shone between the towers of New York City, bouncing with dazzling brilliance off soaring towers of steel and glass. The streets were a bustle of traffic both human and car. Marc stood entranced by it all, framed by the curtains of his hotel window. He could hear the random shouts and honking horns far below even through the double-pane glass. He'd been away a long time from any big city. Even so, New York was unique. Its seemingly endless man-made peaks and canyons stretched interminably like the Dolomites, only to end abruptly at the island's edge. He liked to imagine what it had been like before the being purchased from the Indians by the Dutch for 60 guilders. He envisioned dense green forests with deer darting like spirits between the trees. The only thing that saved New York City was Central Park—a gasp of green in a landscape suffocated by concrete. The park was just a dozen blocks away. He wanted to go for a run there. He needed to clear his mind, to try to wrap his thoughts around a world suddenly transformed. Believing in magic was a casualty of childhood lost, and yet suddenly here it was again. It was an intoxicating idea. The solid grey towers outside seemed to crumble with uncertainty. *Nothing* was impossible again. *Nothing* was as it seemed. He glanced at his watch. No time for a run. Damn it. He'd have woken earlier if he hadn't had that last glass of wine.

"We need to get going," said Diane as she straightened her hair in the mirror.

"I know."

Without turning around, she looked at him reflected. Marc was still wearing his pyjamas. "You need to change."

"Yeah."

The observation lounge reminded Marc of a luxury box seat at a sporting event, the kind he'd only been in once as the guest of an oil executive in Dallas. For some reason, it was decidedly citrus. The carpet was orange. The luxurious leather swivel armchairs and sofas were tangerine. The plump pillows were peach and lemon yellow. Marc was reminded of some trivia his friend Don had told him once—that orange, the colour, was named after the fruit and not the other way around, as most people assumed. Don had told Marc this while explaining how presumptions can be one-hundred and eighty degrees wrong. They had just discovered that the most corrupt people in Kuwait weren't the locals, but the American oil executives.

Most of the furniture in the lounge faced a curved floor-to-ceiling glass wall. This allowed the occupants to observe the gateway floor below in comfort. That decidedly industrial concrete space below was the complete opposite of the decor here. On his initial visit, Marc had failed to notice the observation area windows looking down from above. Of course, he'd been somewhat distracted by the presence of the trans-dimensional portal. Against the back wall were tables of breakfast sandwiches, croissants, juice, and fresh fruit. Some of the guests, including Bob Crosby and his wife Bea were adding items to their plates with silver tongs. Sam Dooley was in one of the arm chairs, talking loudly with his mouth full to a woman Marc had not seen before. There were other guests, some of whom Marc recognized from the banquet, and others he did not. Most notably, Roland Griff himself was present, along with Antoine and the still-startling presence of General Bragad'oc. While Griff and Antoine wore suits, no one was as formally dressed as the night before. The General took this to an extreme. He wore leather and steel armour, as if girded for war. A thick crimson cloak draped his shoulders, and a heavy iron broadsword hung from his belt. While the dress was completely out of place in this modern lounge, the orc seemed more at home in it. His clawed green hand rested comfortably on the pommel of his weapon as he gazed grimly down on the bustling Arrivals Floor. Despite standing with Griff, he paid no heed to what the billionaire was saying. Instead, his yellow eyes were focused expectantly on the platform. Griff wasn't addressing him. He was animatedly discussing something with John Boshain, and Tania Greely, the two executives Marc had seen upstairs. A few feet away, Antoine was talking to a security guard. The guard was dressed more like a soldier. He wore a helmet, flak-jacket, and boots. He also had a gun holstered at his belt. Everything he wore was black, save for a gold battle-axe emblem stitched on his shoulder. As Griff finished speaking, John and Tania nodded in acknowledgement. Griff clapped his hands loudly to signal he was done, and turned away. His gaze happened upon Marc's. Griff broke into a grin and strode over, as if Marc and Diane were just the people he'd been looking for. "Good morning! So glad you could join us!"

"We're honoured," said Marc.

"Amazed is more like it," said Diane with a nod towards the gateway below.

"This is only the beginning," Griff promised. As he spoke, the billionaire stole a glance over to Antoine, who nodded grimly. The armed guard had gone. "Now, I must apologize in advance. My attentions will have to be on the operation itself. Help yourself to food and coffee. I hear the danishes are delightful. Then, have a seat and watch the show! Oh, and please, don't be alarmed by the amount of security on the floor. There will be *no* problems. It's just a necessary precaution. I subscribe to the Powell-doctrine."

Before Marc or Diane could respond, Griff turned and walked away to join Antoine, who had moved to the glass wall.

"Did he say the Powell doctrine?" said Diane.

"Remind me what that was?" said Marc, reaching for a croissant.

"Peace through a display of overwhelming force."

On the far side of the lounge, General Bragad'oc had also moved to the glass wall. He did so off in the corner, away from the other guests. Below, the gateway chamber was now busy with workers rushing about in preparation. Amid the hubbub of activity, the orc's eyes settled on a single Griff employee standing in the corner, beside a stack of crates. The man wore an orange jumpsuit, the uniform of those responsible for loading and unloading goods. When the worker looked up and saw the green-skinned figure watching him through the glass, he briefly lifted his palm to reveal a cell phone concealed there. It was a risky move—cell phones were not permitted on the receiving floor. Not by low level workers, anyway. The guests had been required to check theirs at security on the way in. This was more a precaution against the use of built-in cameras and recording capabilities than the use of the phone itself. General Bragad'oc nodded almost imperceptibly, then walked over to join Griff and Antoine at the center.

"Mom, Dad—check this out!"

Marc and Diane looked over to where Naomi and Jack had been glued from the moment they'd arrived. They stood at the glass wall, with their faces pressed up against it. Diane paused to snatch some banana bread slices for each before heading over. She'd tried to get them to eat when they'd first arrived, but they were simply too excited.

"Here," she said, "eat these, at least." Naomi and Jack each accepted the food before turning back to the window. They ate without tasting.

"Jesus..." said Marc breathlessly.

Diane followed his gaze.

The population of the floor below had shifted considerably in the past few minutes. Most of the workers in orange and blue jumpsuits had vacated. In their place was what could only be described as a small private army. At least a hundred men dressed in the same uniform as the guard they'd seen earlier had replaced the workers. Black flak jackets and helmets now filled the chamber. They bristled with machine guns and rifles. A few even had what Marc recognized as grenade launchers. Among the soldiers were vehicles—hummers, jeeps, trucks and scout cars. Several of these featured mounted weaponry. All were lined up before the ramps to the raised round disc of the gateway platform. The concrete dais was now bathed in white floodlights, but was otherwise empty. Above it, the countdown clock displayed the time remaining: 0:00:04:05.

"Four minutes left!" said Naomi eagerly. Marc had never seen her so excited. Not since she was little, anyway.

Jack gripped his mother's leg. In his other hand he clutched his blanket. The boy too was aquiver with nervous excitement. He stared down at the ring below as if expecting a circus to begin. Diane petted his light brown hair to calm him.

"Sure doesn't look like they expect to be welcomed with open arms does it?" said a familiar voice. Marc and Diane turned to see Sam smirking impishly over a cup of coffee.

"No, it does not," Diane agreed.

On the floor below, commanders walked the lines of troops, doing final inspections and barking orders.

"Well, I suppose you need to be cautious," said Marc. "I mean, Namibia was supposed to be friendly too, but we kept a sizeable security force there just is case."

Sam snorted. "Yeah, well, that's a hell of a lot of 'caution' down there."

Several feet away, General Bragad'oc rejoined Roland Griff as he gazed down on the gathered troops. The billionaire glanced up at his off-world ally. "So, General, this is your last chance to reconsider. You're quite sure that these will be enough men?"

"Absolutely," said the orc. "As you know, my people are primitive and uneducated. Once they see the technology you wield, they will quickly surrender to your control."

Antoine looked at General Bragad'oc with a raised brow. "But there are thousands—millions of orcs, are there not? What if you're wrong?"

"I'm not," said the General. "Your British conquered India with fraction of the forces did it not? Besides, this is an amicable enterprise."

Antoine, undaunted, frowned back.

"Enough," said Griff, raising his hands. "If the General is confident, then so am I!" The tycoon shot Antoine a silencing stare. He then presented him with his empty coffee cup. "Do you mind?"

The grim faced servant opened his mouth to object. He then closed it, and took the cup.

"Me too," said General Bragad'oc, handing over his cup.

"There's still coffee in it," said Antoine.

"It's gone cold."

Vitriol spat from Antoine's eyes. Once more he opened his mouth to speak, and once more he closed it. He accepted the general's cup with a silent snarl. The General showed no sign of noticing, instead he turned his attention back to the final preparations below. Antoine handed the cups off to a caterer. He'd communicated his distrust of the General to Griff on several occasions. Each time, his employer had responded with the same reasoning. "I never trust my partners, I trust their ambitions. I learn what they want, and I exploit it." Lately, Griff had grown weary of his underling's concerns and no longer answered them at all. Was it his lackey's place to question him? After all, Griff had accomplished far more in life than Antoine ever could. Antoine did it out of loyalty. Griff had hired him when no one else would. He'd given him wages no ex-con had any right to expect.

Antoine knew Griff trusted him to be loyal, but that did not mean he trusted him to be right. He only trusted himself on that.

The Arrivals Floor was abuzz with activity. The troops were now assembled in neat units around the platform. Each soldier clutched a weapon at the ready.

"Gateway opens in one minute and counting," said a woman's voice over the loudspeaker. "Repeat, gateway will open in one minute. Units take your places."

"Fall in!" shouted one of the commanders to the few remaining men still engaged in other activities. The commanders completed their inspections and moved to the front of the battalions.

By now, all of the occupants of the Observation Deck were standing at the windows watching with breathless anticipation. Bob Crosby had found his way to Marc and Diane. "So what happens when the timer hits zero?" he asked.

Sam jumped in, "Well, from what I heard Griff say, we waltz in and start setting up shop in The Fourth World, as he calls it. O'course, all we'll see is the soldiers step onto the platform and disappear. Should be right *kif*."

"Really?" said Diane. "Sounds like a magic trick!"

"Poof!"

"So we're really just seeing them off?" said Marc.

"Perhaps they could name it Roanoke," said Sam with his customary smirk.

"What?"

"Never mind."

The Observation area glass wall began to darken considerably. Casting a shadowy veil across the chamber beyond.

"What's going on?" said Diane.

"I can't see!" said Naomi.

"I can!" said Jack.

"It's for our protection," Marc explained. "When the gate opens there's a big flash—really big. When I was here the other day, I had to wear special glasses. Trust me, it's for your own good. I think we'd all be blinded otherwise."

The lounge lights dimmed as well. This made it easier to see through the now heavily tinted glass barrier to the well illuminated arena beyond.

"You know—I just don't trust that guy," said Bob with a glance towards General Bragad'oc. His usual sunny demeanour was overcast with concern. "What y'all think he's doin'?"

Marc looked at the orc, who had wandered away to talk on his cell phone. Marc shrugged. "Looks like he's making a call."

"It's weird."

"What's so weird about talking on a cell-phone?" said Diane, leaning in. "I mean, besides the fact that he gets to keep his phone and we don't."

"He's an orc from an alternate universe. Who exactly is he calling?"

Marc had to agree that Bob had a point. Still, Griff presumably had approved the orc's access to a phone, so...

"Mom! Dad! It's about to happen!" shouted Naomi. Jack also looked at his parents with wild eyes.

On the Arrivals Floor, one hundred armed guards stood at the ready. Black fingerless gloves gripped shiny black gun metal. Teeth gritted behind opaque visors.

"Juncture in 10... 9... 8... 7..." said the loudspeaker, "6... 5... 4... 3..."

The plan was simple. The gate would open. The soldiers would step onto it. The gate would close. They would then be inside the orc world. Colonization would begin. Once more, the black orb in the center of the platform had begun to glow with a cool blue-white light.

"2... 1... 0... Juncture initiated."

Inside the observation lounge, the guests gasped. With a *WHOOMP!* the orb flashed like a magnesium flare. Despite the dark glass shielding them, all were briefly dazzled by the brilliant luminescence.

On the concrete Arrivals Floor below, private security contractor Paul Kenzie saw blurry blobs. Despite the protection of his helmet glass, he knew he would have to wait several anxious seconds for his eyes to recover. It was not his first time seeing the gate open. It *would* be his first time going through it. He had been waiting for this moment. They had all trained months for it. Each were paid many times what they could make in security anywhere else. Their wages were easily double even the most lucrative contractor jobs in actual war zones of this world. The only special stipulation was that they tell no one. Money for silence was a common requirement for such work. This time, the repercussions were even harsher than the Pentagon's. Each contractor signed strong NDA's with bankrupting financial punishments and clauses ensuring they could in no way reap financial rewards by revealing secrets. They also couldn't sue for 'wrongful death' or other injuries. That was all okay. The pay was worth it. For a long time, it all seemed too good to be true. It certainly seemed too fantastical. Of course, there had been forays into The Fourth World by small contingents since the beginning. These were the pilot expeditions—envoys sent to set up the initial trade deals. The handfuls of early recruits who were veterans of such missions now served as squad and unit commanders. Still, even they had seen little of the world they were now set to invade. "It's enough," Paul's squad leader Daryl had declared. "After all, in the land of the blind, the one-eyed man is king!" Paul had pointed out that it wasn't an analogy that necessarily boded well—drawing his commander's ire. It was an odd phenomena of the gate that photographs and videos failed to survive transit. The media would survive, but oddly wiped clean. Blank memory sticks, Paul could understand, but the erased print photos were just plain weird. Consequently, they had only pencil drawings and descriptions to prepare them. Daryl, as an expedition veteran, had described a lush green world surprisingly similar to Earth, albeit with many grasses and trees that proved alien on close inspection. Not totally alien, another veteran named Dave had observed, "There are oak trees, maple and pine! Other plants too that are exactly or nearly the same as ours." Their similarities are more surprising than their differences, he'd argued. The denizens of The Fourth World, were not so reassuringly familiar. They had all seen General Bragad'oc. He was scary enough in himself. The idea of hundreds, or even thousands of such fanged monsters seemed like something out of a nightmare. Still, their commanders assured them, the orcs were 'backwards' compared to themselves. Captain Michaels, who considered himself a student of history, had promised, "We're the British, and they're the Zulus. We offer them the chance to move into the twenty-first century. They'll welcome us with open arms—freeing them from the yokes of primitivity. It's only right we get rewarded for that." Paul was gleeful. He loved the idea of finally being in charge of something, even if it was just a tribe of green-skinned savages. He'd been born into a poor family in Memphis to a single mother. Paul's childhood had consisted of more evictions than he could count. He'd joined the army at eighteen, but never made officer. Even here, he was still treated as a low-level grunt. In The Fourth World, however, the lowest foot soldier would belong to the uber-class *homo sapiens*. It wasn't just the idea of venturing into a foreign world that made Paul excited. It was the idea of becoming someone who mattered. Paul's vision began to clear. What they were expecting was for the concrete dais to once more be terraformed into a slice of The Fourth World. The surface would be grass and mud, perhaps a few puddles if it had been raining. Paul had seen it many times before, during training and on guard duty in the arrivals floor. This time, the ground was to be empty. There would be no incoming shipments today. Instead, it was they were to be *exported*. They would step onto that foreign soil, and wait to be transported into another universe. For Paul, it was like waiting to be crowned king. He had no reason to doubt this. Thus far, everything had gone exactly as Mr. Roland Griff had predicted. The billionaire was Paul's hero. He was the perfect capitalist—a champion of the American dream. When he spoke, it was as if he spoke to Paul directly. When Roland Griff promised, Paul knew he could deliver. "All Americans are potential billionaires," Griff liked to say, and Paul knew it was true. What Griff said would be, would be. Or so it had always been, thus far. Paul was therefore dumbfounded when, as his eyes adjusted, he could finally see. This was not the empty platform they'd been told to expect. Instead, it was packed with shadowy figures clutching every type of medieval weapon imaginable. What drew his eyes, most of all, were the rows upon rows of gritted tusk-like teeth.

11

"Into the valley of Death, rode the six hundred..."
–Alfred, Lord Tennyson

Despite their months of training, the humans on the floor were surprised. The orcs on the platform were not, and that was enough to decide the battle that followed. Up in the observation room, mouths hung open. Some guests assumed the massive contingent of orcs was what was expected. Others were simply confused.

"What in God's name?" shouted Roland Griff. "General, what the Hell is going on here?" The billionaire cast about, looking for the orc commander.

General Bragad'oc stood several feet away. For a moment, their eyes met. The General still held his cell phone to his ear. *"Now."*

The lights flickered once and went out, instantly plunging both the

Arrivals Floor and Observation area into total darkness.

The soldiers were supposed to be arriving in The Fourth World during daylight hours, early morning to be precise. Consequently, their night vision goggles were buried deep in their packs, far out of reach. The orcs, on the other hand, were as often subterranean cave dwellers as not. Their eyes could see clearly into the infra-red end of the spectrum. To them, the elimination of other light waves only helped to highlight the warm vulnerable flesh of their foes.

In front, a tall, lanky orc captain named Kragg swung a notched battle axe and cleaved Paul's head from his shoulders. The soldier's briefly still functioning brain tried to understand what had happened as it hurled over the heads of its comrades before landing with a wet thud. 'Griff had promised they would love us...' it thought, then died. All around the dais, orcs poured onto the floor with axes hacking, swords thrusting, and clubs bludgeoning. Meanwhile, a volley of arrows and jagged spears rained down. Many of the missiles clattered as hail off of the soldiers' helmets, but a few found the soft meat of shoulders and necks. All of this happened before a single shot was fired. By the time the soldiers began shooting, the dais was nearly deserted. Soldiers in front found themselves in close quarter edged-weapon combat they hadn't prepared for. Soldiers in back, began a barrage of semi automatic weapons fire. Several orcs flew backwards, riddled with bullets. Even more humans in front fell from friendly fire. Boot steps grew sticky as a slow tide of blood began to seep across the concrete. The smell of iron tickled nostrils.

The orcs charged, hacking and slashing with brutal glee. The nightmarish battle was visible only by the intermittent strobe of gunfire. The result was a series of illuminated stills: contorted faces; arcs of blood spatter; and lopped limbs hanging mid-air. All of this was set to a crescendo of human screams and orc battle cries. Mixed in to this symphony of horror was actual music. Someone had programmed Wagner's *Flight of the Valkyries* to play when the gate opened. It was meant to be ironic.

In the observation deck above, Marc and Diane dove to where they had last glimpsed their children, groping about desperately. Around the room people screamed in terror. They began crashing into each other and tripping over furniture in the dark.

"Mummy!"cried Jack.

"Jack, Naomi, where are you?" screamed Diane.

"Kids!" yelled Marc.

"Mum!" shrieked Naomi. "I can't see!"

Someone shot a flare into the air on the Arrivals Floor below. The white hot light was intense, though less bright than the portal opening earlier. The windows had automatically switched off their tinting and the scene beyond was displayed with horrific clarity. For a several seconds, the room was cast into high relief. Shadows leapt and bent across panicked faces and scrambling bodies. Marc and Diane used the moment to grab their children. Diane lifted a petrified Jack. Marc grabbed Naomi by the arm. The thirteen-year-old's eyes were wide with terror. Across the room, Marc caught a glimpse of General Bragad'oc. The orc commander stood, towering like a totem of ancient evil above the cowering figure of John Boshain. The Griff Corporation CFO stared aghast as his fate was made manifest. The General raised his broad sword high, its blade crimson with the blood of others, and brought it down. The flare died. The final blow was lost to darkness. Diane had seen the strewn bodies at the orc's feet. "We need to go!" she shouted.

"This way," said Marc. He tugged at her sleeve, hoping to guide her towards where he believed the exit to be. "We need to stick together."

Below, the sounds of battle continued, but slowed considerably. There was little gunfire now. Mostly came the sounds of hacking flesh, like one might hear in a meat rendering plant. A stray bullet struck the gas tank of a jeep on the Arrivals Floor. The jeep exploded upwards in a bright yellow fireball, tossing the vehicle up into the air. Orange light now flooded the entire chamber. The Observation windows shattered inward, showering the room occupants with glass. The jeep crashed down, engulfed in orange flames.

"Ah! I got somethin' in ma leg!" shouted Bob. The big man fell to the floor clutching his shin. Several feet away, his wife Beatrice lay motionless, face down on the carpet.

Below, the Hellish glow illuminated the grisly remains of conflict. There were dozens of orcs standing amid heaped bodies in black body armour. The inferno raged. All at once, emergency lighting flickered on, filling both rooms with half-light. At the same time, sprinklers triggered and water gushed from the ceiling. The fire began to die. The indoors took on the appearance of an outdoor battlefield in the rain. Water ran in rivulets off the helmets, armour and weapons of the orcs. On the concrete, water and blood mixed in red swirling clouds and ran to the drains.

The battle of the floor below was decided. The battle in the Observation Deck was not. General Bragad'oc, no longer enjoying the advantage of darkness, was better armed and better able, but still out-numbered. He stood amid a heap of corpses, sword ready. Antoine faced him, bearing a long bladed knife. "He can't take us all," Griff's henchman snarled.

The General grinned. While there were still over a dozen humans in the room, he knew Antoine was the only real threat, and he was poorly armed. The other humans had no training, nor weapons.

"General, what have you done?" shouted Griff from the shadows.

General Bragad'oc laughed, "Reaping what you sowed."

"He's right," yelled Sam. "This is your fault, Griff!"

"We need to go," said Diane. She looked toward the now visible exit. Marc nodded. All that mattered now was his family.

"Here!" yelled General Bragad'oc through the shattered window to the orcs below. "They're up here!"

The green-skinned warriors below roared and rushed to find a way up. Kragg, the orc lieutenant, knew about elevators. The elevators, however, had been disabled by the fire system. Stymied, the orcs rushed the stairwells, only to find they required pass-cards. The orcs began to hack and smash at the steel doors.

General Bragad'oc stood ready to slash down any human that approached him. If enough rushed him at once, he knew they could overwhelm him. He also knew that time was on his side. The orc warriors would soon be through the doors and all the humans would die.

"Retreat!" yelled Marc, "We need to get out of here!" As he said this, he picked up a piece of bent metal from the floor to use as a weapon.

"Sir, we need to go," Antoine whispered to Griff. The billionaire stood frozen in the grip of shock. He stared numbly at the ruinous massacre his dreams had become, mouthing incomprehensible words. "*Now, sir.*" Antoine pulled the lanky Griff stumbling towards the exit.

"I need help!" shouted Bob.

"I got ya," said Sam, as he helped the big man to his feet.

"Where's Bea?" asked Bob.

Sam looked at the body of Bob's wife a few feet away. "She's..."

"Bea! We have to help her!" He fell to his knees and rolled over his ample wife. Her front had been cleaved open from neck to hip by a single stroke of the General's sword, exposing an array of pink organs. "Oh gawd!" yelled Bob. He vomited onto the orange carpet.

"She's dead, Bob—come on!" shouted Sam. Marc helped Sam drag the anguished Texan from the eviscerated remains of his wife and back to the lounge exit. General Bragad'oc watched them go, knowing that none of it would matter in the end.

12

"Let the weight of the axe guide your hand."
– Lord Darkoth

The disheveled refugees spilled out into the hallway. They were men and women, all in states of shock and horror. The angled light cones from the emergency systems made even this undisturbed corridor seem otherworldly and unreal. Jack and Naomi were the only children. Diane remembered spying another little girl with a young couple when they'd first arrived. She saw no sign of them now. She hoped that somehow they were still alive. Perhaps hiding, she thought. Jack clung to her. His face was buried in her shoulder. He didn't want to see anything, and neither did she want him to. Naomi gripped her father's hand desperately. Bob limped with one arm over Sam's shoulder. Sam struggled to support the Texan's weight. Roland Griff stood frozen in the middle, as useless as a statue. He gazed with glassy eyes, as if unable to fathom what had occurred. How had his lifetime of ascension come to this?

Marc slid the metal bar he had been holding under the door handles, barring them. It wouldn't hold long once the orc troops reached them, but any delay might help. He could see the calculating grimace of General Bragad'oc now studying him through the safety-glass window. The General had a darkly amused expression on his face. Like a cat with a mouse, Marc thought. "Where do we go now?" he said, turning to face the others. "The elevators?"

Sam tapped the Up button several times. It failed to light up. "Come on, come on!"

"It won't come, not on emergency power," said Antoine.

"Well, we have to do something!" said Diane.

"The executive stairwell—it leads directly to the top floors," he replied.

"Wait, what?" said Marc. "Not to the ground floor?"

"No. It was about access, not safety."

"But, surely the fire code–"

Antoine smirked. "You think the fire marshal approved any of this?"

"I see."

"There are other stairwells and the loading docks, of course. But there's the slight problem of a small army of orcs in between. So, yes, it's going to be a long climb."

"Well then," said Marc, looking about the frightened, motley gaggle of survivors, "we better get started."

"I don't understand what happened!" Griff blurted, as if awakening from a trance.

They all turned to stare at him. The celebrated entrepreneur had lost any semblance of composure and control. Instead, he looked lost and confused and suddenly smaller.

"Hubris" said Sam between gritted teeth. "What else is new?"

General Bragad'oc turned expectantly at the sound of orcish boots on steps. He stood in the wreckage of what had once been the Observation Lounge overlooking the Arrivals Floor. He alone had slain everybody that lay heaped amid over turned furniture and smashed glass table-tops. No, he remembered, there was one exception. The little girl whose body lay still clutched in her dead mother's arms. She had died when a shard of glass had pierced her neck from the exploding windows. Her mother had then approach the General, begging him to kill her too. Ever merciful, the General had obliged. The orc wiped the hot blood from his sword blade with a lacy table cloth. It would only be drenched again soon, but military discipline required it, if only to keep the scabbard interior clean. He smoothly re-sheathed the weapon as the doors burst open and the contingent of orc soldiers charged in. The lights came on all at once. The hum of air conditioning resumed. Power was restored. The carnage was suddenly well lit and visceral. General Bragad'oc smiled.

The General's lieutenant, Kragg, cast about the room as he approached his commander. "Survivors?" the lanky orc growled in guttural Orcish.

General Bragad'oc nodded towards the double doors that lead to the hallway. "They're barred."

"After them!" shouted Kragg at the soldiers.

"Wait," said the General. "They've taken the executive stairs to the top floors." He made a quick head count of the troops. Many more remained in the stairwell, but he needed every orc he had. He pointed at the first line of warriors. "You six should be plenty. Break down the door and pursue them."

Kragg scowled. Of course, the General could overrule him, he just didn't like it happening in front of the troops. "Now!" he barked, trying to make the order his own.

The gang of orcs leapt to the steel doors and began hammering it with axes and clubs. The strong steel dented but, for now, held. The General glanced about the lounge for something that could be used as a battering ram. There was nothing. It's going to take a few minutes to get through, he decided, there's no way around it. He looked to the remaining force of soldiers. "The rest of you, take the other stairwells, spread throughout the facility and kill every human you see."

"Kill them all!" Kragg roared, raising his battle axe high.

"Not you, Kragg," said General Bragad'oc, catching the warrior by the arm. "You and I need to manage the gateway to bring in the rest. There's a whole city of humans around us. We'll need all of the forces we can get at our disposal if we're to achieve our main objective."

The straggling line of eight plodded slowly up the relentless steps that led from landing to landing. The grey concrete walls were featureless save for large painted numbers indicating floors they could not access. Forty-six, Marc counted to himself, as he climbed. He held Jack in his arms, having taken over carrying him to give Diane a rest. Naomi trudged between them. "Are we there yet?" she asked.

"Not yet." He had been carrying Jack since floor thirty. The boy seemed to grow heavier with each step. In front of him, Antoine led with his knife at the ready. Behind them were the others, including Sam desperately half-carrying Bob, his back straining from the effort. The big Texan was pale and delirious from blood loss and climbed with ponderous, faltering steps. He had spent the first half of the climb, wailing and crying out for 'Bea'. Since then, he had fallen silent, save for the occasional moan of agony. Roland Griff and his CMO, Tania, trudged like zombies behind them. Tania, no longer appeared the razor sharped executive she'd been before. She had tossed aside her designer suit jacket and high heels. She wore instead an expression of sheer fury. A top Harvard Business School graduate, she was used to setting the pace, and having things go right. This was not going right. Stopping was not an option, however. Echoing up the many floors from the basement below came the relentless pounding of the orcs. *Bang! Clang! Bang!* They had broken through the initial doorway Marc had barred. Now they were battering the locked stairwell door itself. After that, there was nothing left between them and the humans they sought, but several flights of stairs.

"That door's not goin' to hold them for long," said Marc. He shifted his son's weight. He was tempted to make Jack walk, but the boy had crumpled the last time he'd tried. "Now I know what a sherpa feels like!" he joked.

"Actually, carrying your kid is what being a Dad feels like, but you wouldn't know that would you?" muttered Diane.

"Ouch! And I thought my back hurt!" winced Sam.

"Mommy?" said Jack. The boy had opened his eyes for the first time since they'd begun their ascent. He turned his small head to look at his mother as he spoke.

"Yes, honey?" said Diane.

"Can you and Daddy not be like that?"

Diane, her face already red from climbing, nevertheless flushed with embarrassment. "I—I'm sorry honey," she said.

They continued to walk.

Forty-eight, read Marc.

Clang! Clang! Bang!

Sam stumbled trying to lift his foot over a step. Bob, whose arm was over Sam's shoulder, lurched backwards, nearly taking them both over. Diane, who was in their path, reached up and pushed back. The two men regained their balance. After taking a moment to right themselves, Sam took the step successfully, heaved Bob along with him, and the procession continued. "I don't understand this. Where are the doors to the different floors?" he growled.

"It's the executive stairwell," said Griff, speaking for the first time since their climb had begun.

"What the hell does that mean? You don't need doors? You just walk through walls perhaps?"

"Mr. Griff had this stairwell accessible only from a few select private floors," said Antoine. Unencumbered, he had already reached the next landing and stopped to look back down. "Most are at the top, but we'll reach the museum floor shortly."

"Another brilliant idea from our fearless leader," spat Tania.

Griff turned on his CMO with eyes of venom. "You were happy to follow my 'brilliant' ideas when they lined your pockets, Tania," he scoffed. "I didn't see you start a multi-billion dollar company on your own!"

"I also didn't bring in a bunch of marauding monsters from another dimension!"

"She's got you there," said Sam.

"Enough!" snarled Antoine.

"Antoine's right," said Marc. "Enough. There will be plenty of time for recriminations later."

"And criminal investigations," muttered Sam.

Griff turned his rekindled anger on the diamond prospector. "What did you—"

"We're here!" announced Antoine. The stocky body guard pointed to the grey doorway inset in the wall on the landing above them. Next to it, in large block letters, was painted '50'.

"Finally," breathed Diane. She paused to lean against the bannister, while rubbing Jack's back.

"So do we stop here or go higher?" asked Marc.

"There are weapons in there," said Antoine.

"Swords and spears," said Griff. "In my office, I have a pistol."

"Thirty more floors up," said Tania.

"Twenty-seven," said the billionaire, peevishly.

"Seriously?"

"I'm not sure Bob here, can make five more floors," said Sam, matter-of-factly.

All looked at the wounded Texan. Bob had his eyes closed and teetered unsteadily on his feet. "Bea..." he pleaded.

"Ever wield a sword before?" said Antoine to Marc.

"Actually, I used to fence in college. So did Diane—it was how..." Marc's eyes met Diane's. He smiled weakly. "...we met."

A loud crash reverberated up the length of the stairwell. It was the sound of the door far below crashing in. Orcish cheers and yells came next, followed by the stomp of boots pounding up steps.

"Might be how you die too," said Sam. Marc and Diane turned to stare at him. "Just sayin'.".

"That settles it then," said Antoine. "We stop here."

13

"The aspirations of men are the mirth of gods."
– Prophet Abdas

The fifth floor of Griff Tower was a sea of cubicles. This was the data entry floor. One of the costs of being so secretive was that more of the housekeeping needed to be done in-house. Once they went public, CFO John Boshain's plan was "a major RIF," or reduction-in-force. Data entry would be out-sourced. Employees on the fifth floor would be terminated. At least, that was the plan before John himself had been terminated by the orc general. One of the other drawbacks of the deep secrecy and 'information partitioning' in the organization, was that none of the above ground employees knew what had just occurred in the basement. Other than the thirty minute power outage, it had been a fairly typical morning. They continued to sit at their desks, typing away on computer keyboards. One of those employees was Leanne Dithers. Leanne had moved to New York from Albuquerque, New Mexico six months earlier. She had been told she would have a tough time finding work for more than minimum wage, owing to her total lack of skills. She had therefore been delighted to land the job here at Griff Corporation. Griff paid double what other data entry jobs did. All she'd had to do was sign a pile of documents saying she would not tell anyone what she knew about the company. That was easy. She knew nothing. She knew she wasn't allowed access to any of the other floors and that was fine with her. She assumed it was all boring financial stuff. If it was some sort of Bernie Madoff pyramid scheme, as her friend Harmony believed, then it was just as well she knew nothing. What Leanne did was boring too. Fortunately, she had developed a knack for being able to clean up the data records without consciously reading them. This allowed her to talk to her friend Kathleen on the phone at the same time. Kathleen worked in IT, on the third floor. "I know," said Leanne, pausing to take a sip of her Dunkin' Donuts Vanilla Bean Coolatta. "Doug does the same thing, he promises his bosses the earth—then leaves at five. We're here until ten and he doesn't care. Jerk." She took another sip as Kathleen commiserated. Leanne wondered how it was she couldn't lose the weight she wanted when all she ever had was coffee for breakfast. A note of alarm in Kathleen's voice caught her attention. Something about noises. "I don't hear anything here, hon, but we're on a different floor. So, y'know." In a glassed-in meeting room across from Leanne's cube, Eliza Chang, one of the managers was giving a powerpoint presentation to a group of employees. The current slide said 'Thinking Inside-the-Box is the new Outside-the-Box Thinking (and vice versa)'. It was followed by twelve bullet points too small for Leanne to read. The presentation had been lifted from a recent TED Talk called *Inside*

Outside In. One of Leanne's friends, Paul, was in the room. From her angle, Leanne could see he was playing with his phone under the table. The others looked stupefied with boredom. Perry was actually drooling. "Sure hon, you go see, I'll wait." While Kathleen went to investigate the sounds of disturbance, Leanne went back to her computer. She was ahead of schedule, so she opened up a browser window to continue her game of *Powder-Pop* instead. She moved a strawberry onto a mushroom. Suddenly, there came the sound of shrieks and loud crashes over the phone. "Green monsters!" she heard someone yell. Kathleen was surprised, then laughed. "Very funny," she said and hung up.

Brandon in the next cube looked at her quizzically. He was the fastest typist on the floor. He was always done his work first. Sometimes that meant he annoyed Leanne with distracting questions when she still had work to do. He also kept his cube a mess, decorating its wall tops with plastic blue Smurfs and various Pokémon figures. Still, when Kathleen was ahead on her work like today, he was someone to talk to. "That got me for a moment," she said.

"What?" asked Brandon, playing with Papa Smurf on his knee.

"So Kathleen puts the phone down, and suddenly I hear all this screaming and stuff about 'green monsters'."

Brandon snorted. "Norm must be playing one of his stupid computer games again. He doesn't care about anyone else."

"For a sec, I thought someone had gone Columbine on us!"

"Yeah well, someone is gonna go Columbine on him if he isn't careful."

"He's gonna get his ass fired, if he keeps—"

A scream pierced the office. Kathleen, Brandon and dozens of other workers looked up from their cubicles like a warren of prairie dogs poking their heads from their holes. Barry from accounting lurched out of the kitchenette area with a crossbow bolt lodge in his sternum, spilling coffee and blood everywhere. He gurgled and vomited a mix of both. He collapsed to his knees, then fell forward, dead. The shocked office workers stared aghast.

All at once a group of orc warriors burst into the room. The office workers stared in shock at the sight of savage green and grey skinned monsters clutching swords, axes, and spears. One tossed Suzanne Waterly's decapitated head into the air. The office intern's cranium rebounded off the ceiling tiles and landed right on Leanne's desk. For a moment, Leanne simply stared at Suzanne's contorted face. Somehow, the intern was still wearing her glasses. Lately, Leanne had been telling people that Suzanne only wore them so people would take her seriously. Suddenly, that didn't seem to matter anymore. Leanne screamed. All at once, the orcs began hacking and bludgeoning their way through the floor. They dragged workers out from under their desks, and beat their skulls to pulpy masses. They easily batted aside rulers and staplers raised in defence. The soaked carpet turned from mocha beige to blood red.

"Kill them all!" roared Garak, the orc sergeant, in orcish. "No time for scalping, flaying or dismemberment! Kill smarter, not harder! They all must die before word gets out!"

Bang! The door to the stairwell shuddered under the impact. The banging was relentless. The orcs would not stop until they were through. *Bang! Clang! Bang!*

"It should hold for a while," said Antoine. "They're security doors."

"What exactly does 'a while' mean?" asked Sam. He was sitting exhausted on a large mahogany table top, on which lay the unconscious form of Bob Crosby. Sam had tried to keep the wounded Texan awake once they'd stopped to rest. He'd failed. "I said, what does—"

"I don't know."

The disheveled group were at odds with their surroundings. This was the same area Jack and Naomi had escaped to the night before. The museum was full of pristine glass cases, neatly arranged on dark hardwood floors. The objects were barbaric orc relics from 'The Fourth World'. Here they were contained so antiseptically as to make them appear harmless. *Tamed,* thought Marc. *They're anything but!* Diane sat nearby with her arms around Jack and Naomi. Jack had his eyes closed. Surely he couldn't be asleep through that racket, thought Marc. Naomi stared blankly ahead, seemingly in shock.

Bang! Bang! Clang! Skree!

Crash! Tania, and Antoine smashed several cases containing weapons. They then paused, surveying the haul. Marc lifted a dull grey broadsword. It appeared crude—made of iron, not steel. That meant it could break more easily. He took a few practice swings. Despite its primitive workings, it was surprisingly well balanced. "This is a good weight for Diane," he said. Holding up the blade, he looked at his wife. She nodded. He slid the weapon across the floor to her. He then turned back to the case and lifted a heavier long sword. He held it out by the hilt. This one's for me, he thought.

Bang! Clang! Clang!

"That's too heavy for you," said Antoine.

"What?" said Marc. He then saw that the dour henchman's comment was directed at Tania. "Oh." The CMO was holding a massive battle axe up to the light. Tania assessed the sharpened steel edge. It was clearly more sophisticated metalwork than the swords. A engraved pattern of knots decorated the handle. They also provided grip if the weapon were to become wet, she noted, with blood for example. "I can handle this just fine," she snorted. She lifted the heavy blade high and brought it down fast. It smashed easily through the display case, sending wood and glass flying. "This is the name people around here had for me anyway, 'The Battle Axe'. Of course, they thought I didn't know. Idiots."

"If it makes you feel any better. They're likely all dead by now," said Sam.

Tania considered this a moment, then nodded. "It does."

A thunderous *BOOM!* reverberated around the room. All turned to the stairwell door. The upper right side had buckled and was now bent into the room. Despite this, the door held.

"How long 'til they get in, Mummy?" said Naomi. Her hushed voice was audible in the momentary silence. They all knew the answer. Marc knew that the orcs on the other side were making the same assessment—not long.

The hammering resumed with renewed vigour. *Bang! Clang! Bang!*

Diane cast about frantically for some avenue of escape. Antoine had confirmed that the elevators were still out of commission. There were two other stairwells, but both were already loud with orcs working their way up, floor by bloody floor. These contingents were many more strong than the six orcs behind them. The decision had been to stand and fight. Now, that notion seemed ridiculous. How were they to defeat six trained warriors? They didn't have a choice, but the children...? Diane's eyes came to rest upon a short cabinet on the opposite wall. Too small for an adult certainly, but not for two kids. "Quickly children," she said, pulling them towards it. Diane yanked on cabinet doors until she found two that were unlocked. Inside there was only a roll of paper towels and a bottle of Windex. She tossed these aside. It'll be tight, she thought, but they can both squeeze in. "Get inside!"

"I don't want to go in there, Mummy!" pleaded Jack with tears in his eyes. Naomi simply stared at the open cabinet as if unsure what to do.

"You have to," said Diane. "They may not find you there."

"But..."

"Please, Jack! Do as Mummy says!"

"But, what about there?" he said, pointing urgently.

Diane turned to see the door in the corner. Painted to match the walls, they had all overlooked it upon entry. It was the same door the children had noticed the night before. Locked and re-locked with padlocks, bolts and chains. "It's locked," said Diane, "We can't get in."

"But he'd have the key," said Naomi, looking squarely at Roland Griff.

"Huh? What?" he said as if stung. "No, not there!"

"Sir, it might help!" pleaded Antoine.

"No!"

Sam jumped to his feet to face the tall reedy businessman. "Listen, you maniac, you lost the right to decide anything here."

"I'd rather die."

"That can be arranged," said Tania, with her axe on her shoulder.

Marc stepped between them, with hands raised. "Roland, if there's anything that can–"

With a *KRANG!* the door to the executive stairwell flew off its hinges and onto the floor. Six orc warriors piled through behind it. Their green skin gleamed with sweat. Their black eyes twinkled with malevolent pleasure. Their fanged mouths grinned. *"Gratha!"* roared the sergeant. There is no single word in English for the Orcish utterance. Instead it requires three. *"Prepare... to... die!"*

14

"The ocean forgives nothing." – The Oracle of Seasgate

The black and white NYPD cruiser rolled to a stop at the foot of the steps leading up to Griff Plaza. Despite its being business hours, the steps, plaza, and glass-walled lobby appeared oddly deserted. No one exited or entered the six sets of revolving doors. Aside from a gyro cart salesman on the corner, there was no sign of anyone. Rizzo, a veteran officer with fifteen years on the force, nibbled his thumbnail as he eyed the building. "If anything, I'd say it was quiet for a work day."

"A call's a call," said Joe, with a shrug. Joe was Rizzo's partner. He was also a rookie. They'd been assigned together six months ago, after Rizzo's previous partner, Barry, had retired. Of course, six months spent in the close quarters of a cop car was plenty of time to get comfortable with each other. Joe talked more than Barry, which Rizzo didn't like, but always did the driving, which Rizzo did. So, it more or less balanced out.

"Yup," said Rizzo. He opened the passenger door and stepped out. Joe slid out from behind the wheel and followed. The two police officers headed up the steps. Joe jogged. Rizzo took his time, sidling up slowly.

Usually, when there was a 911 call from an office building, security was there to meet them. A building like this would have several guards on duty. As they pushed through the glass doors, they saw only one—the guard at the front desk. Otherwise, the great foyer was also deserted. Its only occupants were the square columns that lined the interior on either side. The only sound was that of an elevator door closing somewhere. Rizzo could just see the nearest bank of elevators beyond. Odd, he thought. For the first time, a faint alarm of *wrongness* sounded in his ears.

As they approached the security desk, not only did the guard fail to greet them, he appeared to be asleep at his post. The guard lay perfectly still, face down on his desk with his arms tucked under him. They'd caught guards napping before, but this was a first for the day-shift.

"Excuse me?" said Rizzo, as they approached.

The only answer was the sound of the as-yet-unseen elevator door. It was on repeat, trying to close, hitting something, re-opening, then trying again.

"Yo," Joe chimed in with his thick Brooklyn accent, "NYPD!"

The guard continued to do nothing.

The two cops reached the desk. Joe was perturbed. Rizzo felt a growing sense of alarm.

"Yo, rent-a-cop, wakey-wakey!" said Joe.

"Hey, we're talkin' here!" shouted Rizzo. Rizzo, his instincts now *buzzing* loudly, leaned forward to take a better look at the elevator lobby.

Doing so, gave him a clear view of the stuck elevator door. The doors closed once more, only to stop with a thunk as they struck a woman's arm extended on the floor from within. At the same moment, Joe caught sight of the two crumpled guards' bodies now visible just behind the security desk.

"Jesus," Rizzo breathed.

"Sweet mother..." said Joe.

Both cops reached for their guns. At that same moment, the 'security guard' lying prone across the desk looked up. His green orc face and jutting yellow tusk-teeth briefly stunned both officers. The black-haired human scalp tumbled from the orc's head and landed on the desktop. This released them from their trance. They drew their weapons as one. It was too late. The orc warrior swung out the broadsword he'd been concealing and sliced open a one-foot gash across Rizzo's chest. The veteran officer spun under the impact and splayed across the polished marble tiles. His bright blood flooded the floor around him. Joe raised his revolver to shoot, only to be struck by seven crossbow bolts at once. His pistol clattered on the floor. Joe stared down at the wooden shafts suddenly suddenly protruding from his torso like quills. A moment later, he too fell dead. The archers now stepped from behind the columns where they'd been concealed. Four of the orcs grabbed the dead police officers and dragged them to the growing pile behind the desk. Two more orcs rolled the mop and yellow washbucket they'd found in the janitor's closet after killing him and taking his keys. They began to swab the floor.

One orc lay in a heap at Antoine's feet. It was the first kill and had surprised both sides into a moment of reassessment. No one had expected one of the orcs to be the first to fall. No one, except Antoine himself. The muscular henchman turned the sword hilt easily in his hand, keeping his grip ready but loose. It wasn't so different from the long bladed knives he'd wielded in his youth on the streets of Morocco. The invading marauders had assumed a slaughter. Even orc soldiers don't *want* to die. The orc was the first death, but not first blood. Sam had immediately received a gash in his side and retreated. The wound wasn't fatal, but deep enough to disable him. Muscles had been severed and hot blood soaked his shirt. The adrenaline surging through his veins dampened the pain, but could do nothing to re-knit sliced sinew.

At the battle's front, the two sides, now equally wary, continued to face off. For the humans, this meant Antoine, Marc, and Tania. A feint here, a feint there—they tested each other, looking for weaknesses. Griff stood back, seemingly disinterested in their fate, or even his own. Distracted by his own thoughts, he gazed up at one of the coloured glass murals on the wall. Diane was also away from the fray. She was in the corner, physically forcing Naomi and Jack into one of the dozen cabinet doors that lined the wall. "Get in," she hissed. She desperately hoped the orc warriors, distracted by battle, hadn't seen the children.

"But, mum..." Naomi protested, pushing back.

"No arguments!" their mother snarled. Seeing the mix of terror and unshakeable determination in her mother's eyes, Naomi relented. Jack had no wish to argue. He eagerly crawled inside. Naomi had to be crammed in with her knees bent up to her chin. Diane just barely forced the cupboard closed then, with keys borrowed from Antoine, locked it. The children, he'd explained, would be able to open it from the inside. "Under no circumstances come out, until all the orcs are gone," she hissed. From within the two children could see out through a small slit hole that served as both decoration and handle. They watched as their mother picked up her short sword from the floor where she'd left it, and went to join the others. Her presence would narrow the margin against the five remaining orcs.

The wounded Sam dragged himself alongside Bob. The Texan lay on the floor with his back against a display case. Sam clutched the growing red stain on his shirt's side and winced. "Guess I'm joinin' you on the bench, bra," said Sam through pain-clenched teeth.

Bob said nothing. His head lolled in an unnatural way. Sam laid his fingers across the big man's neck, feeling for a pulse. Nothing. Sam sighed. He reached over and drew closed Bob's heavy lids. He then slumped down beside him, to witness whatever would follow.

Seeing Diane approaching, one of the orcs barked a guttural command. He lunged forward towards Antoine. While the orc soldier wore leather armour, Antoine wore only dress pants and a white shirt with the sleeves rolled up. This afforded him no shielding, but allowed for nimbleness. Knowing this, Antoine side-stepped the lunge, deftly pirouetted on one foot, and drove his sword through a gap in the armour between the orc's shoulder blades. "Ar-ah!" the orc screamed. It vomited blood, as it crashed to the floor with a dull *thud*.

Meanwhile, the orc facing Marc swung with a side-swipe. Marc's fencing skills kicked in. His brutish opponent's muscle and body movement telegraphed its move, allowing Marc to bring his own sword up to parry. The two weapons clanged then slid with a rasp of iron. Seeing his opponent off-balance, instead of pushing back as expected, Marc abruptly dropped his blade. The orc fell forward. Marc brought his sword around for the killing blow. Despite years of sword fighting, he'd never experienced the feel of his blade cutting into flesh. It startled, but did not stop him.

At the same time, another orc faced off against Tania. The marketing executive gripped her battle axe ungainly with both hands. The orc also held an axe. His weapon was cruder and simpler, but bore the notches of battle. The green warrior scoffed in accented English, "Human female, can you even lift your weapon?"

Tania, responded with a sudden downward strike across the handle in the orc's hands. The impact drove the weapon from the orc's clutches, breaking two of his fingers in the process. "Yeah," she said with a sneer, "I can manage. Thanks for your concern."

A second orc, seeing Antoine distracted, lunged forward. The iron sword cut across the human's left arm, slicing shirt fabric and skin. Antoine, unable to bring his blade around, hammered the orc's exposed cranium with the pommel of his sword. The blow brought the crunch of bone. His brutish opponent collapsed, blood leaking from his eyes.

Diane, rushing to join, was forced to parry a hack from another orc. Not ready, she did so one-handed. The impact deflected the attack, but also knocked the sword from her grasp. Terrified, she faced the snarling green humanoid unarmed. The orc's lips curled with gloating glee. Marc, dove forward and thrust his sword tip up under the orc's barding and deep into its belly. "Cah!" the creature spat, before crumpling to the hard marble. At the same moment, an orc head, freed from its shoulders by Tania's battle axe, flew through the air and shattered a glass display case.

The humans stared in shock and disbelief. They panted from the heart-pounding exertion and fear. All were amazed that the battle had ended so swiftly in their favour.

"Thanks," said Diane.

"No problem," said Marc, with a smile. "You know what they say, families that slay together..."

"And *still* with the puns."

A loud crash reverberated through the museum chamber. They turned to see the large double doors that lead to the elevator lobby flung open. The bold figure of General Bragad'oc stood framed in the doorway. A hoard of fifty orc warriors followed.

"Oh Hell," said Sam.

The General now wore a bright crimson cloak clasped with a gold lion claw to a gilded chest plate. The cape billowed dramatically around his broad shoulders and armoured form. Any illusion of being a subservient lackey to Griff was gone. Instead, he gazed boldly into the room as the commander he was. Still, his grim visage briefly betrayed surprise at the sight of the six slain orcs strewn across the floor. He reassessed the motley band of humans, and gave a curt nod of respect.

Sam rose unsteadily to his feet. "There's no way we can take them all," he muttered, "Not even close."

"We have to retreat to the executive stairwell," said Tania.

Diane looked desperately to the row of cabinets on the far wall. She knew the cupboard in which Jack and Naomi were hidden. She thought she could just make out the whites of Naomi's terrified eyes staring through the shadowy recess of the handle-hole. The orc battalion had effectively cut her off from reaching them.

General Bragad'oc strode further into the room. A dozen orcs followed. The commander raised his gauntlet to halt them. Marc briefly fixated on the rows of yellow teeth jutting from his bottom lip overbites. The tusk-like fangs were more inhuman than the primal green faces behind them.

He supposed the orcs would eat them after killing them. They would have no more compunction of consuming us, he decided, than we would of eating a cow. "Surrender and your deaths will be swift," said the orc commander.

"We can't go—" Diane pleaded to Marc under her breath, *"the children!"*

"We can't leave Mr. Griff," said Antoine.

The billionaire stood alone, midway between them and the orcs. He still wore his dark designer suit jacket and tie. He glared at the invaders with a special kind of loathing he reserved for those who betrayed him.

"Sam and Tania are right—we have to go!" said Marc.

"You'd leave your own children?" gasped Diane in disbelief.

"If we try to reach them, the orcs will know where they are and we'll all die. If we retreat, the orcs will follow us and maybe, just maybe, Naomi and Jack have a chance."

Diane stared at her husband with tear-filled eyes. She nodded.

"I won't leave Mr. Griff," said Antoine.

"He betrayed all of us, including you!" said Tania.

"The only reward for your loyalty will be death, Antoine," Marc agreed.

Antoine looked to his employer, who now faced down the orc contingent with arms crossed, as if daring them to advance. Antoine looked to the orc general, who returned his gaze with a smug sneer. The burly bodyguard turned to Marc. "If my reward also includes the death of Bragad'oc, I'll consider myself well-paid," he said. With that, he turned again to face the orc line.

"Let's go!" said Marc. He grabbed Diane's arm and half-dragged her into the executive stairwell. Reluctantly, she followed. Tania helped Sam through the doorway behind them.

Antoine strode boldly forward to stand between his employer and the bristling phalanx of orc warriors. As he walked, his gaze remained locked with the General's. Roland Griff appeared satisfied to have his champion in place. For a moment, Antoine and the orc commander studied one another. Finally, Antoine spoke. "Well, General. You've managed to bring down a much greater man than you'll ever be."

General Bragad'oc snorted. "Considering I'm an orc, that's not saying much, is it?" He nodded after the departed humans. "You know, their fate is only being momentarily delayed. Your sacrifice, along with everything else, means nothing."

Antoine raised his sword and grimaced, "Enough talk. Let's do this, you, and me."

General Bragad'oc lifted his own weapon. An amused smirk played across his thin green lips. Without stepping forward, he swung his blade to the floor. It was a signal. A line of orc archers fired. All at once, Antoine was a porcupine of crossbow bolts. The surprised adjutant twisted in a slow, agonizing dance. General Bragad'oc calmly re-sheathed his own unsullied sword. "Again, you mistook me for a human, Antoine. We orcs don't bother with such quaint notions as 'honour'. You always know where you stand with an orc..." Griff's bodyguard collapsed to the floor. The impact spattered blood on the white marble in a tattered crimson star about him. "...or *don't* for that matter." The last light of life guttered and died in Antoine's eyes. Bragad'oc pointed to a line of soldiers and barked in orcish, "Kill them!" Two dozen orc warriors charged towards to the stairwell door. Roland Griff looked down at his henchman's body in dismay.

"Griff!" shouted General Bragad'oc.

The billionaire businessman gave no indication of having heard him. "Human!"

Griff appeared deaf to the orc's command. Bragad'oc leaned in close and spoke in a whispered snarl. *"Slug."*

The billionaire turned his head to gaze at the orc commander with burned-out eyes. Bragad'oc drew his sword once more. He raised it back over his shoulder, as if readying to deliver a decapitating blow. Griff's gaze failed to flinch. "You thought to subjugate us orcs. Instead, us orcs have subjugated you," General Bragad'oc growled.

"How did it happen?" said Griff, as if only vaguely interested. "How did you know you could win?"

The General smiled. "Your arrogance. I knew it could be used against you."

Griff looked away, chewing his thoughts. "So this is it? This is how it ends?"

The orc commander's grin broadened. He opened his lips as if to reply. An *Arthur's Theme* ringtone began to play from the phone on Bragad'oc's belt. The general lowered his sword and turned to his awaiting troops. "Take whatever's of value!" he ordered.

The orcs sprang to action. They fanned into the room and began smashing display cases. Some tore orcan arms and armour from the walls. Four unpinned the massive map tapestry from the wall and began rolling it on the floor. Two more began wrenching open the doors of the long row of storage cabinets. Most of the cabinets were locked and needed to be pried from their hinges. Once opened, the orcs spilled any contents onto the floor and kicked through them in search of items of value. From within the last cabinet, Naomi could see the progress that would inevitably lead to their own place of concealment. Her heart raced. Jack, petrified with fear, pressed close to her chest, eyes clenched shut. Naomi, mechanically, stroked his back. Death, she hoped, would be quick.

"Yes?" said the General in orcish into his phone. "Ahh!" he roared, yanking it from his ear. Guttural yelling issued from the earpiece. Bragad'oc held it from a safe distance and shouted back. "You don't have to shout into it Krag! Just speak normally." There was the sound of keys being pressed. The orc commander snarled in frustration, "Idiot, I showed you how to use it! Just put the end to your ear." After a moment, he added with strained patience. "The *other* end."

"They're going to find us?" Jack whispered, opening his eyes.

His sister considered lying. There was a loud '*Crack!*' as a cabinet door, feet away, was torn from its hinges. "Yes."

"What do we do?"

"We run for it."

"Will we make it?"

"Probably not. But run like Hell anyway. Don't look back."

In the bar of light from the cabinet handle-slit, Jack nodded.

The orc general was now on the opposite side of the room, engaged in a now manageable phone conversation with his lieutenant. The once pristine museum was a wreck of shattered glass, splintered wood furnishing, and strewn artifacts. Several orc soldiers tried on helmets, or tested pillaged weapons. The cabinet door next to Naomi and Jack's was yanked open. The two orcs systematically spilled its contents of papers and bindings. Seeing nothing of interest, they reached for the next cabinet. Thick, clawed fingers reached into the handle-slit, roughly brushing Jack's cheek. He stifled a cry. The fingers pulled. The locked door held. Knowing what came next, Naomi pushed Jack's face hard to the side. "Sorry," she whispered. An orc sword-tip jutted into the hole. The blade tilted as the orc warrior prepared to pry. Polished cabinet wood splintered.

"Enough! We go!" shouted Bragad'oc. "Now!"

Naomi and Jack stared with astonishment as the sword tip vanished back through the handle-hole. The soldier could have opened the door with a moment's more effort, but his obedience was absolute.

"Take him—*alive!*" General Bragad'oc barked as he headed for the exit. Two of his soldiers briskly grabbed the still-discombobulated billionaire. The other soldiers snatched what items they wanted, dropped the rest, and followed their already-departed leader.

Seven seconds later, the room was deserted.

In disbelief, Naomi lifted the inside lock latch of the cabinet door. Brother and sister spilled out onto the cold, hard floor.

The two children picked themselves up. Jack immediately clung onto his sister's waist. Naomi stared at the entranceway through which the orcs had departed. She was astonished at their good fortune, but wary the monsters might return. The museum itself was a mess of smashed and plundered display cases and cabinets. Antoine's corpse lay where it fell.

"Look!" said Jack, tugging on his sister's shirt.

Naomi turned, following his gaze to the mysterious locked door in the corner. The orcs had been hard at work trying to open it. The chains and padlocks were gone. The steel of the door itself had been badly dented. It was partially torn from its hinges. As with their own place of concealment, it had been dutifully abandoned mid-effort when the order came, despite being very nearly breached. A single bent hinge held it in place. Part of the door had been pulled from the frame and, from the gap between, the children could clearly see a pulsing yellow glow.

15

"Discipline is the infantry's best weapon."
– Soldier's proverb.

The air in the Arrival's Floor stank of orc sweat. The large chamber was packed with green-skinned soldiers from wall to wall. Since the initial assault, more and more waves of warriors had arrived on the dais. The last contingent were still trying to find room to clear it, forcing the already crammed orcs below to press still further back. There was one more unit to arrive, then that would be it. This had been the plan, to maximize the landing force before venturing outside of Griff Plaza. As a result, the ornery goblin-folk were pressed skin to skin. They grumbled, grunted, cursed, and belched. It was hot, musky, and uncomfortable. The orc soldiers were used to close quarters in the Caves of Korrum, and the Barracks of Dis Hüme, but nothing like this. Turning around meant negotiating elbows and arms with your neighbours, and orcs weren't known for peaceful negotiations. High on a stack of crates, Kragg, the Lieutenant Commander, or *Ilk Brow* in orcish, scowled. Despite his position of relative comfort, he too was sweating from the stifling quarters and running short on patience. The last crew had landed thirty minutes ago, what was taking so long? All at once, a shoving match broke out right below him. One orc, tired of feeling his neighbours breath on his neck, had pushed him away. This had driven the other orc into his opposite neighbour, who pushed back. A violent tussle erupted between two sides. Kragg swiftly drove his pole axe between them. He then pointed to the most aggressive of the soldiers, an orc with arm tattoos and long, braided black hair. "You! Stop it or you'll be wearing your intestines for boot-straps!" he growled in orcish. "There'll be plenty of humans to kill, soon enough."

Knowing the evisceration threat was real, the orc quickly bowed his head in supplication. "Urosh," said the orc.

Kragg glanced about at the remaining combatants. They too gazed earthward. "Better." Despite his projection of confidence, Kragg knew they must move out soon. Orcs could not be so constrained for long. In the corner, a troop of orcs rummaged through a pile of dead Griff mercenaries. The human corpses had been dragged there to make room for orc troops, and for future sustenance, if needed. Some of the bodies still wore flack jackets and assault rifles. One of the orcs lifted an HK 416 and began swinging it about like an axe. A second orc, with a top knot of fiery orange hair, tried to snatch it away, with a shout of "Fool! You know nothing—it's a stabbing weapon!" The two orcs began a tug of war over the gun, until the first orc's clawed finger slipped over the trigger and a burst of gunfire slew the second orc and two more behind him. "Who's the fool now?" he chuckled, gaping admiringly at the gun. A rush then ensued among the others to grab any remaining weapons. Dozens of the green-skinned marauders were now armed with guns. The first wave, which included 'The Igrock' elite guard, had most of them. Only two more managed to shoot themselves before figuring out where the bullets came out.

The last of the orcs found room on the floor, leaving the dais clear once again. On the dais, the grass was obliterated, stomped into mud by hundreds of hobnail boots. Up in the control room, the goblin sappers readied the gate once more. Bragad'oc's detailed descriptions and smuggled sketches had enabled them to build a crude, non-functioning replica of the controls to practice with in The Fourth World. The engineers had no comprehension of how the gate technology worked, but they knew how to use it. At an orcish command from Agdhal, the lead sapper, dongle-keys were turned. A second command was shouted out to the orcs below. Despite their irritation, the soldiers had enough sense of self-preservation to listen. They lowered black blindfolds over their eyes and waited. Another starburst of light flooded the chamber. Grass and mud vanished. Once more, the smooth surface of the Arrivals Floor dais was visible. The orcs remained still, with blindfolds in place. They knew what to do. One orc in the first wave had forgotten and was now blind. He was promptly executed for both failure to obey orders, and for being a burden. Three minutes passed. This afforded time for the orcs in The Fourth World to enter the circle. Failure to do so completely might mean the loss of a limb or worse. One orc had arrived bisected from head to toe. Dongle-keys turned again. The automated human countdown voice spoke calmly as if it were just another workday at Griff Corporation. "2... 1... 0... Juncture *initiated*." Light flashed—dazzling the soldiers even through the three layers of sack cloth.

A new contingent of orcs stood on the again-muddy dais top. They yanked off their blindfolds and gazed about in wonder at the packed chamber, as others had before them. They had all been trained, but mere grunts could not be fully prepared for world-leaping. No one could. Unlike the previous waves, there was nowhere for them to go.

The door to the chamber swung open, somehow pushing back the throng. General Bragad'oc stood framed, red cloak settling. He nodded approvingly at the gathered troops. Griff stood sullen beside him, with funereal eyes. The bedraggled executive was held by an orc at each arm, although he showed no inclination to flee.

Kragg raised his fist in salute and shouted above the din. "We're running out of room! They can't keep pushing more through unless we can send more up the tower."

"No time," the General shouted back. "The guards upstairs have killed human police. More will come to look for them. We will act now, while surprise is ours."

The orc troops let out a *roar* and began banging their weapons in approval. General Bragad'oc raised a palm to signal for silence. Despite their enthusiasm and close quarters, the brutish warriors quickly complied. Their commander gazed about the chamber, using the long pause to marshal their attention. Only when near total silence reigned did he nod his approval. He then spoke in clear, punctuated orcish. "Brethren," he began. "Once we faced extermination on our world. The Elves, the Dwarves and, worst of all, our human cousins, drove our great race to the edge of extinction. Then one human, the Wizard Griff..." The General sneered at Roland Griff, who paid no notice. A murmur of growls filled the chamber—halted by Bragad'oc's raised hand. "...who came to us with his magic talismans—the *technologeze*.

He gave us the tools to defeat our enemies, though he knew not what he did. And now?" The general snorted with amusement, "Now, he gives us a whole new world to conquer. Let us show our appreciation for his gift." At this, General Bragad'oc lifted his arms in triumph. The orc troops roared their approval, and once more banged arms and armour. Above the din, the general shouted. "Prepare then. Prepare for the coming of our lady of darkness, *Ul Du-eth,* with a fitting festival of blood and carnage. Go ye forth and lay all to waste!" The shouts and roars grew louder. Gunfire sprayed the ceiling, showering concrete dust. The General stepped aside. A flood of orc soldiers poured through the chamber doors and down the hall towards the main stairs, bellowing with bloodlust and battlecries.

16

"The snake looks foolish when he tries to stand."
– Elvin proverb

Normally, Alphonzo's hot dog and gyro cart were parked in his usual spot every day by 10 AM, in time for the earliest of the lunchtime crowd. Today, Alphonzo had arrived late owing to a dentist appointment he could no longer put off. He'd arrived at 11:00, with a novocaine-frozen jaw that felt more like a hunk of raw meat than part of his own body. Still, he was here. So where was everyone else? It's not like the street was empty. There had been customers, but none, not a single one, from Griff Plaza. The tall black tower was what made this location so desirable. Every day he could count on a steady stream of workers, too busy for anything other than a quick bite. Alphonzo wondered if it had something to do with the police cruiser that had arrived shortly after he had. It was parked curb-side with no sign of the officers. Still, despite the strange lack of people leaving the tower, there were some customers from the neighbouring buildings. "Here you are, sir," said Alphonzo, handing a foot long beef dog over the cart. "Condiments right there."

"Thanks," said the customer. He was a tall man, wearing glasses, a chocolate tie, and full length wool coat.

"That'll be $3.50."

"Oh, I seem to have forgotten my wallet," said the man, feigning to search his pockets.

Alphonzo grimaced. Handing over the food before payment was a rookie mistake. His mind was not on his work. He could not afford to lose money, not with a two thousand dollar dentist bill to pay. "Then you must give it back, sir."

The man took a bite, then managed a smirk even while chewing. "You fink someone wanzit mow?" he mumbled with his mouthful.

This made Alphonzo's blood boil. "If you don't pay, you must give it..." Alphonzo stared in surprise at the top of the Griff Plaza steps. Over a hundred green-skinned monsters had appeared there. They carried battle axes, spears, pole arms, and war hammers. The hot dog vendor dropped his tongs and fled across the street.

Turning to leave, the man did not see Alphonzo run. He wiped mustard from his lips and gloated. "Yeah? You gonna make me? You an' what..." He halted at the sight of the orc battalion assembled on the steps above. "...army?" The man's brain tried to comprehend the strange assembly and reconcile it with all known reality. It could not. The orcs roared as one, banged shields, and rolled like an avalanche towards him.

Moments later, with the hot dog customer's head on a pike, the front line of orcs rushed along 37th Street. Humans ran shrieking from the advancing army. Some fell with arrows in their backs, while others were cut-down where they stood. Drivers tried to cower in their cars, locking the doors and calling 911. Windshields were smashed, and occupants were dragged out by clawed hands. Parked cars burned. A entire office building was set ablaze with torches. A city bus rocked and swayed from the butchery taking place inside. Atop an overturned mail truck, Kragg waved a battle standard of a cracked white skull on a black field and bellowed his approval. "Kill them! Kill them all!"

Three blocks away, in the Javits convention centre, 'Sci-Fi and Fantasy Con 6' was underway. The floor was filled with booths from movie studios, comic book publishers, book publishers, video game producers, and companies that were some or all of these things at once. Under colourful banners and between the booths, rivers of visitors flowed. Here and there, at the edges, were eddies of conversation. Many of the attendees wore costumes of their favourites characters. All wore lanyards and carried plastic bags stuffed with swag—comic books, t-shirts, and cheap plastic trinkets to be tossed into drawers later. In the back of the massive hall was Stage #12. There, a cosplay contest was underway, sponsored by Gin & Tonic Press. Everyone on stage was in some sort of costume, ranging from *Hulk* villain 'The Abomination', to 'Fluttershy' from *My Little Pony*, to every regeneration of Doctor Who, to Charlie Chaplin, to 'Brisco County Jr' from the obscure 90s science-fiction TV series of the same name. Most of the audience were in costume as well. Supporters shouted cheers as each of the finalists were announced. The two judges stood to one side. Actor, Tom Jacobs, who had played character parts on several cult shows from the 60s, was the M.C. He flashed a smile and brushed back his thinning shoeblack hair as he addressed the crowd. "Ladies and gentleman, wizards and wookies, these are your finalists. The judges will make a last pass, before declaring our new 'Best Costume' prize winners!

The judges, an editor and a director, began to solemnly walk down the long line of elaborate characters. They paused before each, occasionally stopping to peer at some minute detail. The excited contestants posed or shouted catchphrases on queue. Further down the line, the backing blue curtain parted. A lone figure stepped out onto the stage. It was an orc, who had somehow gotten ahead of the advancing forces and entered through an open backstage door. Dazzled by the bright stage lights and surprised by the massive crowd and strange costumes, the green skinned warrior simply stood and gawked. He held his battle axe loosely at his side, where it dripped red spots on the carpet. The orc was so stunned that he only looked back when the judges reached him and began assessing his 'costume'. "Excellent make-up," said the publisher, tugging on the monster's long black forearm fur. "Feels almost real."

"Yes, but I'm not sure if he's LoTR orc or WC orc," said the other judge. "Not really canon either way."

"Mmm, way too scrawny to be *Warcraft*," said the first. The publisher peered into the orc's cirrhosis-yellow eyes. The orc scowled back, but still did nothing. "Definitely *Lord of the Rings*."

The judges passed on to the next contestant who was, by amazing coincidence, a human dressed as an orc. "Make-up's not as good," said the publisher, noting a trace of pink below the contestant's eyes.

"Yes," the director agreed, "but the emblem is exactly right." He pointed to the insignia on the painted paper maché shield.

The orc, baffled by this treatment, glared about at the audience and growled. Furthering his confusion, the crowd were delighted by his snarls and menacing looks. Several lifted phones to photograph or livestream him. The judges conferred a moment, then turned to address the crowd. "Do we have a winner?" asked the first judge.

"We do!" said the second judge. At this, he stepped forward and pinned a 'First Prize' ribbon on the chest of the man dressed as an orc. The crowd cheered. The judge raised the winner's arm high in triumph. The excited contestant yelled out a battle cry in an 'orc' language he'd spent six months learning.

The real orc recognized the celebration of victory. He decided that, somehow, he had been insulted. With an animal roar, he swung his axe around and lopped the fake orc's head from his shoulders. A gout of blood splattered the first several rows of onlookers. The decapitated head rolled off stage and landed at the feet of those in front, where it looked up in surprise. The crowd gasped. Some laughed and cheered, assuming it to be a staged stunt. The horrified publisher judge knew it was not. For a stunned moment, he held the dead contestant by his arm. He then let go, and the headless corpse collapsed to the floor. The orc then swung again, disembowelling the judge. All at once, the audience realized this was no performance. People shrieked and ran. Six more orcs, drawn by the screams, burst through the curtains. Leaping from the stage, they began hacking, and clubbing at attendees. Some attempted to defend themselves with plastic weapons and Star Fleet phasers that didn't fire. More orcs rushed from emergency exit doors and joined in the steady slaughter of the panicked crowd. A six-foot tall, obese Papa Smurf, was skewered on a pike and heaved from the upper level balcony. The orcs chanted, *"Ra-ka-sha! Ra-ka-sha!"*

137

17

"A man sees in the world what he carries in his heart."
– Goethe ('Faust')

The steel door shook under the impact of an orc hammer blow. *Bang! Clang! Bang!* Marc and Diane pushed Roland Griff's heavy glass desk against the door to buttress it. Sam collapsed in Griff's chair, gritting his teeth in pain. Tania knelt beside him, tying a makeshift bandage with five-hundred-dollar neckties she'd found in a desk drawer. New York City sprawled around them behind panoramic walls of glass. It was a multi-million dollar view, and it represented freedom just a sixty story drop away. Inside, Roland Griff's minimal, but elegant office had become a spacious prison cell on death row. *Bang! Clang!* The pounding continued. The door shuddered, but held—for now.

"Again, we find ourselves just one doorway apart from an orc horde," said Marc, as they nudged the desk tightly into place. "This is becoming a habit!" He noticed again the arrangement of shields on the wall. Their pedigree was no longer mysterious. It was horrifying.

"And again, it's just a matter of time before they break through," said Tania. "Whatever paranoia drove Griff to install steel security doors throughout the building like this, still only postpones the inevitable."

"Only this time—," Sam winced, and paused for breath. "This time, there are more of them and fewer of us."

"As long as they don't find Naomi and Jack, I don't care," said Diane.

"Speak for yourself, sister," said Tania. "I mean, I hope your kids survive too, but I have no intention of dying." Tania yanked the ends of a necktie tourniquet. Sam winced again. "That hurt?" she asked.

"Kinda?"

"Sorry, I'm not really the nurse type."

Sam managed a wan smile. "You're doing okay."

Abruptly, Diane began to cry. Wiping hot tears from her cheeks, she turned away. Marc moved to comfort her, putting his arm around her. "We're going to die aren't we?" she said.

Marc glanced at the battered office door. *Bang! Clang! Bang!* "I—I don't know..." he stammered.

"If this is how it ends. Well... I need to tell you something." As she said this, she leaned in close and lowered her voice, so that Sam and Tania could not hear.

"Okay..."

Clang! Bang! Clang!

Diane exhaled, then began, "While you were away, I..." She

hesitated and averted her eyes. "I was so angry at you for leaving me alone for so long." Marc looked at her with sudden alarm. "I was so angry and... lonely."

Marc took his arm away. Despite everything, an acid feeling swept through his body. He stared into her eyes. "Diane, what did you do?"

"I..." Diane looked away, "...well, there was this guy. This guy from the gym. I'm sorry, but... well, you were away for so long."

Bang! Bang! Bang!

Marc stepped back.

"Marc, I... we..."

Bang! Bang!

Abruptly, the pounding stopped. There was silence in the office. All turned with held breath, waiting to see if the assault would resume. One minute... Two minutes...

"They've stopped," said Sam.

"That makes no sense," said Tania. "A trick maybe? To get us to come out?"

Sam frowned. He thought he heard the faint sound of commotion and gunfire from outside. The height of the tower and the thick window glass all but muted any sounds from the streets below. His eyes went to the TV mounted beside the door. He tapped a button on Griff's armrest. The set powered on. There was no need to change the channel. The words 'News Alert' flashed across the bottom of the screen. It was coverage of a *war zone* —a live feed from the streets of New York City just a blocks from Griff Plaza. A woman reporter wearing a flak jacket and helmet, shouted into a microphone. "...complete panic. Early reports suggest a street gang uprising. Some claim an alien invasion. Fox News is reporting that the assailants are secretly Antifa activists in disguise. Breitbart News are calling them 'illegal aliens'. Meanwhile, several US Senators have expressed outrage, citing 'highly-credible' 4Chan sources that the alleged monsters are, in fact, 'BLM protestors wearing green-face'. Others says it's all just some kind of internet hoax 'like 9/11'. This is no joke." Behind her, over-turned cars burned out of control. Panicked people ran, screaming. The reporter was knocked aside by the rushing mob. "Help us!" someone screamed.

Coverage cut back to the studio. News anchor Noel Peters couldn't conceal his shock. Beside him, a cellphone photo was shown. It was a blurred image that was baffling to anyone *not* inside Griff Tower. To Marc, Diane, Sam, and Tania, it was clearly a shot of a dozen orcs charging down a city street butchering bystanders as they went. Marc remembered hearing once how the human brain doesn't so much 'believe it they sees' as 'sees what it believes'. "Thank-you, Joan and stay safe!" said Noel with a curt nod. "Um, we too have received conflicting reports. We do know that dozens are dead, caused by assailants armed with what appears to be axes, swords, and spears. They are dressed in bizarre costumes and maybe connected with the Fantasy Convention being held at the nearby Javits Center. Police have descended on the area and are preparing to face down the perpetrators."

Tania walked to the glass wall of Griff's office and gazed down upon the streets below. She could clearly see the smoke and fires. Dozens of bodies littered the pavement. "Oh... my... God," she breathed. The sight of her city in ruin shook her. Somehow it now seemed both more real and unreal. For the first time, Tania choked up. The others joined her at the window.

Sam, struggling to his feet, put his hand on Tania's shoulder. "Well, I guess we know why they left. The bigger fight is down there."

"The police will stop it, or the army," said Diane.

"Of course they will," Marc agreed.

Tania's face was a mix of grief and anger. Tears ran down her cheeks. "It wasn't supposed to be like this," she said. "Griff told us there was no danger. He said it was 'another world'. He said, there was no chance of it effecting us in ours. Now look! There are people dying on the streets of New York. How could this happen?"

Diane embraced Tania. Both wept.

"Hey! Look at this!" said Sam, pointing back to the TV. He turned up the volume.

The coverage had cut back to video from the street. It was of a different location, where the NYPD had set up a roadblock. The anchor continued, "...where police are preparing for a showdown with the so-called 'monster mob'."

High above the city streets an ABC News helicopter swept between buildings, then angled lower for a closer view. Multiple twisted columns of smoke rose from burning cars and storefronts set ablaze. One entire office building was engulfed. Flames belched from its windows and a thick cloud of grey smoke hung across the sky. The fire was out of the reach of firefighters and would soon spread to neighbouring buildings. The reason was the army of orcs packed into the main thoroughfares and side streets. They bustled about, forming into clear battle formations facing the police blockade. NYPD cruisers and riot cars had assembled at the intersection. This, the chief had decided, was as far as these strange invaders would get. Officers crouched behind vehicles with shotguns out. Others wore riot-gear, with shields and canisters ready. Snipers appeared on neighbouring rooftops. A police helicopter hovered overhead, a scant hundred feet from the news copter. Reporter Tad Cummings half-shouted into his head piece to be heard above the roar of the rotors. "So like a western gunfight, police are preparing for an apparent showdown. Despite the large numbers of assailants, the police, armed with guns and tear-gas, should have little difficulty subduing them."

On the ground the police officers had set aside their astonishment at the strangeness of their foe. Official word was that they were gang members in make-up. It sure as hell doesn't look like make-up, thought Police Deputy Chief Anna Phelps, surveying the scene from the front seat of her police car. Still, it didn't matter who these green-skinned people were. They were criminals that needed to be arrested or stopped with lethal force. Their numbers were intimidating. Estimates stood at six thousand. The NYPD had over thirty-six thousand officers on the force, but hadn't had time to gather more than three thousand here so far. Their edge was in terms of weapons. The monsters held swords, shields, and spears. Their body armour looked like something from the dark ages: metal plates, scales, and leather bands. It made the scene even more surreal and mysterious. It also meant they had an 'out'. If the monsters did not surrender, she had ordered her men to open fire. The rules said 'no choke holds', they said nothing about assault rifles. It would be a blood bath. Afterwords, there would be inquiries. The bleeding hearts would question if it was necessary to massacre the green-skinned attackers armed only with blades. They would demand to see body-camera footage. But I won't see my people get killed to save these humans, animals, or whatever they are, Anna vowed. Whatever they were, she had to admit as she watched them marshal under the shouted commands of their leaders, they did seem to know what they were doing.

At the rear of the orc army, General Bragad'oc arrived. Two hundred more orc warriors trailed in his wake. These were the fresh arrivals from the gate at Griff Plaza. The general stepped onto the hood of an abandoned yellow taxi. A second step over the smashed windshield took him to the roof. Here, his crimson cloak settled about his shoulders as he inspected the assembled formations. The roadway made for a narrow line of columns. It was not ideal, given that numbers favoured them. Still, it was anticipated. One of his lieutenants, Agg-Dah, jogged towards him. The orc was wiry, and smaller than most, but a capable officer. Bragad'oc had picked all of his invasion field commanders personally. "All Orcs have been called to join the fight?" asked the General.

"Yes, sir!"

"And Krag?"

"He's ready, General."

General Bragad'oc nodded and strode boldly into the packed mass of orc soldiers. Despite their numbers, the soldiers moved quickly out of their supreme commander's way. Pressing back, a corridor opened so rapidly in front of the General that he was not required to slacken his pace. The ranks closed again in his wake. In minutes, the General had reached the front line. His dramatic advance had gained the attention of both the police and the news media. He raised both arms, palms forward towards the police blockade. Silence fell, save for the beat of overhead helicopter blades and the crackle of nearby fires. "Humans," he began in crisp English, "I know that you have hoped that if someday you met creatures from another world, they would say to you, *'We come in Peace'*..." He then paused, for what appeared to be dramatic effect. It had another purpose.

In the shadows of the sewer tunnels, Kragg crouched, listening. In his hand he clutched a modified rifle with bump-stock for full automated fire. Behind him, in the tunnel, were the Igrock—over two hundred elite orc soldiers. Each carried firearms taken from the dead hands of Griff security forces. Automatic weapons at the front, followed by pistols and rifles. Unlike the bulk of the orc forces, these soldiers had been thoroughly trained in modern armaments. The flanks of the first two lines of the orcs in the street above also had automatic weapons, concealed beneath heavy robes, or in shoulder sacks. "That's it. That's the cue," growled Kragg to the orc behind him. The message was rapidly relayed backwards through the tunnels.

On the street above, the police waited, cautious but confident they could easily crush these primitive creatures.

Finally, General Bragad'oc continued. "Let me assure you, humans..."

Twenty-feet behind the last row of police, a man-hole cover tipped open. It was then slowly pushed back by a pair of clawed fingers.

General Bragad'oc grinned malevolently and added, "...we come in war."

For a moment, nothing happened, as if the General's message was somehow unclear. Hearing the scrape of iron on asphalt, a lone officer in the last line turned toward the sound. His eyes went wide as he saw the line of thirty orcs with guns now standing behind them. A steady stream of orcs climbed from the open manhole cover in back to join them. Kragg roared, "Araq Dal!"

General Bragad'oc echoed the command from the front, "Araq Dal!"

At this both lines of orcs attacked. It was coordinated and rehearsed. In the rear, the first line of orcs dropped to their knees and opened fire, while the second line stood and shot over their heads. In the frontal assault, orcs drew their concealed arms and opened fire. Many leapt atop the roofs of nearby parked cars, dumpsters, and anything else available to gain height. Others appeared in windows of nearby office buildings where, having butchered the human occupants, they had been lying in wait. They now rained death from above upon the suddenly sandwiched police line. At the same time, a volley of crossbow bolts arced overhead, and landed amid the stunned officers. Many found gaps in riot gear armour. A police lieutenant screamed and fell from a van roof as an arrow pierced his eye. Brandishing axes and swords, the remaining orc infantry charged, barreling down the road at the panicked NYPD. Before they could close the distance, dozens of them fell from police fire. The orcs had known many would die from their tip-of-the-spear attack and were unfazed by it. *Death by battle is glory.* The humans, seeing the rush of enemy forces closing in, panicked utterly and broke ranks. Even veteran officers had no experience in this kind of brutal hand-to-hand combat. In the confusion, the front line of NYPD had not understood that the rear was also under attack. Both police lines attempted retreat. The result was madness and chaos. The orc onslaught rolled over both ends, slashing, hacking, stabbing, and hammering. Primal kill-or-be-killed instincts took over in a desperate adrenalin and blood fuelled melee where it became impossible to tell man from orc. Accustomed to armoured foes, the orc warriors found openings in kevlar vests, or simply crushed the bones inside. Red drenched asphalt and sprayed walls. Purple gore ran in rivulets into the cracks, gutters, and gurgled down storm drains. Battle cries and screams filled the air.

General Bragad'oc marched solemnly back through the orc lines. Even in the heat of battle, the soldiers parted to make way for him. He did not watch the fighting. He already knew the outcome. He had other matters to attend to. As he passed, two orcs armed with rocket launchers fired at the police helicopters above. One exploded and crashed into a nearby building, before falling in flames to the streets below. The second, its tail rotor blown off, spun out of control and disappeared over the roof tops of nearby buildings. An instant later, a massive fireball erupted. Buildings shook. Windows shattered. On the rooftops, orc commandos descended on surprised SWAT snipers—killing them and tossing their corpses to the street below. Ever so slightly, General Bragad'oc smiled.

18

"Take as you will be taken." – the Priestesses of Death

The private museum in Griff Tower was a mess. Overturned shelves and smashed display cases were the grand chamber's only occupants. Their ransacked contents lay strewn where the orcs had dropped them. The body of Bob Sutherland lay on its side, pushed over as an impediment to a closed cupboard which had proved to be empty. The bodies of the slain orcs likewise lay where they fell. Orcs had little interest in the dead, even their own. According to their faith, the Demon Orc Ulrogg devoured the souls of the dead. Great warrior orcs became his muscles and flesh, while weak, cowardly orcs became excrement. It was a true compliment to tell an orc soldier that someday he would be worthy of Ulrogg's arm. There was only one change since the orcs' departure. The door in the corner, still hanging from a single twisted hinge, had been pushed aside to make the gap below a little wider. "You see that?" said an old man's voice excitedly. "That means 'knowledge', so it reads 'Plunder only knowledge, for whatever the taking, the giver loses none.' Roughly translated, that is."

Behind the door was a spacious apartment. Inside were hardwood floors and wallpaper made of William Morris prints. The furnishings were likewise of the 'Arts & Crafts' movement, with comfortable armchairs and solid wood tables. This was a sitting room, complete with cheerful gas fire, wireless surround sound, and a mounted 4K TV. The bloody battle scenes from the streets below played on repeat on CNN. The sound was switched off. A large mahogany desk in the corner was piled high with papers and manuscripts of alien origin. Some were ancient, while others were far more recent. On a black board behind were scrawled strange letters and runes. Beneath these were words in English, *'The Eldow did settle there, and named the city Caros.'* Sitting on the edge of the desk, with an unfurled parchment in his hands, was Professor Giles Pinchent. For the past four years, this had served as his apartment. It had also served as his prison cell. The professor looked up from the paper and smiled at the two children seated opposite him on the sofa. "Of course, you understand, ancient elvish doesn't translate exactly."

"That was really written by elves?" asked Jack with amazement. Despite just having been nearly killed by orcs, the idea of elves being real was fantastic and wonderful to the boy. Naomi was still in shock, and wary that at any moment, the orcs might return. Being so young somehow meant that Jack was able to both accept these amazing things more easily, and get over the terror of them. *He doesn't understand,* thought Naomi. *He thinks the danger is over now.*

"Absolutely. Beautiful is it not? Beautifully spoken too. You see elvish is more of a composed language, rather than organically evolved like our own."

"Huh?"

The Cambridge professor was delighted to have someone genuinely interested in his studies for once, not simply looking for a way to exploit them—even if that someone was a seven-year-old boy. "Well, let's see... in English we say the words 'up' and 'down'. They're opposites, but you wouldn't know that from just the words. In Elvish, 'up' is *'eiro'* while 'down' is *'orie'*—the same word *backwards*. Makes sense right? It also makes the language very lyrical. Almost like singing." Professor Pinchent then began to musically chant strange foreign syllables.

"What're the words for 'in' and 'out'?" asked Jack.

"Ha! You make me feel like a teacher again, Jack! 'In' is *'kal'* so 'out' is—"

"*Lak!*" shouted Jack.

"Exactly! You're a natural linguist," said the professor. "And let me tell you, once I figured that out, it made translating these elvish texts a lot easier!"

"You've really been a prisoner here for five years?" said Naomi, gazing in wonder about the room. Despite the pleasant decor, she could see no windows or other exits.

Professor Pinchent, remembering himself and their situation, grew sombre. "Well, no, not exactly. Initially I was free to come and go. Roland Griff was my benefactor."

"What's a benefactor?" asked Jack.

"It was my work that enabled... well, all of this! I'm the one who discovered the way to open a gateway to The Fourth World. You see, many

150

years ago, I realized that all of these common stories about elves and dwarves, goblins and trolls, weren't pure fantasy. They were stories from another world that really existed."

"Like *Dragons of Yorru?*" asked Jack.

"I'm sorry?"

"It's a game he plays." Naomi explained. She'd already discovered that the grey-haired old man, with his crinkly eyes and kind smile, spoke to them as adults, not children. This was a delightful change from being spoken down to as they usually were. Except, that is, when he failed to explain things that they really didn't understand yet.

"Oh I see," said the Professor, pausing to remove and clean his reading half-glasses. "Well, the point is, once I stopped treating these stories as fiction, I found there were clues as to how to open a gateway to one of these other worlds."

"So why'd you give it to Griff?" asked Naomi as she strolled to a nearby bookshelf. There she began to read the spine of the thick tomes with half interest. *Language and Linguistics... The Origins of Words...*

"I didn't," said the Professor, replacing his spectacles. "I still don't know how he'd learned of my work. It was just theory then. Nothing published, and only a few promising, but inconclusive experiments. He offered to fund my research and acquire the very expensive artifacts and materials I needed to forge the Lodestone. That's the black sphere you see in the middle of the dais that makes translocation possible. He made me believe his motives were altruistic."

"Altru...?" asked Naomi.

"I thought he was being nice. Griff is a very smart man, with real vision. He was about the only person who ever recognized that my crazy ideas, weren't so crazy. Unfortunately, where I saw the potential for knowledge, he saw only the potential for profit. Once I'd opened the gateway for him, he quickly showed his true colours." The old man gazed about sadly, "As prison cells go, it's very comfortable. Still, I'm rather tired of it."

"Griff's a jerk!" said Naomi flatly.

"Yeah!" Jack agreed.

Professor Pinchent smiled. "I couldn't have said it better myself. You see, I..." The Professor paused, as he noticed Jack was no longer paying attention. The young boy was staring at the mantelpiece. There, a small black orb hung from a chain on a hook. Naomi saw it now as well. Despite its plain obsidian surface, there was something beguiling about it. The gleaming surface winked reflected candlelight. "You have a good eye, lad."

"Is that a marble?" asked Jack.

"He collects marbles," Naomi explained.

"Not quite." Professor Pinchent rose from his chair and lifted the orb by its chain. "Would you like it?"

"Yes, please," said Jack.

"Very well. It's yours, as a thank-you for rescuing me," said the Professor, lifting the chain over Jack's head. It hung neatly as a pendant, although on Jack's small frame it reached his navel. "Let's keep it safe, though, shall we?" With this, the old man lifted the small black stone and lowered it past Jack's collar. The orb, chain and all, disappeared from view under the boy's shirt. "Excellent."

"Now what?" asked Naomi.

"Now?" said the Professor, thoughtfully. "Now, I suppose it's time to end what I started."

Several minutes later, the two children and the old man cautiously descended the concrete steps in the tower stairwell. Emergency lighting cast the stark stairs in cold blue white luminescence. Peering between the railing bars, Jack could see the seemingly endless drop to the basement levels below. They moved slowly, in part, because of the Professor's age. "Arthritis in my knees, makes them creaky," he explained. Also for fear of encountering orcs at each landing. "One good thing that fink Griff did was to give me a decent hearing aid, and orcs aren't known for being stealthy."

"Jack," said Naomi.

"Yeah?"

"Jack!"

"What is it?" asked the young boy, stopping to look at his sister.

"You forgot this in the professor's room." Naomi tossed Jack his blanket. She had been carrying it, curious to see when he would realize his mistake. He had not.

Jack caught it and stared at it in wonder. How could he have forgotten it? "Thanks."

It took over thirty minutes to reach the bottom of the stairwell, with several rest stops along the way. "Thank God we're going down, not up," said the Professor. "I doubt I could have done it."

Professor Pinchent had explained that he could destroy the portal if only he could gain access to it.

"How?" asked Naomi.

"Simple enough," he explained, "Just overload the Lodestone and *Kablooey!*"

"Kablooey?" Jack responded.

"You prefer Ka-boom?"

Jack nodded and grinned. Naomi smiled as well. It was good to see her little brother happy.

They reached the doors leading into the Observation Lounge. These were the same ones they had fled through hours earlier. For whatever reason, the power here was still off, and the emergency lighting gave the corridor stark shadows and an aura of menace. There were no bodies or signs of conflict, save for a discoloured swath on the grey concrete floor. It looked as if something, or someone, had been dragged. The double doors to the lounge were ajar. That was good. A simple locked door could have stymied them. "Could you?" said the Professor.

Naomi nodded.

"Be careful," he added. "We don't know what's on the other side. Be prepared to run."

Naomi nodded again, grimly. She knew what she expected to find— dead bodies, lots of them. And that, she thought with a shudder, was the best-case scenario. She leaned close to the doors and paused, listening for signs of the movement. Any sound of orcs and they'd need to abandon Plan A. Plan B, they'd already agreed, was simply to escape by any means available. As Naomi strained her ears, Jack put his hand in Professor Pinchent's. The old teacher looked down in surprise, then smiled kindly and gave the boy's hand a reassuring squeeze. He and his late wife had never had children, but he enjoyed their curiosity and openness to ideas. Naomi heard nothing. She gently pushed the door open an inch and peered inside. She could see a narrow view of the lounge through the gap. Overturned tables and chairs. Broken glass. She pushed the door further open and stuck her head through, half expecting to have it chopped off. The dimly illuminated lounge was a mess with broken chairs, overturned tables, and shattered glass. There was strange graffiti on the walls, consisting of skulls, axes, and bizarre crude symbols. Most surprising was the lack of bodies. There were plenty of blood stains to evidence the carnage which had occurred, but all of the corpses had been removed. "Very weird," she said.

"What's weird?" asked the Professor.

"It's surprisingly clean. I mean, all the bodies are cleared away."

"It's not about being clean."

Naomi wasn't sure what that meant. She pushed open to the door to show them. She had been afraid of how seeing victims might affect Jack. She'd been afraid for herself, as well. Everything that had happened earlier, while traumatic, had happened so quickly that it seemed like a dream. The idea of finding butchered corpses lying about had filled her with dread. So it was with a sense of relief that Naomi entered the room. Jack and Professor Pinchent followed. Jack still held the professor's hand with one hand, and his blanket with the other. He was opening his mouth to speak, when a flashlight beam swung into view through the smashed windows overlooking the Arrivals Floor. All three dropped to the floor. "There's someone there!" Naomi hissed.

They listened and could hear now the sound of activity. This was followed by growls of conversation. "Orcs," the Professor confirmed. The three approached the window in a crouch, so as to remain unseen by those below. As they drew closer, they were forced to drop onto their hands and knees to remain out of sight. Naomi was surprised to see the Professor crawling along beside her. "You okay?" she whispered.

"Not really."

They reached the rim of the broken window and peered over cautiously. The floor below was in near darkness owing to the emergency light fixtures having been shot to pieces during the battle. It was also empty relative to the throngs that had packed it earlier—but not entirely so. A few figures were visible on the dais. These were illuminated by four orc sentries holding military-style flashlights in stark contours of light and shadow. A dozen more orcs soldiers stood by as guards. Four small goblin engineers worked at the console, making adjustments. Presiding over it all was General Bragad'oc. He watched with arms crossed, crimson cloak draped over shoulders, grimacing with impatience. Roland Griff stood a few feet away. Even from here, the rueful expression on the billionaire's downcast face was apparent.

"Amazing really," whispered Professor Pinchent.

"What?" asked Jack.

"Well, these primitive creatures don't know how a light bulb works, but somehow Bragad'oc taught them to work an inter-dimensional gate, based solely on his descriptions of it, I assume. You have to admire the ingenuity of it."

"Admire them?" said Naomi. "They slaughtered dozens of people here!"

"Mmm, yes, well there is that."

"They invaded our world and plan to conquer us!"

Professor Pinchent looked thoughtful for a moment, studying the orc General from afar. "That's what's baffling," he admitted. "I'm not sure what they're planning to do. Bragad'oc is smart. Smart enough to know that a few thousand Orcs will be no match against the U.S. Army once they arrive."

"So what—"

"Oops! Cover your eyes," said Professor Pinchent, raising his hand to his face as he spoke. "They're opening the gate!"

Naomi and Jack shut their eyes tightly and covered them with their hands. On the floor below, the orcs had all pulled protective eyewear into place. A brilliant flash of white light filled the chamber, flooding every nook with blinding illumination. Even with their eyes covered, the trio were dazzled by the light that shone through. Blinking, they gazed down on the floor below, to see what had occurred.

As each of them blinked away the spots in their eyes, the orcs on the floor below removed their own blindfolds and goggles. On the dais, stood four figures on horseback. Each was dressed in obsidian armour from head to toe. Their mounts likewise wore barding, black in every detail. Despite their faces being hidden within narrow-slitted helms, Naomi could tell they were not orcs. Orcs had a decided body type, hunched at the shoulder, with long, lanky arms. These figures were tall, and rode erect in their saddles. They commanded the room instantly with their presence. Each held a shield bearing a different insignia in red—a worm-ridden hand; a grasping claw; a dead tree; and a skull. The four riders radiated a palpable sense of ruination. "I dreaded this," said the Professor.

"What?" said Naomi. She was suddenly in the grip of near all encompassing terror.

"The Grūshank Knights."

"Groo-shank?"

"An order of dire lords, sworn to the forces of darkness. They are evil made flesh. They cannot die."

"They can't die?"

Professor Pinchent nodded, both fearful and fascinated. "They have been here before."

"What? When?" asked Naomi. She couldn't imagine such figures arriving unnoticed.

"A long, long time ago," said the Professor, still unable to the draw his eyes from the scene below. The riders rode down the dais steps in stately fashion. Orcs scurried aside to make room. Only General Bragad'oc remained where he was. As the first of the knights reached him, he crossed his arms across his breast plate and bowed his head in respect. Beside him, the great Roland Griff gawked. "In Biblical times." Professor Pinchent continued. "We called them '*The Four Horsemen of the Apocalypse*'."

"Per-fessor?" said Jack.

"Not now, Jack," said Naomi.

"Yes, *now*," said Jack firmly.

Sensing the alarm in her brother's voice, Naomi turned to see Jack facing the other way. Turning further, she now saw a contingent of a six orc warriors standing behind them with spears aimed. "Um, professor?" she said.

19

"Truth is real, but fleeting." – Elvin proverb

Professor Pinchent, Naomi, and Jack, knelt at spear point. They had been marched as prisoners from the Observation Lounge to the Arrivals Floor. General Bragad'oc had been surprised, but pleased to see them. "It is very convenient of you to drop in on us like this, Professor. I knew Roland had you hidden away somewhere." The orc commander smiled darkly. The Grūshank Knights had moved to the corner of the chamber, where they stood immobile, heads bowed as if in silent consultation. The space around them, Naomi noticed, seemed to ripple like air over dessert sand. The orcs scurried about, packing up equipment as if readying for departure. Six warriors gathered about the glistening black orb in the center of the dais. They clutched iron poles, ropes, and crowbars. A scrawny goblin sapper barked orders in orcish. Four of the orcs immediately began wedging their tools into the seams between the stone and the platform itself. The two other orcs stood ready with their ropes. On a shrill cry from the sapper, the warriors heaved and began to lever the orb loose. "Anyway, you're just in time." General Bragad'oc continued. "It seems we have need of your services." With a loud scrape of steel on cement, the shiny black sphere popped from its socket. The orcs with ropes immediately looped them under it to form a cradle. All six then lifted the heavy magical rock from its nest onto an awaiting tarpaulin that had been laid alongside. "Oo-gaug," cried the sapper to General Bragad'oc.

"Arak." The orc general raised his hand in acknowledgment. The soldiers nodded, then carefully wrapped and tied their treasure. "You see, Professor," said General Bragad'oc, "I thought I only needed the lodestone to create a new gateway. Griff informs me it's more complicated than that."

Professor Pinchent's eyes lit with fury. He glared at the unrepentant billionaire. "You shouldn't tell him anything, you fool!"

"Don't you dare speak to me like that, old man," spat Griff.

Bragad'oc chuckled. "Griff has always known to ally himself with the winning side. It just took a while for him to realize he was no longer on it. Now he has, and has made appropriate adjustments. In any event, it seems that if we are to open a gateway in a new location, there is required some sort of ridiculous ceremony where some Elvish gibberish must be said." Professor Pinchent had continued to stare down his former captor. Griff, as if pleased to have someone he could feel superior to again, sneered back. The orc commander roughly grabbed the old man's neck in his gauntlet. "And, it seems you're the only one on this entire ape-besotted plane that knows how to do it!"

Professor Pinchent's frail form seemed hopelessly vulnerable in the orc's armoured clutches. Still, he managed a look of proud defiance. "Then you're in a bit of a pickle, because I won't help you!"

"Really?" said the general. With a fluid motion, he drew a long dagger from his belt and pressed the point below the Professor's ear.

"Never."

"Then it seems we have no further use for you." Where the dagger's tip met flesh, a drop of bright red blood appeared.

"Fine," said the old man adamantly.

Bragad'oc's olive green face showed a look of surprise. "I didn't expect bravery from a wizard."

"I'm not a wizard. Besides, as you like to point out, I'm an old man. My race is almost run."

"Brave for yourself, perhaps. But what about..." The orc general released the Professor's chin. He then reached over and grabbed Naomi by the hair. She screamed as he yanked her to her feet. Jack screamed too, in new found terror. Bragad'oc laid the flat of the dagger's blade against the trembling girl's throat. He yanked her head back, exposing her windpipe. One twist would cause the well-sharpened edge to bite through. "...the little ones?"

"Professor!" Naomi shrieked. Tears streamed from her eyes.

Jack tried to run to her. He was cuffed to the floor by a nearby orc soldier. The boy sobbed uncontrollably.

Professor Pinchent stared in shock. Despite his scholarly knowledge of all the sordid dealings and barbarism of the orcs, none of it had prepared him for the brutal reality of it. He knew what logic dictated. He should sacrifice all of them for the greater good. Logic, however, was a poor counterpoint to the fear-filled eyes of a pleading child. "Okay, I'll do it."

"Excellent," said General Bragad'oc. He threw Naomi to the concrete floor like refuse.

"But why?" cried the Professor. "Why close this gateway only to open it somewhere else?"

The General barked in orcish to a nearby sergeant, *"Bind them. They'll be coming with us."*

The four Grūshank Knights, who had remained motionless on their mounts throughout this entire exchange, now turned and cantered towards the loading dock exit. Despite his terror, Jack could not help but gawk at the tendrils of red flame wafting from the horses' nostrils as they rode.

20

"The downtrodden form the steps of power."
– Nirish Gamba

Evening fell. The darkness served the orc invaders who were naturally nocturnal. Their eyes caught the light, reflecting back as pairs of blinking orange dots in the dark—predatory and full of cunning. Along with most of Lower Manhattan, Times Square had been evacuated of civilians. As many as possible had been cleared by truck, helicopter, or ferry to the New Jersey side. The rest were told to 'shelter in place'. Despite these orders, there continued to be *incidents*. A group of drunken day traders, out for a 'liquid lunch', had found themselves trapped in a bar for two hours. They had decided to 'make a break for it', only to turn a corner and rush headlong into an orc battalion. Their well-quaffed heads now decorated the lampposts on 39th Street. A separate 'posse' of New Jersey tough guys had decided to take on a patrol of "green-skinned freaks." After surprising the orcs with baseball bats, they discovered their weapons were no match for actual battle axes and morning stars. A CNN news-copter caught the ensuing slaughter on live TV. For the most part, the streets were now deserted save for the orc units, patrols, and 'plunder and kill' squads working their way door-to-door. Behind human lines, Times Square was free of civilians, but abuzz with activity. The US Army had designated the famous intersection as both basecamp and battle-line. Troop trucks, humvees, scout cars and tanks, had replace the usual evening traffic. The normally neon-lit avenues were day-bright as a result of mobile units with floodlights on poles. Soldiers rushed about, gathering into units and unloading equipment. The earlier rout of the NYPD meant the orcs were to be taken seriously, whatever their weapons. Too many innocent people were dead in the streets. Numerous fires burned unchecked, including a skyscraper on Park Avenue. The monsters needed to be stopped, and stopped quickly.

"The main force is here. It looks as if they're waiting for us," said Major Kasai, tapping a glass screen. He was inside a mobile command unit, facing a row of video monitors. Some displayed status and overhead maps. Most displayed live video feeds of the enemy positions. Despite what happened that afternoon, it was hard to accept the opponent they faced as real. Green monsters with swords? There was no explanation for it, but it was what it was. It wasn't Major Kasai's job to explain the enemy, only to destroy it. He furrowed his brow, studying the orc barricades. The enemy had overturned cars, buses. They had piled up mailboxes, hotdog stands, and anything else they could find. Some kept watch, with guns, crossbows, and spears. Others organized in a primitive counter-part to the US Army's own preparations. The orc front was just a few blocks from their starting point at

Griff Plaza, and few more blocks south of the Times Square. Intelligence had estimated six thousand of the alien marauders in all. Two thirds were at this one location, Major Kasai noted. Recently, they had been joined by four figures on horseback. None of the other invaders used horses at all. Army sharpshooters on roofs had noted that these figures seemed different from the rest, beyond just their mounts or armour. Major Kasai studied the feed, trying to discern what it meant.

"Who are the cowboys in black hats?" said General Heimlich. Major Kasai jumped in his seat. He hated when the General snuck up on him like that. General Heimlich spoke with a Southern accent that always made him sound relaxed. The Major knew he was anything but.

"No idea. They weren't there before," said Major Kasai.

"I think they're humans," offered Sergeant Dale flatly over the radio. He was watching 'live', through a sniper scope from a nearby rooftop. "Or sumpem like 'em—er, us."

"Pfft, they're all humans. Or, maybe Mexicans." General Heimlich sucked on his teeth. It was a trick he used to draw moisture into the plug of chewing tobacco he kept tucked in one cheek. "Well, if they're waiting for us. It would be rude to disappoint them. Let's show 'em what American hospitality is like!"

Major Kasai turned to look at his superior officer with concern. The General wore a big white moustache that made him look like a Kentucky colonel. Major Kasai looked doubtful. "With all due respect, General, the last time that was tried..."

General Heimlich turned and spat expertly at a trash can several yards away. Tobacco-stained yellow saliva struck and ran down the inside of the can. The General turned and gazed contemptuously at his operations

165

officer. "That was the NYPD, Major. We're the U.S.-God-Damn-Army. You think that's the same thing?"

"Yes sir—I mean, *no* sir."

"Good." General Heimlich turned back to study the monitors before them. "Besides, if we wait, they'll only spread further out into the city. That'll make them a harder target and cost more civilian lives. Nope, I think it's time these illegal immigrants met the United States cavalry. Prepare to roll out!"

"Yes, sir!"

Despite the General's customary bravado, Major Kasai still struggled with a nagging concern. As a veteran of the Iraq war, he knew far too well the dangers of urban fighting. There too, American troops had every advantage in terms of weapons and armour. Close quarters and ready concealment, however, were powerful levellers. Add in the high probability of civilian casualties—*American* civilian casualties, and the prospects for a serious snafu multiplied. The real question, of course, was how this bizarre army got here in the first place. They were hardly inconspicuous. They hadn't arrived by Greyhound bus, or the Montauk train to Penn Station. Someone would have noticed. The FBI and CIA knew nothing. It was unsettling to say the least. Techs bustled about the mobile command centre, monitoring chatter, and gathering status updates. The brightly lit interior of the narrow van office was crammed tight with computer and communications technology. In contrast, on screen, the green monsters were rolling a line of real-life, thirty-foot tall trebuchets down to their front-line on 6th Avenue. It should, by all rights, be a slaughter—twenty-first century vs. twelfth. Still, Major Kasai couldn't shake the nagging feeling there was something more going on. It was something to do with the four midnight-black figures on horseback trotting blithely down 45th Street towards the barricades.

21

"Love is a beautiful waste." – Ach Noor (poet)

"Looks like no one's home," said Sam.

The Arrivals Floor was now deserted. Marc, Diane, and Tania walked among the wreckage and debris. Somewhere came the sound of water drizzling from a pipe with a bullet hole leak. Sam sat on the driver's seat of an abandoned forklift, his hand resting on the freshly bandaged wound in his side. They'd replaced Griff's silk neckties with gauze and tape rifled from a First Aid Kit they'd found en route. The stench of burnt gasoline and hubris still hung in the air, causing the four to cough and cover their mouths. Intermixed, was the distinct metallic odour of blood and gore that stained every surface.

"They've stopped bringing orcs through," said Marc.

"Maybe all they had?" Tania suggested.

Marc hemmed thoughtfully. None of them knew how many orcs there were, so it was possible that was the case. "Or perhaps, all they need."

"Didn't there used to be some sort of ball thing there, in the middle of the platform?" said Sam, pointing.

"The lodestone," said Tania, noticing the vacant slot for the first time. "It was what made the gate work."

For a moment, all paused to consider the portent of the missing black orb. Marc's attention was drawn by something else in the corner of the chamber. He hoisted himself over a shell of scorched black metal that used to be a truck, to take a closer look.

"I guess the good thing is, we're probably safe for now," said Sam. "With that thing gone, there's nothing to interest the orcs here anymore. 'Course, there's still the problem of a lot more green meanies between us and safety."

"We could wait it out," said Tania. "Let the police or army or whoever take care of them."

Sam pulled his hand away from his bandage. This revealed that the fresh white linen was already stained bright red. "Not sure I have that luxury, sweetheart."

Tania had once decked a man for calling her that. Sam was too badly wounded to hit. She had also grown to like the acerbic diamond prospector. Despite, or perhaps because of, his big mouth. Her previous partner had been a woman, but she'd dated men before. Gender was not the first thing she considered in a relationship. "Okay," she found herself saying with uncustomary softness, "We'll figure it out."

"We can't wait around here either," Diane blurted. "We have two children to rescue!"

"Ho!" shouted Marc from the other side of the cavernous chamber. "I think I may have an idea to help with that." He was holding in one hand an orc breastplate and a helmet with hinged face guard in the other. At his feet were more pieces of discarded gear. These included brigandines, cuirasses, weapons, and more helmets. These had all belonged to orc foot soldiers slain in the initial invasion. Their surviving fellows had looted the best items and tossed the rest in a heap on the floor. Marc pulled the helmet over his head. It was snug, but fit. He then carefully closed the face plate like a little door and hooked it into place on the other side. The crude covering was poorly fashioned, but effectively concealed his human features. "Well? What do you think?"

"I think it's bloody bonkers. It's like something out of a *Laurel and Hardy* movie," said Sam. "But, we got nothin' else."

22

"Ideas are breaths." – Elvin saying.

Fours years earlier

"Is this it?" said Roland Griff, with a jab of his thumb and a smirk of ill-concealed amusement. He was wearing a grey Tommy Hilfiger parka and hiking boots instead of his customary suit. He was chewing gum. "This is what keeps her in?"

Frigott, the orc captain, nodded. He saw no humour in the situation. He scowled under his horned helmet. A low growl rumbled in his throat.

"They did tell us it was invisible," said Professor Pinchent, tamping down his pipe. "We've seen enough to believe it." While his employer might scoff, he felt nervous. It wasn't just the thought that their orc escort would happily slit their throats if their orders changed. This was a sacred place to them and, unlike every other sacred site he'd visited in his lifetime, its so-called deity was present and they were there to meet her. He looked once more up the amazing place they'd come to. It was a gate cut into the very mountain top. The entire mountain was unnatural in appearance. Its sheer cliffs of black stone rising abruptly out of the surrounding landscape made it seem more like mountain-sized rock dropped from Heaven, or thrust up from Hell. It had taken their expedition three days to scale, despite the well-cut pilgrim's path that wound around it and the pulley-drawn basket-lifts where needed. The gate itself, fifty-feet high at its apex, was decorated in the distinctive style of the orcs—capable but crude, without finesse or even the attempt at it. This was an art whose medium was anger. Each graffiti-like element was a collection of chisel-scars celebrating defiance against a universe that had birthed them and now disowned them. The Professor had learned some of that history already from found artifacts, as well as his conversations with orc officers. The present 'peace' between the orcs and the other races had been in place for just over sixty years. The war before it had lasted eight centuries. The truce, however, contained the seeds of further conflict. The orcs, near defeat and disastrous in the art of negotiation, had agreed to punishing, largely dictated terms. The elves had ignored their own philosopher prince, Asofos, who cautioned in his essay *Equos* (trans. *Armistice*), "Just because a deal is struck, doesn't make it fair. Enforcing the law as written in such circumstances is not the same as justice and provides an opening move for evil." He had actually been discussing marriage at the time, but the implications were the same. Discontent was rife. Skirmishes and local uprisings were common. Even as the threat of new war rose, the humans, elves, and dwarves had refused to renegotiate. The orc armies now marshalled in the name of their last 'living goddess'. They had ceased paying the crippling reparations required by the treaty but, it was argued, that 'water cannot be squeezed from sand'. The tribes were divided into separated ghettos and territories, so united resistance was 'impossible'. In an effort to appease them, the orcs had even been permitted access to their holy site and their goddess in her cell. The only stipulation was that they remain orderly and make no attempt to free her.

The assembled entourage gazed up at the yawning gateway before them. Faux blocks had been carved directly into the black basalt that formed the archway of the entrance. A pantheon of igneous orcan visages leered down from above. To the humans, they appeared as gargoyles. To the orcs, they appeared as gods. Wrathful gods and all dead but one, thought the Professor. In this world, the wars rage on many planes at once, each impacting the other. Or so says the lore. In truth, the Professor wasn't sure she was a god. Can true gods die? One thing was certain, she was no orc. Above the gate was an inscription in Elvish. This had been added a mere twelve years prior when she had first been entombed. Its lithe delicate strokes were at odds with the architecture around it. Its presence was a sacrilegious stain to the orcs, but one they could not remove. 'Here, the worst of you is made flesh.' Who, Professor Pinchent wondered, is 'you'?

"Are we going in?" said Antoine. Griff's henchman's hands rested on the AK-47 slung from one shoulder. This was not a random habit. Except when otherwise needed, his hands had been placed there steadily since they'd arrived. As always, his eyes were busy, darting from side-to-side for dangers without or within. He also wore a parka, albeit to the waist only. His bald head was covered with a black wool hat that could be pulled down to become a balaclava.

In addition to Griff, Pinchent, and Antoine, the human contingent included twelve heavily armed Griff security contractors. Dressed in fatigues, helmets, and flak jackets, the small force could easily able to take on even a small army of the medieval combatants. This was a good thing. The orc contingent numbered more than forty and no one, not even Griff, was foolish enough to trust them. The current arrangement with the orcs was tenuous at best. This pilgrimage was meant to change that. Measured latitudinally, their arrival point was not far from where they now stood, being less than a mile from the mountain's base. Altitude was the issue. The arduous ascent had exhausted them. The Professor in particular was ill-equipped for such a journey. He'd detested sleeping in tents as a boy, and old age hadn't made him more amenable. His benefactor had insisted, however, and truth be told Professor Pinchent wouldn't have missed it for the world. Griff had asked if they couldn't simply open the gate to here where they wanted to be. "No," the Professor had explained, "there's a certain parallelism between worlds it seems. Where a gate is opened in one world, is relative to where it will open in the other." Griff's basement location in New York was practical for many reasons, but in part because it opened in a gully in The Fourth World. This had saved them excavating the site. Upon first arrival, they had secured a sort of understanding with the orcs. That understanding had cost them three trunks of assorted trinkets and the deaths of eleven men. Griff, however, needed to secure more than promises of safe passage from the orcs—he needed them to work for him. He required their submission. For that, they needed the blessing of 'she who must be obeyed', as the professor liked to called her in his best brow-beaten British barrister voice. Since *she* could not come to them, they must go and pay homage. Professor Pinchent ascertained what he could from the very limited texts in Elvish and Dwarfish. There were no orc writings. Theirs was an oral culture.

So he interviewed them instead. "It seems that she is either a kind of witch or goddess, or 'pit fiend' depending upon who you ask. Not an orc, they all seem to be male-ish. How they reproduce, and in such numbers, is still a mystery to me. But she is their leader, nonetheless. She is last surviving of their leaders. It seems the wizards of elves and men, were unable to destroy her. They were able to imprison her instead, in her own domain. A sort house-arrest, as it were. Despite this, she still holds sway over the orcs and they will do as she bids. If you want to get anything of substance from them, you need to convince her." After a flurry of messages, they had received authorization from an Orc general they had yet to meet, but who had recently seized control of all of the orc forces.

Griff paced back and forth before the invisible barrier, eying it skeptically. "So, what happens if we step through?"

"Nothing," said the Professor. "Its magic works only on her. She is permitted visitors, but cannot leave. They can come and go as they wish. Few do. She has a tendency to kill any who disturb her unnecessarily." He'd explained this before, but now faced with the reality of the situation, Griff was actually listening. Beyond the entrance were the suggestions of a vast interior, although blotted out mostly in shadow. It was as if the whole mountain top had been hollowed out. The floor was of square marble tiles that went on until vanishing into darkness blacker than night. Marking every seventh grid point were great round pillars, ten feet in diameter, formed from stacked cut basalt discs. If nothing else, it was a temple to darkness and despair. Captain Frigott had led them to a thin line of inset gold that delineated the invisible barrier.

"Why can't they just dig it out? Or under it for that matter? They're not the brightest bulbs, maybe they just haven't thought of it."

"The gold is just a marker. The barrier, they say, is a ward-spell cast by a dozen eminent wizards over thirty days and nights. It is a sphere, eternal and unbreakable. If she were to dig straight down or somehow fly up, she would still be stopped. Again, it will do us no harm."

"Well then, we'll just have to chance it" Griff said bravely, standing straight and staring into the abysmal lair. "Antoine, step inside."

For an instant, the burly henchmen's face betrayed surprise. He then simply nodded, and stepped over the gold line. All held their breath, half expecting him to vanish or burst into flame.

Nothing happened.

"Is that it?" said Griff, chuckling. "There's nothing there! It's just a lot of mumbo-jumbo."

"I don't think so," said the Professor.

"I did feel something," said Antoine.

"You just think you did," scoffed Griff. "Because you expected to. Like the placebo effect or such."

"I did not imagine it," said Antoine. "It felt like... shifting sideways, without moving."

"I believe him," said the old man.

"One way to find out," said Griff. The billionaire strode confidently through. A look of delight crossed his face. "Whoa! Yes, you're right. A little like vertigo. Harmless though. Magnets, I expect. Coming professor?"

Professor Pinchent steeled himself briefly, then he too stepped over. "By Jove" he said, "that is a queer feeling. Not horrible."

Griff turned to face the others. "All right men, let's have the rest of you then."

The contractors started to walk forward. Captain Frigott raised his clawed hand. "No."

"What?"

"Igta," said the orc officer looking for the right word. He had been placed in charge precisely because he had picked up English so quickly. Still, there were many words he did not yet know.

"Orders," Professor Pinchent translated.

"Orders like Hell," roared Griff. "We had an agreement. I'm not going in with just the three of us and all these orcs."

"Igta sae val," said the Captain, "No orcs."

"He means, just us three. Only orc priests, I expect, can enter."

Griff's eyes narrowed with suspicion. "Why didn't you tell us this before?"

"Bara-ca ta daff."

"You didn't ask," translated the Professor. He then added, "I don't think this is up for debate."

Griff chewed on this briefly, unhappy but unwilling to turn back. "Fine," he said. "All right then, let's go find the bitch."

Captain Frigott frowned. "What is that word?"

"It means 'female'," the Professor assured him. He wasn't sure the Captain believe him, but saw that Griff had already begun striding off. Antoine trod briskly behind. "Back soon, I hope," said the Professor, as he too followed into the looming darkness.

Despite the size the gate, it was soon small behind them in the all encompassing interior of the mountain peak. It became a postage stamp of daylight, while they floated on the disc of light cast by Antoine's flashlight beam. Occasionally the beam would search out in the endless gloom, only to reveal more of the grid of black tiles and evenly spaced basalt columns. It was also cold. Frigid enough to turn their breath to faint plumes in the air. Professor Pinchent was glad for his tweed jacket and clutched it tightly. "I must say, I don't like this," he said. "I don't like this at all!"

"You never liked it," said the billionaire. "That's the problem with you academics. You're all well and good when it's just theories. You want nothing to do with reality."

"Is this reality?" said Antoine gruffly. It wasn't a philosophical question. The burly henchman didn't suffer those. So unreal were their surroundings, he genuinely wondered if it might be some kind of illusion or hallucination. Antoine raised his high-beam flashlight and shone it in a slow circle about them. It cast out a long cone of light that revealed many more yards of flagstone floor and ten-foot diameter columns, but nothing else.

Griff stepped boldly forward with a confidence Professor Pinchent could not understand. Antoine dutifully followed. The Professor hurried to keep up, as best as his aged frame could manage. "If we lose sight of the gate, we may never get back!"

Griff snapped his fingers. Antoine produced a small can of reflective spray paint from his jacket pocket. It had been brought expressly for this purpose. He sprayed a large neon green 'X' on the floor. He would continued to do so every fifty feet. Professor Pinchent worried what the orcs, or goddess herself for that matter, might think of them defacing her sanctum.

Abruptly, Griff paused. He surveyed the scene. He then turned ninety degrees and resumed walking. He gave no explanation. All directions led to darkness. It was as good as any. Somehow, it *felt* like forward. Antoine dutifully followed. The Professor looked reluctantly back at the X on the floor. He didn't want to stray too far. He also didn't want to be left alone in a place whose inky blackness could conceal anything. He didn't know for certain if a goddess dwelt here, but *something* did, something capable of building such a place.

For a while they walked—their footfalls swallowed by the vastness around them. Griff halted. He looked annoyed. "Well, this is getting us nowhere. You're sure she's home?"

Professor Pinchent adjusted his hearing aid. Griff's voice seemed small and distant. "She has to be," he nodded. "She's a prisoner."

"Mmm, yes. Hollowing out a mountain top is impressive, I'll admit. But it's also annoying. It's like JFK, you have to walk forever to get anywhere. Still, they did quite a job."

"Oh, I don't think they did, if you mean the orcs. They're not capable of it. The elves and dwarves, maybe, but why use it thus? No, I expect she did it herself."

"By herself? She built her own prison?"

The professor shrugged. "It wasn't built to be a prison."

Griff shrugged and continued his march into darkness. By now they had lost sight of the entrance altogether. The only sure way back was the trail of regularly spaced neon Xs on the floor.

The Professor suddenly knew this was a mistake. "Look, Roland, I think we should–"

At that moment, Antoine's flashlight fell upon a rectangular stone encasement set upon a low dais. The black obsidian was featureless, save for three strange runes engraved on the side. For a moment, the men simply stared at it in surprise.

"Is that a...?"

"Sarcophagus. Yes, I believe so," said Professor Pinchent. Despite the danger, his archaeological passions were aroused.

"Hers?" asked Griff.

"No... no, of course not." The Professor sounded out the strange writing as best he could. *"Hoo-ro-goth.* Or is that *go-et?"*

"All right then, where is she?" said Griff gazing about for something that wasn't more of the same. "Hello?" he shouted.

As if in answer to this, came a low guttural growl like that of a giant tiger roused from sleep. Eyes darted anxiously about. Antoine raised his gun. *Where? What?* The sound had seemed to come from every direction.

"We should leave," urged Professor Pinchent. *"Now."*

"Nonsense, I didn't come all this way to run off empty-handed."

"The books say she is 'evil itself'."

Griff scoffed. "And what exactly is 'evil' anyway?"

"Evil? Evil is... is..." Professor Pinchent gasped and pointed. *"That!"* Next to the sarcophagus, a sickly green light appeared. It was not a verdant green, but a toxic hue of decay and suffering. It infused a roiling cloud of darkness that swept across the dais and onto the tile. The flashings of that storm outlined the silhouette of a tall female figure in its midst. The figure's head was crowned with a fan of bent blades, and a cloak fell about its shoulders like folded wings. The figure's left hand rested on the stone coffin's lid, as if seeking comfort there. For a moment, none could speak. Even Antoine was struck with awe. The orcs they'd met on their initial forays into this world had been savage but primitive and simple to subdue. It had given them a sense of superiority. Now, all that was suddenly called into question. What was this?

"Gira Koth Nä?" came a shriek like rent steel. An icy wind followed, buffeting them and freezing flesh on bone.

"What is it saying?" shouted Griff over the cacophony.

"I don't know!" yelled Professor Pinchent, half-guessing the billionaire's words.

"How dare you enter my sanctum?" came a voice made of vapour and nails that issued both from the figure itself and from all about them at the same time. No, realized the Professor, it's inside our heads. She's realized we can't understand her words and is speaking to us directly in thought, which our brains are interpreting as words. The undulating cloud halted its forward motion. Its internal writhing continued. It seemed to be waiting, he thought, for their response. It's deciding whether or not we die.

Griff gathered himself and stood straight. "I apologize for the interruption. I'd thought your, uh, minions, had told you we were coming." He paused to allow the figure to speak. It said nothing. The smoke at its feet, however, seethed and muttered in a contrivance of voices. "I've come to offer a business proposition," he explained.

"A what...?"

Professor Pinchent noted, the being was clearly able to understand them now as well. He wondered if it had somehow acquired English or, more likely, was ignoring the spoken words and reading their minds. That was a concerning proposition on many levels. Never play cards with an opponent who can see your hand. Especially if, knowing Griff, you plan to cheat. Either way, it still struggled with words or concepts that were foreign to it.

"A... uh, a deal... " Griff explained, "a bargain... a mutually beneficial arrangement." With this, Griff drew an envelope from his inside coat pocket. Fearing they might not find *her*, he had drafted, with the professor's translation, a letter detailing the offer. "No need to commit now. Look it over, discuss it with your people, lawyers, monsters, whatever, and get back to me."

"Get back... to you?"

"Uh yes, exactly. I'll just leave it here," said Griff. He lowered to one knee and carefully laid the envelope on the floor. "Take your time."

At this, the light and cloud seethed. It then began to roll towards them again. At first, they stood locked in place, then all, including Griff, lost their nerve. The pulsing entity surged towards them with increasing speed. They turned and fled.

Griff took the lead in retreat, his long legs sprinting full-tilt across the stone tile. Professor Pinchent came next, carried on by adrenaline despite his advanced age and arthritic joints. Antoine came last, by choice, running backwards with gun raised to guard their retreat. In far less time than had taken to leave it, they bore down upon the neon-green 'X' that marked their turning point. There, they stopped. The entrance, no longer blocked by arrays of pillars, was again visible along the straight corridor that lay between. It was still some distance, but reassuring in its present. Heartened by this, the three men turned to face the nightmare that had been barreling down upon them.

Except it wasn't.

The figure and its entourage of darkness had stopped at the point where Griff had dropped the letter. Outlined by the virescent glow, it lifted the envelope in long slender fingers. It turned it over to examine it. In its silhouetted hands, the letter appeared as a tiny paper chit. It must be twenty feet tall, thought the Professor. Previously, distance and lack of reference had made it impossible to gauge its size. Or perhaps it has grown, he thought.

"We should keep going," Antoine said, "while she's distracted."

"Read it and let me know," shouted Griff. "The terms are negotiable!"

The black outline looked up. Green aurora eyes studied them. Below them, Professor Pinchent swore he could make out the outline of a smirk.

Antoine tugged firmly on Griff's arm. His employer, having regained some of his poise, was torn. "Better to let her stew on it, sir," Antoine urged.

"I agree," said the Professor, trying not to sound panicked.

"Hmm, yes, you're probably right," said Griff. "We don't want to seem desperate." Relenting, the lanky businessman turned and walked towards the exit. The opening was dazzlingly bright in the field of darkness. The effect was to make it seem otherworldly in itself. Antoine relaxed very slightly. He knew his employer wouldn't stop now, if only because of the optics. Better to make a bad decision than appear indecisive. Griff nodded as he walked. "You know, I think she'll agree. I have a feeling about these things. When a deal is close, I can smell it."

The old man stole a glance over his shoulder. There was no sign of their strange host. She had vanished completely, rejoining the stifling dark that seemed close in behind them. "You're fool to make a deal with that... that thing!"

Griff whirled on the old man, his face a mixture of fury and delight. "And you're a fool to challenge me, Gilles! Your doubts are getting to be annoying. You're just lucky I'm feeling good tonight or I might just have you locked away in a tower."

"Roland, please. You don't know what you're dealing with there. This isn't a tough guy on Wall Street, or some foreign business rival."

"Yes, yes, I know. She's not very nice. But there's tremendous power there and I, for one, intend to harness it."

The old man grabbed Griff's arm. "If you try, you may just find it's you who gets harnessed in the end. Evil, real evil, isn't a resource to be tapped. It multiplies. *It becomes.* Don't you see? You cannot use evil without being used by it. They are one and the same."

"I see that I'm wasting my time talking to you old man. Philosophy has no place in business." With that, the tycoon roughly pushed the old man aside, and strode into the daylight. The orc and human soldiers waited there, soft silhouettes against the blue sky. As they crossed the line, the human soldiers cheered and gathered about, delighted to see them return. Griff accepted them with open arms and a look of triumph. The orc captain and his soldiers betrayed looks of momentary surprise, but also acceptance. If the humans were spared by their goddess, who were they to argue. Professor Pinchent himself felt palpable relief to be the daylight once more. Somehow, the invisible barrier had felt more real than iron bars. He looked up once more at the Elvin script that defiled the archway above. He saw then that he had mistranslated it. Those sing-song phrases still confused him at times. It did not say '*Here, the worst of you is made flesh.*', but rather, '*Inside, you become that which you disdain.*'

"Old man," Griff shouted at the professor over the heads of his men. "I still don't believe there's any such thing as evil, but if there is, I promise you, we'll find a way to package, market, and sell it!"

23

"Freedom isn't always good. When blood is freed, people die!"
– King Archos I

The square of Griff Plaza was unusually crowded. Unusual because normally by this time in the evening most of the office workers would have gone home. More unusual, was the nature of tonight's occupants. The black-marble tiled public space was packed with orc warriors itching for a fight. Most stood or sat in their units, waiting for the call. Several milled about, making arrangements, scrounging for food, or sharpening their weapons. The low grumble of orc chatter was held in check by the occasional sharp glances and muttered reproaches of sergeants. Amid the gathering, stood four orc warriors who appeared to be lost. While the rest of the soldiers had removed their heavy helmets, these four wore theirs. They glanced about, as if nervously looking for someone, or something.

"I sure hope Orcs aren't like dogs," said Tania, under her breath. The heavy head gear concealed her human features and blond hair. It also made her sweat and blinkered her peripheral vision. This required her to turn her head from side-to-side to allay the feeling of being 'snuck up on'. Surely a liability in combat, she lamented.

"What do you mean?" asked Marc. His helmet had a bright blue symbol painted on each side. Tania wasn't sure what it meant in orcish. Right now, it simply meant 'Marc'.

"You know, when they meet other dogs?"

"You think they might sniff our butts?" said Sam. He chuckled, then immediately regretted it as his pain worsened. The South African stood behind her, leaning heavily on a spear he was using as a cane.

"No! I mean how dogs just know if you're friendly or not."

"Or scared?"

"We'll know soon enough," said Marc. "If they can sniff us out, it's game over."

Tania glanced back at Diane. She too was looking about, risking some orc seeing her human eyes through the slit in her visor. Tania resumed her own wary scanning. They were in the midst of the hornets' nest, hoping not to be stung. To one side, a warty-faced orc sat on a black marble planter contentedly picking his nose. To the other, three orcs gorged on a box of Cinnabon cinnamon rolls they'd pillaged from a nearby food court. The sticky pastries smeared their green cheeks and chins. When a fourth orc attempted to join in, he was offered the point of a dagger instead. The rejected soldier shrieked obscenities, but backed away.

"So far, so good," said Sam.

"There!" said Diane, pointing urgently.

"Shhh!" whispered Tania, grabbing Diane's arm. Despite her speedy intervention, the Cinnabon-eating orcs looked over with interest. One stood up. Licking his fingers with a black tongue, he approached to take a closer look at the four helmeted 'orcs'.

"Crap," muttered Sam.

At that moment, the previously rejected orc lunged forward and sucker-punched one of the others. He snatched the box of cinnamon rolls, turned, and ran off. All three of the robbed soldiers dashed off in pursuit, bellowing threats and waving weapons.

"That was close," said Sam, with a sigh of relief.

"Too close," said Tania, glaring at Diane reproachfully.

Marc looked where his wife had pointed. "It's the kids," he said. Diane nodded anxiously. On the street below the square, a small contingent of orcs surrounded Jack, Naomi, Roland Griff, and an old man Marc didn't recognize. "At least we know they're alive."

Diana nodded dumbly.

"That scum, Roland," snarled Tania. "Why haven't they killed him?"

"For the same reason they didn't kill the kids," said Sam. "They think they might have a use for them. They certainly kill everyone else."

"What about the old man?" said Marc. "Who's he, and why is he alive?"

"That is Professor Gilles Pinchent," said Tania grimly. "A British professor who first proposed the idea of The Fourth World in a thesis he wrote. More importantly, he also proposed how to get there. Most thought his ideas were crazy or a joke. Not Roland Griff. I'm not sure he ever had an original idea in his life, but he sure knew how to capitalize on the ideas of others."

"I wondered how he did it," said Sam.

Tania nodded ruefully. "He's a narcissistic amoral bastard, but smart as a whip. He understood that Pinchent was no quack, and offered to fund his work. When the Professor realized that his benefactor was planning to exploit the denizens of The Fourth World, he rebelled and threatened to go public. Griff locked him up and made him keep working for him."

"That's kidnapping!" said Marc, shocked.

Tania, shrugged. "One of Roland's lesser crimes. And I knew of it, so that makes me an accomplice."

Marc and Sam stared at her. Diane remained focused on her children. To her relief, she could see that they appeared to be unharmed. She also noted that Jack was holding the professor's hand. Good, she thought, at least someone is watching out for him. At that moment, a shirtless orc wedged a crowbar into a manhole and, with a quick push, levered the cover off. Three orc soldiers roughly grasped the children and Professor Pinchent and began shoving them towards the open hole. Marc, his hand still on her arm, could feel his wife's body tense. "What are they doing with them?" she asked frantically. She started forward. Marc tightened his grip, stopping her. Diane spun about, eyes burning. "We have to get them!"

"And do what?" said Marc. "Die together? Diane, look they're my kids too! Whatever's happened with us—or whatever will happen, we both want what's best for them."

Diane searched Marc's eyes. Her arm relaxed somewhat. She looked back at the prisoners. Jack was now being lowered into the sewer, passed from one set of orcs above, to awaiting green clawed hands below. They treated him like baggage, but did not harm him. Diane saw that Sam was right. The orcs had a use for the children and were sparing them. For now, anyway. "So what now?" she asked.

"Now?" Marc watched as Naomi was lowered next through the manhole. She was cursing at her captors, and tried to bite one on the hand. Marc tensed as the orc reacted by cuffing her on the head. Naomi stopped struggling. They rudely shoved her below. "Now, we follow them," said Marc. Such a course of action, he knew, would be incredibly dangerous. Every minute spent with the orcs meant the risk of detection. The close quarters of the sewers multiplied that risk and left no avenue for escape. Still, abandoning the children was not an option. Death was a very real possibility, but the alternative was not a life he wanted.

Tania caught Marc's eye. "I'm not sure Sam's injury would do too well in sewage water," she said. She put her hand on Sam's shoulder. Sam, to Marc's surprise, put his hand on Tania's.

Marc studied Sam a moment. The wounded diamond prospector leaned on his spear shaft like a drunk clinging to a lamp post. His wisecracks had grown more infrequent since coming up from the Griff Tower basement. Even through the narrow gaps in Sam's visor, Marc could see the pain on his face, and the perspiration on his dark skin. Sam smiled weakly when he saw Marc looking at him and winked. "No, not you guys," Marc agreed. "You just try and sneak through the orc lines." He then turned to look at Diane. "Diane and I will go. This is a family problem."

Diane looked into Marc's eyes, and nodded in agreement.

At that moment, a murmur of excitement rippled through the orc ranks like wind across tall grass. While the four humans could not understand what was said, the source of the excitement was obvious. The troops attention turned towards the east. Diane, Marc, Sam and Tania all turned as well. Being taller than most of the orcs, they were able to gaze over their heads. Still over a block away, but rolling up the street towards them, was a line of six US Cavalry Division Abrams tanks. The massive steel vehicles rumbled at thirty miles per hour, with guns raised, flattening debris, obstacles, and an abandoned gyro cart in their path. The orcs, who had never seen such mechanized might, leapt to their feet, swords, axes, and spears in hand. "Okay, we all better move," said Marc. "It looks like things are about to get explosive here!"

24

"The perfect ambush is more satisfying than breath."
– Orc proverb

General Heimlich marched briskly along the line of National Guard soldiers. He made a show of inspecting each, as if having a bent lapel was a an impediment to battle. All stood sternly at attention, staring ahead, giving little indication of whatever mixed brew of bewilderment and excitement they felt. None felt fear. Why would they? The assignment was baffling and bizarre, but all had confidence in their ability to meet and crush the strange backwards foe they faced. The General had left Major Kasai back in the mobile command unit, where his unnecessary fretting would do the least harm. The last thing soldiers needed before a battle was the sight of a nervous CO. Instead, Colonel Winston was accompanying him. The Colonel was a true leader and was always in agreement with whatever the General wanted. "You've got a stain on your shirt, son," said General Heimlich, tapping a young private on the chest.

The eighteen-year-old glanced down in surprise. "Um, I think that's a camo mark, sir."

"Are you questioning the General?" snapped Colonel Winston. The Colonel, like many redheads, flushed easily. His pale complexion turned pink as he shouted. The troops called him 'Tomato-Face' behind his back.

"No, sir, it's just, um... no sir."

"Go change your shirt, Private," ordered the General. "This fight's going to be on cable, satellite, and live-streamed around the world so we need to look sharp. We need to show the world that the US military knows how to dress for a fight."

The soldier ducked out of formation and ran back towards the supply area. A soldier from the next row stepped forward to close the gap. At the same time, a lieutenant jogged towards the two commanders. He was carrying a cardboard tray with a pair of Starbucks coffee cups. Colonel Winston plucked the cups from the tray and dismissed the junior officer. He peered at the names written on the containers in black sharpie and frowned. One was labeled 'Jerry', the other, 'Colin'. After a moment's confusion, he realized the first was supposed to say 'General', the latter 'Colonel'. He handed the first cup to his superior officer. General Heimlich took a sip and nodded thoughtfully. "That's one upside to fighting a war on the streets of New York City."

"What's that, sir?" asked the Colonel.

"Starbucks vanilla lattes."

"Yes, sir!"

"If our boys had these in 'Nam we'd have won that war."

"Yes, sir."

General Heimlich looked approvingly at the line of tanks that had rolled into position up the street. They awaited his signal. Likewise the rows of infantry, each with live ammunition, stood by. There would be no second debacle like what had occurred earlier with the NYPD. Nor would it be like that incident in Jersey a few years back. This was not the first time General Heimlich had faced down medieval style weaponry*. He wouldn't make the same mistakes again. There would be no pulled punches. No media-coddling. These aliens were clearly killers that needed to be stopped. Let the scientists and news pundits analyze it all later. Right now, they needed to take back the streets of New York. "Your men ready?"

"Yes, sir. Ready and awaiting the call, sir."

"Excellent. We'll start with a barrage of artillery, then we'll just roll right through them. That'll break up their ranks like watermelons at a hoedown. It should just be a mop-up operation from that point on." General Heimlich turned to face the troops once more. As he did, he paused to take another sip from his coffee drink and nodded approvingly. The commies didn't have anything as good as all-American coffee grown right here in the USA, he was certain of that. Damn Vietnamese probably didn't even know what coffee was. "Attention!" he shouted. The soldiers, who were already at attention, tried to snap even more so.

Colonel Winston, standing beside the general, cleared his throat pointedly. He leaned forward to catch the commander's eye. The General frowned at the interruption. Colonel Winston tapped his upper lip. He was trying to let the general know he had white latté foam on his moustache. General Heimlich, failing to understand the gesture, scowled and continued. "Men. Today we face a foe that is unlike any we have faced before. Make no mistake. These green-skinned freaks, whether they be men in make-up, or invaders from Mars, are the enemy. They have killed American citizens, and burned the buildings of New York to the ground. Do not hesitate to kill as needed. You are defending your country, our honour, and the very streets of America. The world is watching. *Do your duty.*"

The soldiers, in chorus, responded with a loud, enthusiastic, "Yes, sir!"

"Sir! General Heimlich, sir!"

General Heimlich and Colonel Winston turned to see Captain Ambrose waving at them from the cab roof of a parked troop-truck. The captain, a tall thin black man in his twenties, shouted anxiously, "They're advancing sir! The enemy are advancing!"

Excitement coursed through the lines of soldiers like an electric current. General Heimlich jogged to the troop truck. The Captain helped him climb atop the cab to see for himself. "Uh, General, you have something on your..." he gestured to his own upper-lip.

"It's called a moustache, son. Maybe, you'll be able to grow one yourself someday."

Captain Ambrose started to object, but was motioned to silence by Colonel Winston. The General, finding his balance on the now-crowded truck roof, turned to survey the battlefield. From here, he could gaze over the heads of the soldiers and row of M1 Abrams tanks, down the broad New York City avenue. He spat out a gob of yellow tobacco juice, took a drag on his cigar, and lifted his binoculars to his eyes. Just leaving the orc barricades, the four horsemen approached. They rode abreast. One held an axe. One held a three-headed flail. Another clutched a jagged-edge sword. The last carried a massive spiked mace. They started out at a brisk walk then broke into a trot. They rode directly towards the line of tanks.

"They must be mad!" laughed Colonel Winston, struggling to balance on the hood of the truck.

General Heimlich nodded in agreement. "This is a chance to show those freaks what they're up against. Blow 'em up!"

"You want to shoot a half-dozen tank shells at four guys on horseback?" asked Captain Ambrose incredulously.

"Not enough?"

"Um... it should be plenty, sir!" Captain Ambrose raised the radio on his lapel to speak.

"And Captain..."

"Yes, sir?"

"Aim at the riders. This is on live TV. Folks don't like to see horsies get blowed up."

"Good thinking, sir. I'll get right on it!" said Captain Ambrose. He relayed the order. In unison, the line of six massive tanks lowered their cannons to aim directly at the approaching horsemen. "Fire!" shouted the Captain. *BA-BA-BOOM!* Six heavy cannons fired. The mobile artillery heaved with the recoil. Instantly, the horsemen vanished in a cluster of explosions. Concussions shook the buildings and shattered the windows in adjacent buildings. The street between the two forces was hidden behind a thick brown cloud of smoke, raining particles of pavement and other debris.

"Looks like the four horseman just met *their* apocalypse," General Heimlich scoffed. Tossing aside his still-lit cigar, he casually unfolded his pouch of snuff. He considered walking away Iron-Man-style, but decided against it. He took a snort instead. The National Guard soldiers watched in silence, waiting to see the mangled remains the dissipating haze would soon reveal.

There was no need to wait.

While billows of smoke still swirled, four shadowy figures emerged from within. They were now walking their mounts. They appeared otherwise unharmed.

"Oh my God," said Captain Ambrose.

"It's like... all that we did was knock them off their horses!" said Colonel Winston.

"Well, I'll be," said General Heimlich.

A wave of panic seized the American soldiers. None of their training had prepared them for this. Curses and whispered prayers stole among them. Some claimed that all six tanks had somehow missed their marks. Others believed it to be the Devil's work. The four riders paused to almost casually remount their steeds. They then twitched their reins and resumed their unhurried approach. In the stunned silence, the steady clip-clop of the horses' hooves was clearly audible.

"What do we do?" said Colonel Winston. "If tank shells can't stop them..."

"It's—it's—it's like they're magic or something!" stammered Captain Ambrose.

"There's no such thing as magic, Captain. Must be some kind of hi-tech armour they're wearin'. Just roll the tanks over top of 'em an' flatten 'em like pancakes!"

"Yes, sir!" shouted the captain. He raised the radio to his lips and relayed the order.

The massive armoured vehicles lurched forward and began to roll directly toward the approaching knights. Thick caterpillar tracks clanked over black asphalt, cracking pavement under seventy-three tons of steel. It was a moving wall of armour. The riders showed no apparent concern and continued to ride toward it, undaunted. At the same time, a second order was given. Flanking troops positioned along the sidewalks, opened fire with fully automatic weapons. Bullets ricocheted in sparks off the Grūshank Knights' black breastplates and helms, to no apparent effect.

"Tell them to aim between the plates fur Chri'sakes!" ordered General Heimlich.

The soldiers not too rattled to process the relayed order aimed more carefully. Bullets bounced off the edges where the black metal plates met, and around the helmet visors' eye slots. There was no way some shots didn't find openings. Still, the Knights showed no indication of injury or even irritation at the blistering barrage. Their relentless approach continued unabated. Dozens of shots struck the black maned horses as well, easily finding the large gaps in their barding. Here the bullets could be clearly seen deflecting off of raw flesh. The impacts on the horses' shiny coats appeared like raindrops on water. The tank commanders atop the turrets opened fire as well, emptying entire ammo strips into the approaching foes, who were now just a few dozen yards away.

Behind the Grūshank Knights, strange new figures appeared amid the still rising clouds of smoke. These figures were massive. Man-like in form, but on the scale of elephants. Hulking great trolls lumbered into reality. They had skin as grey as stone, bulging eyes with pin-prick pupils, and arms knotted with rope-like muscle. Their oversized bald heads, as big as boulders, and unwieldy strides, made them look like massive, ugly toddlers. Eight in all, the trolls wore animal fur loin cloths, and carried spiked clubs. They guffawed at the sight of the men arrayed before them,

197

and hooted with delight. The U.S. soldiers recoiled in horror. Sergeants yelled orders at their men to stand their ground, even as they wrestled with the impossibility of it all. These monsters were no men in costume. "Hago-ha!" bellowed the first troll. "Hago-ha!" echoed the rest.

"Take 'em out!" shouted Captain Ambrose into his radio.

The tanks halted their advance, raised their guns, and fired. The massive vehicles rolled backwards. Missiles struck troll bodies full-on and exploded in a gratifying eruption of putrid yellow ichor and gore. The trolls shrieked and yelled. Two lost arms. Another's head was blown clean off, and bounced down the street behind it. A third monster was split asunder, leaving a gaping hole in his middle through which the orc lines could be seen. The orcs seemed undeterred by the apparent decimation of their giant allies. "Mwah?" asked the lead troll, unfamiliar with such weaponry. Even the Grūshank Knights paused their approach to assess the impact.

"That's better," snorted General Heimlich with satisfaction.

Then, the unthinkable happened. In plain sight, one of the troll's dismembered hands began to crawl back towards its owner, dragging its arm behind it. At the same time, all of the grey giants began to writhe and contort. Their skin boiled and erupted with new flesh. Tissues weaved together, yellow gore slurped back inside, and wounds began to close. The headless troll turned and felt about awkwardly for its missing cranium. The decapitated head grimaced and scowled where it lay, as if directing its body remotely, while trying to navigate the reversed right and left. Finally, thick grey hands grasped the head and, turning it around to face the right way, lowered it onto its neck. Instantly, flesh fused. The troll turned to face its enemy. The head began to scowl about once more. Within seconds, all of the trolls were completely regenerated. Their once-mangled bodies showed

198

neither blood nor bruise. The lead troll gave a yellow gap-toothed grin at the astonished human forces and began to chortle. *"Heh-heh-heh!"*

"This is the Devil's work," gasped Captain Ambrose.

The Grūshank Knights launched into a gallup. The trolls charged behind, with giant steps that shook the ground and cracked concrete. The soldiers began to fire, only to see their bullets again bounce harmlessly off the Grūshank's armour, or be absorbed into the trolls' skin that closed the holes like pudding. Riding between the tanks, the knights met the human defenders and began to hack and slice, sending splattering arcs of blood into the air with each swing. The soldiers screamed. None of their weapons harmed the knights. None of their armour slowed their blows. The trolls pile-drove into the mechanized cavalry like line backers in a football game. The impact turtled two of the tanks immediately, crushing the tank commanders in the cupola and trapping the rest of the crew. Two of the trolls stood on either side of a single Abrams M1, grinning down at the horrified commander. The soldier still gripped the M2 .50 Cal machine-gun, which smoked from the rounds fired to no effect. The trolls chuckled in amusement. One reached for the commander, and plucked him out like a doll. "No—please!" shouted the soldier, his helmet flying off, his feet kicking madly. The troll bit off his head. The soldier's body hung limp. The troll chewed thoughtfully as if trying to decide on the taste. The other trolls snatched away the limp corpse and bit off the legs. The first shrugged and tossed the remains away. There was more where that came from. Both trolls reached under the massive vehicle and heaved it over. Wrenching off the turret, they dumped out the three remaining crew. Scrambling to their feet, the soldiers tried to run for the American lines. The gunner and driver were snatched up and gobbled. The loader, a man named Lewis Harvey, better known as 'Butch' made the lines, only to be bisected from behind by the jagged edged sword of a Grūshank. Some soldiers watch this scene play out with the horror it deserved. Most were far too absorbed in their own survival. The Grūshank whose shield bore a worm-ridden hand, swung his three-headed flail with devastating effect. Each landed blow instantly turned iron to rust, cloth to ash, and caused living victims to rot and crumble into heaps of diseased meat. One Abrams tank raced backwards, out of control, its driver brained from an impact with a troll. It reversed directly towards the Grūshank Knight with the grasping claw insignia. The Knight was caught surrounded by National Guard soldiers, including many corpses, packed too deep to wade through in time. With blinding speed, it swung its battle axe and struck the tank—splitting it in half. The sundered steel hulk flattened fifty US soldiers before sliding to a halt. The knight's horse staggered at being clipped by the metal frame, but regained its footing, and shook it off. The Grūshank rode forward to resume the manual labour of slaughtering soldiers, now climbing over one another to escape. With a battle roar, the orcs charged.

The human line broke completely. Even the bravest, most determined soldiers realized they were fighting a foe they could not kill. The orcs poured through their ranks. Green arms raised and fell, stabbing and bludgeoning. In mere minutes, the National Guard troops were either dead, dying, or had fled. Bodies lay strewn everywhere. Blood drained into NYC rain gutters. The wounded screamed and wept, until methodically silenced by orc infantry walking among them. In the center of it all, General Heimlich and Captain Ambrose still stood atop the cab of the troop truck. It was an island in a flood of madness. Colonel Winston had attempted to flee, only to be hacked to pieces in seconds by an orc with a machete. The two surviving officers had expected to be attacked at any moment. Yet they remained undisturbed while the river of death rushed around them. General Heimlich wanted to die. He had envisioned fighting off hoards as they tried to drag him from his perch, before perishing in a moment of glory at the hand of a one of the black knights. Instead, the orcs and knights seemed bizarrely disinterested in them. The Grūshanks sat astride their horses, overseeing all. The orc soldiers mopped up the remains of the battle, assessing dropped equipment and weapons for plunder. "Can they see us?" said General Heimlich.

"I... I don't know," said Captain Ambrose.

"Yes, we can see you," said a gruff voice, in accented but perfect English. The two officers looked to see a tall, commanding orc in a billowing red cloak approach. General Bragad'oc calmly drew a long sword. "Are you prepared to tell us anything useful?"

"Never!" shouted General Heimlich defiantly.

"Well then, you're of no use to us." With a single slash, he disembowelled Captain Ambrose, who wordlessly collapsed to the roadway below, dead. "We don't really need information at this point anyway." The orc commander raised his sword a second time.

"Wait!" shouted General Heimlich.

The orc general paused. "Yes?"

"What *are* you?"

General Bragad'oc grinned, showing his long canines. "*A prelude.*"

---

* See *The Siege of Walter Parks*. Available from booksellers near you.

25

"He ate of the fruit anyway and was set free."
– Book of Orcs

Dorothy was absolutely beautiful. Marc knew he wasn't supposed to notice that. *Not* noticing was impossible. Especially now that they were here together in a hotel. It wasn't his fault. If anything, it was Diane's for choosing Dorothy, or 'Dotty' as everyone called her, to be her maid-of-honour. It wasn't her fault either, of course. Not her fault alone, anyway. Diane and Dotty were equally to blame for being best friends. It's not as if Diane wasn't aware of Dorothy's beauty. She was very aware—painfully so. By any standards, Diane herself was quite attractive. Except, when she stood next to Dotty, who was by those same standards stunning. So, Marc had always made a point of *not* looking at her. When Diane made in some oblique way a reference to her best friend's attractiveness, Marc pretended he hadn't noticed. This was, of course, ridiculous. But it was what he had to do, so he did it. The difference was, Marc was in love with Diane. That was why he'd asked her to marry him. To him, she had that special kind of beauty that only someone you're in love with has. Still, Marc knew these seeming off-hand remarks about her friend were a sort of a test for him. "Did you see those bellhops staring at her?" said Diane, shaking her head. "You'd think a hotel like this would have better trained staff!"

"No," Marc lied. "I was too busy checking out the view, myself." Realizing this might be misinterpreted, he added, "Out there, I mean." He pointed to the large picture window that dominated the bridle suite of the hotel. It provided a stunning panoramic view of Emerald Lake, its icy waters shining bright turquoise in the afternoon sun. The lake's source was the melting glacial ice of the surrounding mountains. It radiated clean, pure perfection amid the towering grandeur of the Rocky Mountains of British Columbia.

Diane paused in unpacking her suitcase and turned to look. "It is beautiful," she admitted. They were staying at the Emerald Lake Lodge, along with members of both their families and the rest of the wedding party. There would be two days of hiking, canoeing, and wedding preparations, before the ceremony itself on the shore of the lake. Following that, Diane and Marc would disappear to Lake Louise, Banff and other places for a kind of road-trip honeymoon.

"Just like you," said Marc. He walked up behind her, put his arms around her waist, and kissed her neck.

"Someday, when we have kids, I'd like to take them up here. It'll be an adventure."

"I'm sure we'll have all kinds of adventures," he said. "Starting with

Kuwait."

Diane nodded and kissed him. Marc's work meant constant travel. It was part of what made the idea of marrying him seem like so much fun.

The rehearsal dinner was the night before the wedding. Marc had spent the day kayaking with Ryan and Chris, his best man and usher respectively. Diane, Dotty, and bridesmaid Allison, had opted to take a long hike along the shore. The idea was for the couple to spend some time apart, leading up to the 'Big Event'. Dinner was a magical affair and a prelude to the wedding itself. As the sun had set, the shadows of the mountains had stolen across the green waters of the lake and surrounding valley. Now, only the peaks of the mountains remained touched with the last gold gleams of day. The deck lamps came on. Their bright glow cast finger-paint lines of light on the water's surface. Marc's father, the host of the evening, raised his glass in a toast. "...and so we finally had our wish. Our wish for a daughter, as well as a son. And a daughter we could not have chosen better for ourselves." All raised their glasses. Ryan shouted "Hear! Hear!" and others joined in. Diane blushed. Marc whispered in her ear.

A short while later, Marc exited the men's room off the hotel lobby. His now untied tie hung at loose ends from his collar. Diane had told him he had no need to wear it, but Marc had insisted. Too many glasses of champagne had begun to have their effect. His fingers fumbled to undo his top button. Finally succeeding, he headed back towards the party. He swayed off-balance and cast a steadying hand on the daffodil wallpaper wall. Balance restored, he started again on his way. As he did, he caught a motion from the corner of his eye. Turning, he saw the unmistakable sight of Dotty, leaning against the wall outside the Ladies room. She was watching him, one corner of her mouth turned up in amusement. Her pale cheeks were flushed with alcohol. A single out-of-place wisp of blond hair fell across her face. As their eyes met, her expression changed from amused to mischievous. "Hello Marc," she said, biting her lower lip.

"Hey there, Dot," said Marc. He stood up stiffly, in an effort to appear less drunk.

"The light's not working in the restroom here. Can you help?"

"Um, sure. I'll go ask at the front desk."

"No, no. It's just loose, and I can't reach. Can you just try it yourself?"

"Oh," said Marc, "sure."

Marc walked to the bathroom door, then hesitated. "There's no one in there is there?"

"No," said Dorothy. She then leaned in close and whispered in his ear. "It's a private one. The door locks." As she said this, Marc could feel her hot breath on his ear.

"Okay," he said. He opened the door and stepped inside. The small room smelled of potpourri. Dotty followed him. Marc flicked the switch on the wall beside the door. To his surprise, the bathroom light flicked on. "It seems to work fine," he said.

"Oops. You must have the magic touch," said Dotty. She closed the bathroom door and turned the lock. "How ridiculous I must look," she said coyly, leaning back against the vanity. Her blouse was now open slightly, revealing a trace of cleavage.

Marc swallowed. Despite his alcohol impaired faculties, the reality of the situation began to dawn on him. "Um, I don't think you could look ridiculous if you tried."

Dotty took a step forward. In the close confines of the tiny bathroom, this meant they were practically touching. Close enough for Marc to feel the heat from her body. She then spoke, her faces inches from his. "You were different from the rest of D's boyfriends," she said, using her own name for Diane. "I'd catch most of them sneaking looks at me over her shoulder, trying to flirt, or even make a pass. You never did. Why? Don't you think I'm attractive?"

Marc's head reeled. Too much booze had left him in a poor state to navigate the situation. Part of him wanted to confess that he'd simply been better at hiding his glances and that, of course, he thought she was beautiful. Part of him wanted to admit that, despite his love for Diane, this was a fantasy he couldn't help but have. Dotty leaned in close. Her chest now pressed against his. "I... I..." Marc's hand fumbled beside him for the door, —finally meeting the knob. The touch of cold brass jarred him from his stupor. "I... I have to go!" he stammered. Opening the door, he ducked into the hallway. He fell against the wall, blinking in confusion over what had just transpired. The door, which had closed behind him, began to open. Not wanted to continue the encounter, Marc turned and stumbled to the main hallway that led back the dining room deck area. As he reached the junction, he walked almost directly into Diane.

"Oh, there you are!" she said in surprise. "I was wondering what was taking so long. If you were all..." she trailed off. She stared in some surprise at the sight of Dorothy behind him. Her blonde friend, uncharacteristically dishevelled, was fastening the top button on her blouse. Marc, drunk, flustered, and unsure what to say, blurted "I'm fine. Sorry." He then side-stepped his wife-to-be and headed back towards the dining area.

"It wasn't what it looked like," Marc pleaded.

"I know," said Diane, scowling at her own reflection. They were in their hotel room. Diane was standing in front of the grand picture window which, in the brightly lit room at night, had become a dark mirror.

"You know?"

"Yes. I know Dotty, and I know you. It's not the first time this has happened."

"It's not?"

She turned and looked at him managing a weak smile. "Well, it *is* the first time she didn't get her way."

Marc stared at her a moment, in disbelief. He then turned and slumped onto the bed. He was still feeling the alcohol, although he hadn't touched a drop since the incident two hours earlier. He now felt tired instead of tipsy. "So why do you stay friends with her?"

"I don't know," Diane admitted. "Not anymore though, not after this. We'll get through the ceremony, then I'm done with her." Diane sat beside Marc, and leaned her head against his shoulder. "I didn't think she'd try it with my fiancé. She just can't stand it when someone else wins."

The following day, Marc and Diane clasped hands on a raised platform before the sun sparkled waters of Emerald Lake. Ryan passed Marc the ring, and Marc placed it on Diane's fingers. "Forever and ever," he whispered to her. Diane mouthed it back.

"Again?" she said, her face a gathering storm cloud of anger. Diane stood in the doorway of the nursery. She was wearing a white knee-length nightie and held their one-year-old daughter in her arms. Naomi's tiny baby fingers were turning over and over a plastic pink hippopotamus toy. She was fascinated by the way her nightlight shone on its rounded surface.

"It's not my fault, I don't decide these things," said Marc defensively. It was ten pm, and he was pulling his empty suitcase from the hall closet. He had just received a phone call, telling him to return to a drill site in Saudi Arabia by Tuesday. That was two days from now, but he'd need much of the intervening time to get there.

"You decide to jump when they say 'jump'."

"I signed a contract. You do know how those work, right? They pay me a bunch of money. The money that pays for this house, and for you to be a stay-at-home mum. So yes, I have to jump when *the contract* says 'jump'."

"Oh jeez," said Diane. "Well, thank-you for explaining what a contract is to me. I forgot since I only used to write them for the TD Bank for ten years. Could you be more condescending?" Hearing the harsh tone in her mother's voice, baby Naomi stopped turning the tiny toy and looked up with concern.

Marc sighed. "Of course, I know you know what a contract is. That wasn't my point."

"And what was your point?"

Marc took a deep breath. He didn't want to fight. He wanted to get packed and go to bed. The flight he needed to be on left at six am, that meant waking at four. "Look, you knew the deal when we got married. You knew what I did and how much I traveled. You knew that when we had kids, you wouldn't be able to travel with me like you used to. We discussed all of this. We agreed."

"You're right, you're a hundred-percent right," said Diane. "I agreed to all of that, I thought our life would be one awesome adventure full of travel and amazing experiences. When I got pregnant I also thought, okay, I want to be a mum, and I can handle all of this, and it will be fine. And you know what? I was wrong. Being a mother is way harder than I thought it would be. Getting left behind is way harder than I thought it would be. So guess what? I want to renegotiate our contract, because this? This isn't working."

Marc stared at her. In some ways, it was the same discussion they'd been having off-and-on for a year. The difference was, previously, Diane had always begrudgingly accepted the situation and the deal they'd made. Of course, that was before Marc's last trip which had lasted over eight weeks. Once home, he'd promised her he'd stay for at least a month. That was a week ago. But things hadn't gone as planned at the drill site. There were geological problems. The oil was there. The issue was getting to it. "Okay, so what do we do? We bought this awesome house in a nice neighbourhood with great schools and a mortgage we can barely afford even with this income. Do you want to sell? Or, do you want to go back to work and have me stay home? Of course, there's the small legal problem of the fact that I signed a damn contract!"

Diane stared ruefully at the wall. Nothing Marc was saying was news to her. She'd run through it all in her own head many times. It didn't change the fact that she was miserable. "Just go," she said. "Pack your bag and go."

"Go...?"

"On your trip."

Marc stared at her a moment. Diane refused to meet his gaze. Instead, she frowned, and chewed on her bottom lip. Marc started to turn towards the bedroom. He stopped himself. "Are you sure?"

Diane shrugged. "Do I have a choice? We have an agreement, remember? It's my own damn fault. Apparently, I was living in a fantasy world." At that moment, Naomi began to wail.

It wasn't as if the next few years were non-stop fighting between them. There were bright spots. Some good family vacations. Months at a time when Marc was between contracts and working at home. Jack was born. As Marc's work picked up and his trips became even longer, they brought in help in the form of Elaine, a nannie from Montréal. Diane got used to the often single-parenting. A strange, resigned peace settled between them. It wasn't the kind of peace that comes from resolution, but rather the kind that came from distance—even when he was at home. Marc watched his four-year-old daughter play with her Christmas toys under the tree, making her new dolly walk. Jack lay in Diane's lap as she sat on the chesterfield. Marc felt as if he were more an observer than a participant. His wife seemed oblivious to him. Instead, she made kissey-faces with their young son, who gurgled happily and blew spit-bubbles back. Perhaps 'benefactor' was a better term, thought Marc. He wondered if he were to get up and walk out of the house that Christmas morning, if they would even notice. As he took a sip from his now-cold coffee, he found Diane's own words ringing in his ears. He wondered if it was now he who was living in a fantasy world.

26

"It takes an army to raze a village."
– Birwaz the Plunderer

Long columns of smoke rose past the lit windows of skyscrapers. Despite the night, the grey black billows remained visible against the ambient light haze that permeated the sky above New York. A trio of military helicopters burst through, shining searchlights on the city streets below. Owing to a no-fly-zone order, there were no more private or news aircraft to crowd them. Even the NYPD was grounded until further notice. An illegal drone, defying the ban, had offered some news coverage until it was shot down by an apparent crossbow bolt. The streets below were oddly deserted. Police and military lines had cordoned off traffic for blocks. Any residents or office workers left were 'sheltering in place'. The only visible humans were dead. Corpses lay where they were butchered or bludgeoned hours earlier—in the middle of the road, a car park, or inside vehicles. Some aerial fire retardant bombers had been called in to douse fires in burning buildings before they could spread. Despite this, many continued to smoulder. Smaller ones burned uncontrolled. The National Guard was on its heels. It never planned for a situation like this. It was a scenario that should not have been possible. How did an entire army simply appear in the middle of America's largest city? How did they possess weapons beyond comprehension? Conventional weapons had failed. Other weapons were unacceptable, given the thousands of civilians believed hidden or captured behind enemy lines. With no clear path forward, the humans had decided to stand down. There was talk of negotiations. Letters had been dropped. Envoys had been sent. The mouse had roared, and the lion was unsure what to make of it.

Despite everything, the streetlights had come on as usual. There had been talk of cutting the power, but it had been determined this would better serve the enemy, who seemed to thrive in darkness. Meanwhile, the trickle of humans still fleeing the area would be hopelessly disadvantaged. Two such humans staggered down 43rd Street, dressed in ill-fitted armour that threatened to come off with each step.

"Ahh!" moaned Sam, clutching his wounded side in agony.

"You can do it, Hon," pleaded Tania. Her arm gripped him tightly around his middle, supporting almost his entire weight. Her arm muscles burned with strain. Her back ached. "Come on now, *step!*"

Across the wide avenue, they caught the attention of an orc patrol. Six warriors watched them with curiosity. Orcs rarely helped other orcs, unless ordered to do so. Even more puzzling was the direction these 'orcs' were moving. Instead of towards the main camp, where the wounded gathered to nurse their wounds or die, this pair were headed towards the front line. While odd, their behaviour warranted no alarms. Then Tania heaved again, trying to push Sam forward faster. The effort hiked up the bottom of her dirty grey tunic, exposing pale human skin beneath. The orc sergeants eyes grew wide. "Humans!" he bellowed.

Instantly the orc patrol sprang to life and jogged across the empty street. Tania and Sam both turned to watch, helpless, as the contingent of soldiers moved to surround them. "Son-of-a..." she muttered angrily. She turned to Sam, "Can you stand?"

"I guess so," he said.

Tania released him and turned to face their attackers. Sam swayed uneasily, but drew his stolen sword from his belt. Once drawn, he found its weight more than he could manage. The weapon fell from his fingers and landed with a clatter on the black asphalt. Sam stumbled forward and fell to the ground. The impact knocked the helmet from his head and sent it rolling. It came to a halt at the orc sergeant's feet. The goblin warriors chuckled with amusement. "Sam!" cried Tania.

"I'm okay. But I think it's time now for you to make a run for it," said Sam. Despite his face being on the ground, he forced a wry smile. "I'll hold them off for you."

The orcs began to make jokes in orcish, and laugh out loud.

Tania, with eyes blazing, stared into Sam's eyes. "Hell no," she said. She drew the battle axe she'd hung from her back, and turned to address the orc sergeant with a snarl. "Go ahead and laugh it up, Chuckles. You think after speed-dating, Yahoo personals and countless blind dates, I'm gonna let some creature with tusks for teeth stand between me and a guy I actually like?" The orcs stared at her in surprise for a moment, before bursting into

214

uproarious laughter. Tania let loose a battle cry and swung the two-handed axe with one hand, knocking the orc sergeant's sword from his grasp.

27

"Don't die with dirty nails." – Dwarf miner creed.

"Keep moving, scum!" shouted the orc lieutenant, his voice echoing down the long, dark subterranean tunnel.

Marc and Diane had no idea what the orcish words meant, but their intent was clear. The forced march was to continue. Dressed in ill-fitted armour, they slogged on through the ankle-deep sewage. The familiar city streets were just feet above their heads, but this felt like another world. They had long accepted the muck which soaked through their poorly cobbled boots. The reek, however, was impossible to tolerate. It permeated every breath, and made it almost impossible not to gag. Even several of the orcs around them had removed their helmets and added their vomit to the waste they trudged through. Diane and Marc had no such relief. To remove their helmets meant death. So, by sheer force of will, they swallowed their bile and marched on. This was greatly assisted by their single-minded focus to get within sight of the children.

Occasionally, behind the lead orc, the long snake of soldiers jammed up and halted. It was either the result of some kind of blockage that needed to be removed, or when Lieutenant Kragg paused to consult his crumpled, soggy map of the Manhattan sewer system. At these moments, Marc and Diane would attempt to move further up the line. They had quickly discerned that 'asking politely' was not the way to go about this. Even had they known the words, and even if their human voices would not betray them, orcan culture simply didn't function that way. Instead, they would barrel forward, aggressively pushing past the soldiers in the way. They did so without question or apology. At the same time, they were careful not to tread on toes or cause any other offences that might have led to an actual fight. Fortunately, the individual orc soldiers were in no rush to get where they were going. They grunted complaints and snarled oaths, but did nothing more to prevent the disguised humans from slipping past. As a result, Marc and Diane had made slow, but steady progress up the line. "There!" Diane hissed, as loudly as she dared.

"Shhh!" said Marc, even as he strained to see what Diane saw. Finally, between a pair of horned helmets, he spotted the pale pink cheek of Jack. The small boy was being carried by an orc soldier. This was not an act of compassion, it was a matter of simple practicality. There was no way the small boy could move through the thick filth as quickly as was needed. Marc knew the orc carrying the boy would as easily kill him, if the order came.

"He's okay!" whispered Diane excitedly.

"Yes," Marc agreed. "He's okay."

"I can't see Naomi," said Diane, concern in her voice.

"They're probably making her walk. She's not as tall as the orcs. So you won't see her until we get closer."

One of the orcs moved, twisting his head to crack his neck. In that moment, Marc and Diane caught a glimpse of Roland Griff, standing next to the Orc Lieutenant Kragg. The officer was distinguishable by his long hooked nose. Griff looked impatient, while Kragg scowled at the many-times folded map.

"You don't think they'll look for us here in the sewers?" said Griff, skeptically eyeing the rounded roof of the tunnel as if able to see through it to the city above. The concrete glistened with layers of black filth built up over decades. "They know you've used them once. Surely, they'll take precautions."

"The humans have their hands full at street level. The General will see to that," said Kragg dismissively, without looking up.

Griff snorted. "You think four guys in black armour will slow the U.S. armoured cavalry division?"

"You don't get to question me or the General, Griff. You get to live for now, be content with that."

"Ha! You need to be nice to me. Your boss and I are about to become like this." Griff raised two fingers, held tightly together. "And I'm not talking about that traitor Bragad'oc"

Now, the orc officer chuckled. "You think you know so much, don't you human?"

"I know one thing you don't."

"And what's that?"

"I know your map is upside down." With that, Griff reached over and took the map from the surprised Kragg, turned it around, and handed it back to him.

The long snake-like procession continued. A few feet back from its head, Professor Pinchent stumbled. Falling forward, he caught himself, by plunging his hand into the cold grey green goo. "Ugh," he groaned. "Simply awful!"

Naomi helped him up, before he could be trampled underfoot by the orc warriors behind. "Are you okay, Professor?" she asked.

"My old bones aren't really up to this," he muttered. As he walked, he shook off what he could of the filth on his fingers. There was nothing he could do about the vile residue. "I am old, Father William..."

"Who's Father William?"

"From *Alice's Adventures in Wonderland*. Although, *Through the Looking Glass* might be more appropriate here."

> *'Twas brillig, and the slithy toves*
> *Did gyre and gimble in the wabe;*
> *All mimsy were the borogoves,*
> *And the mome raths outgrabe.*

"What's that?" asked Naomi.

"Jabberwocky! A poem about a fearsome monster," said Professor Pinchent, stepping down into a waist deep section of chilled sewage.

"Are they real?" asked Jack from over the shoulder of the orc tasked with carrying him. This vantage, allowed him to look back down at his sister and the white haired professor.

"Who knows? Who knows? Anything seems possible now."

Naomi kept her grip on the old man's arm, steadying him, and helping him keep pace. Whatever the orders from the orc they called 'Krag', she didn't want to test the creatures' tolerance should they stop moving. She could sense the pain and discomfort the Professor felt as he struggled. She decided to distract him. "How can they stand it, Professor? The orcs, I mean."

"Oh, they feel it. You can see it by the queasy looks on their faces. But orcs are very different from you and I. They're used to a more... medieval society."

"What does that mean?"

"More filth. You have no idea how recent a thing hygiene is. You have indoor plumbing to thank for that. As well as a basic understanding of bacteria. Medieval noses are, well... more accustomed to stink."

"They smell like puke!" said Jack, wrinkling his nose. "Even before coming down here."

"Um, yes, well. No bathing and hard labour in full armour will do that. They also daren't complain, even if they don't like it. Orc society is one built on fear and dominance. Complaining about the smell would be perceived as weakness, or worse—insubordination. It's a very Hobbsian world they live in."

"A *what* world?" said Naomi.

"One where life is nasty, brutish, and short."

"Oh."

"Are they really evil?" asked Jack. "I mean, maybe they're just misunderstood. We were taught not to judge people because of their race."

The old man nodded. "Yes, but you see, what we call 'races' aren't races at all. Humans are just one race, with a... variety of skin tones and other features. Moreover, the orcs aren't a natural race at all. Tolkien had them as elves corrupted by evil, but according to their own lore that's simply not true. They are were once men, you see. Just like me, or Griff, or even your father. Men so obsessed with conquest and domination that it changed them to monsters. When we opened the gate, we created a bridge between fact and fiction; or metaphor and reality, if you prefer. The orcs weren't transfigured by some 'dark lord'. They corrupted themselves and have been at war with the other races ever since. In a sense, you could say we are fighting ourselves and, it appears, we are losing."

They continued in silence for another moment. Occasionally, the procession passed under manhole covers. These were outlined with ragged rings of light leaked from the street lights above. Any outcry or other loud noises while passing beneath would be met with a swift death. That much had been made clear. Jack tried to breathe through his nose, as the Professor suggested. "It won't help with the stink," the old man promised, "but it's healthier."

"Where are they taking us?" asked Jack. He rose and fell with each step of the orc that bore him.

Professor Pinchent frowned. "I'm not sure. I've been listening to their conversations, but all I've got so far is that we're going to some sort of tower."

Forty-feet down the tunnel, Marc and Diane continued their own hike. While the line moved, advancement was impossible. They could only just keep the kids within sight. Regardless, Marc wasn't at all sure what they would do if they got there. Here in the sewers, even if they did manage to rescue the children, there was nowhere they could escape to quickly enough to avoid prompt re-capture. Better, he reasoned, to get to another location. For now, they would simply keep up, and see what they could do when they got to where they were going—wherever that was.

"Thank God I run," gasped Diane, "this armour is heavy as hell!" She spoke softly enough to be heard only by Marc. "Who knew these green monsters could march so fast?"

"I think they do a lot of it," said Marc. "Plus, I think the ones who can't keep up are, well..."

"Yeah."

"Diane, listen. I've been doing a lot of thinking," said Marc. "I want you to know that I still love you. I still love you, and I want you to know that I forgive you."

Diane stopped dead in her tracks. Marc practically plowed into her. The orc behind him did plow into him, and began grunting and swearing in orcish. More orcs cried out as the sudden halt dominoed down the line. She turned and glared at him through the eye holes in her helmet.

"What the Hell?" Marc hissed.

Diane scowled fiercely a moment more, then resumed her march. Marc quickly followed. The orc behind him, who had been just about to complain, simply muttered and did the same, as did those behind him.

"Do you want to get us killed?" whispered Marc.

Diane spoked without turning to look at him again. "You forgive me? *You* forgive *me*? You complete jerk! I didn't finish telling you what happened back there, but obviously you leapt to your own untrusting conclusion. I didn't cheat on you, but I was sure as Hell tempted to. *That's* what I was saying!"

Marc absorbed this with a confusion of emotions. He was relieved that his wife had not been unfaithful. This released the combination of anger and hurt he had been struggling with. He felt some consternation that she had been tempted. He also felt embarrassed and guilty for the assumption he had made. "Oh, I—I didn't know. I mean..."

"You know who's been unfaithful?" Diane continued. She was loud enough that Marc worried the orcs might hear, despite the sound-dampening effects of the dreary dark tunnel and constant percussion of boots in water. "You! Only *your* mistress is your career. You've been running off and doing whatever you want to do with the idea that we'll just wait in suspended animation until you deign to return."

Marc tried to feel indignant. "We've discussed this before. You knew what I did when we got married. You loved traveling with me to all those places!"

"That was then. Now we have a family. There comes a point where you have to choose between adventure and your family. You have to decide what's important to you and no, you can't have both. We aren't just book characters who don't exist when you're not reading about them. We had an agreement sure, but it sucks and I'm miserable. So what's right about that?"

Marc struggled with the notion that he was the one who had somehow been unfaithful. He thought of how easy it was to simply disappear on an airplane and live a separate life, one devoid of responsibility. He thought of his friendship with Don, who had effectively traded his family life in exchange for that freedom. Marc was thinking about all of this, when the soldiers abruptly halted in front of them. Wherever they were going, it seemed they had arrived.

28

"Worms and kings both die in the dirt." – Ebros Vüm

The curved tip of the pole arm slid into a slot in the manhole cover. The orc soldier holding the weapon then pushed, lifting the cover from the hole. He drew it aside and released. It landed with a dull *clang*. A shaft of mingled headlights, neon, and street lamps shone down on the upturned green countenances of the orcs. Honking, yelling, and rumbling trucks—the cacophony of New York City flooded the tunnel. Thankfully, a gust of cool, fresh night air followed as well. Car tires rushed passed the open manhole which, being at the side of the road, remained unnoticed. Somewhere, a frustrated cab-driver was honking non-stop. A curb-side preacher shouted at passersby, "The end is nigh! The devil's children are among us!" Kragg chuckled. Under the pit-dark shadows of his boney brow, the orc's eyes shone like orange candle flames. Lady Gaga's *Born this Way* blared from his belt. Kragg stared down at the pouch containing the iPhone that General Bragad'oc had ordered him to carry. For a moment, he did nothing.

"Well? Are you going to answer it or what?" said Roland Griff.

"Uh, hmm..." Kragg hesitated. He pulled the still-ringing phone from his pouch and clutched it awkwardly in his gauntleted hand. Removing his other glove, he stared at it. It seemed like a magic item to the battle-hardened warrior, and he'd never trusted magic. The display read 'Daddy Shark'. That was the General's codename. The orc lieutenant had never got the hang of the strange device. He still preferred the simplicity of a signal fire built from the piled bodies of enemy dead. The phone insistently continued its song. Its facial recognition software identified Krag's face and unlocked. His clawed finger tapped the display, making a *tack-tack* sound. The phone continued to ring.

"I'll do it," said Roland Griff impatiently. He reached over and pressed the answer button with his finger. "There."

Kragg put the phone to his ear and listened a moment. He grinned a broad, shark-tooth grin. With arms raised, the hook-nosed orc officer faced the long line of soldiers. *"Eir goth nau!"* he shouted in orcish. There was no more need for stealth. The soldiers roared their approval and beat their weapons on their shields. The words roughly translated to 'They did it!' The soldiers all knew what this meant—victory for General Bragad'oc and the Grūshank Knights. Their long soggy trek was a strategy designed to bring success, whatever the outcome of the above-ground battle. If the humans won, the fight would serve as a distraction, allowing their mission to reach its goal. A win for the orcs meant ultimate triumph was assured. Lieutenant Kragg tried to hang up the phone. Again his curled claw only tapped uselessly on the glass. Annoyed, he flung the phone into the ankle-deep sewage. He drew his sword and pointed to the open manhole cover above. "Ya güt irgost!" he cried, '*Take the street!*'

Sixth Avenue and Twenty-Seventh Street were supposed to be safe. It was some distance to the barricades and, despite the martial law imposed just blocks away, life here had continued somewhat normally. New Yorkers prided themselves on their ability to continue uninterrupted in the face of crisis. This was the biggest disruption since September 11, 2001. Still, the residents of the city couldn't simply vanish. The mayor had told them that the best thing they could do outside of the 'effected area' was to continue spending their money to support local businesses. The front-lines were impenetrable. The primitive invaders would soon be dealt with. Still, there was an excited air about the city. Residents crowded in front of televisions in bars and restaurants for news. Word had just broken of some sort of battle taking place. Owing to the ban of news helicopters, direct coverage was sporadic and sparse. Twitter and Facebook were abuzz with posts from those still trapped behind lines. Hashtags like #xSqrMassacre and #escNY had begun trending. There were so many rumours and false reports, it was hard to know what was real and what was fake news—until now. Now, the four horseman of the Apocalypse galloped up Sixth Avenue. With black cloaks billowing, they swung their weapons about in arcs of devastation. All attempts to stop them had failed. They were invulnerable to bullets and bombs. They rode in a spear tip formation. The flail-wielding Grūshank Knight in the lead, known pejoratively as Pestilence, charged in a mantle of fire. This was the result of a dozen Molotov cocktails thrown by a group of vigilantes from Queens. The flames licked harmlessly about him. His assailants lay as heaps of diseased meat a block behind. In the vanguard's wake, came an ocean tide of marauding orcs killing everything the knights left standing.

Kragg and his men poured from the open manhole. One of the orc soldiers, who had still not fully grasped the concept of 'cars' was struck and killed by a bus. The driver, unsure of what he had hit, then made the fatal mistake of stopping and opening the bus doors to take a look. After that, the slaughter began. Screaming men and women, some fleeing from the advancing army to the south, found themselves facing orcs here as well. The cornered crowd were cut down with swords and axes, stabbed with spears, and bludgeoned with hammers and clubs. Screams filled the night. Car horns honked in a panicked crescendo, before being silenced one... by one... by one.

Amid this butchery, Marc and Diane, still disguised in orc armour, searched desperately. During the surge from the sewers, they had lost sight of the children. "Where did they go?" said Diane, the panic rising in her voice.

"They can't have gotten far," said Marc. "They were just a few feet ahead of us."

Under a street light at the corner, a contingent of orc guards glowered bitterly at the battle taking place around them. Each longed to join in and partake in the simple pleasures of mutilating humans and irrigating the earth with their blood. Orders were orders, however, and so they were forced to stand their ground. They remained in a tight circle formation around their three charges. They did so with weapons drawn, hoping that some panicked person would run by close enough to kill.

"I saw Mum!" Jack insisted. He peered frantically between the torsos and arms of the orc guards surrounding them.

"You *thought* you saw, Mum," said Naomi.

"I did," said Jack. "In the sewers, before they brought us up!"

"If she was in the sewers, the orcs would have killed her." Naomi didn't want to squash her baby brother's hopes, but she also didn't want him running off after a fantasy. It could get him killed. "Tell him, Professor."

Professor Pinchent nodded wearily, adjusting his hearing aid. "Your sister's right I'm afraid, lad. It was very dark down there. Your eyes played tricks on you."

"No!" Jack insisted. "I did see her. She was dressed like an orc."

The professor gazed up at the soaring walls of New York skyscrapers around them. "They said they were taking us to a tower, but which one?"

"Could it be any tower?" said Naomi, resting her hands on her brother's shoulders. Jack continued to search the chaos around them.

The old man shook his head. "They took us over a mile underground to get here, so it had to be a specific one." Suddenly, his snow-white eyebrows lifted in surprise. "Of course!" he said. Raising his hand, he pointed between two of the guards' huddled helms to the instantly recognizable lighted form of the Empire State Building. "But, *why*?"

29

"There are no victims. All would build empires."
– Evrok V

It was Nelson's job to work the metal detector to ensure no weapons entered the Empire State Building. It wasn't his job alone. There were a half dozen guards on duty in the lobby to manage the constant stream of tourists. There were more on the 86th Floor Observation Deck, and on the renovated 102nd Floor Top Deck. Normally, they would all be busy scanning, answering the same questions, or conducting bag searches. Tonight, everything was different. At first, there had been a rush of people coming and going. Those *going* remembered 9/11 and coronavirus. They wanted to leave the tower, and Manhattan, as quickly as possible. Those *coming* wanted to use the landmark tower as a way to observe what was going on below. There they would watch, take selfies, and live stream the amazing scenes below. That was hours ago when no one knew or understood what was happening. Eventually, the police had stopped in and ordered the building shut down to tourists. No one knew what was going on, but at least it was quiet. All of the glass lobby doors were locked. The sign that said 'Tenants Only' had been put up. Anyone wanting to enter needed a passcard with their photo on it. The guards had been told to remain on duty, despite there being little to do. So, Nelson stood by his metal detector, along with his pal, Marvin, waiting for someone to scan. He was bored—bored of the grand art deco interior, bored of the brass murals, bored of standing around. Even Marvin was boring. He'd said nothing for the past hour. If only something would happen, he thought.

The marble floor made the *clackity-clack* of Robyn's footsteps echo eerily as she approached. Robyn was a chubby and attractive black woman in her thirties. She too wore a guard uniform, but with an extra gold band on the sleeve. She was the shift supervisor.

"You guys good?" she asked.

"Sure," said Nelson.

"It's weird," said Marvin. Marvin scratched his head. He'd been scratching it all night. Nelson had noticed the dandruff on his uniform collar. Gross, he thought. "It's like it's closing time."

"Well, that's cuz we're closed," said Robyn.

"I know but, it's weird, this early'n all."

"Weirder are the reports of what's goin' on," said Nelson. He had been following the news on his phone. Normally, they weren't supposed to look at their phones while on duty. Normally, Robyn would have reprimanded him. Nothing tonight was normal.

"Anything new?" asked Robyn.

"Lots of crazy stuff! Big battle down at Times Square."

"I saw that," said Robyn.

"You know who's behind it?" said Marvin. "The Free Masons. And the Jews."

Nelson rolled his eyes. "Always with the Jews."

"I told you not to go on with that crazy anti-semite conspiracy crap, Marvin," Robyn scolded him.

"It's not a conspiracy theory, it's true. The ZOG is trying to take over. For, like, real now!"

"Zog?" asked Robyn.

"Don't ask," said Nelson.

"Zionist Occupational Government."

"Oh right," said Nelson. "Wait, I thought you said they already controlled everything? That they like being all secret and stuff."

"Marvin," said Robyn.

"Yeah, well all that's changed. Maybe, they done decided—"

"Marvin!"

"What?"

Robyn looked at him squarely in the eyes. "Cut it out."

Marvin shrugged. "Fine, fine... but don't say I didn't warn you."

"Robyn?" shouted one of the other guards. It was Alex, a skinny Irish kid with red hair, who was posted by the front doors. It was his job to check the passcards of anyone claiming to be a tenant.

"What?" shouted Robyn. She was still locked-eyes with Marvin. She wanted him to see that she meant it this time. All it took was for the wrong person to overhear one of his racist rants to get them all in hot water.

"I... I think they want in."

"Well, check their passcards, Alex. No passcard, no entry."

"I think you better take a look..."

Robyn's first instinct was to be annoyed. Checking passcards wasn't rocket-science. Still, there was something in the young guard's quavering voice that made her turn. *Fear?*

The row of doors created a glass wall between the marble lobby interior and the cement-grey sidewalk outside. Standing behind the glass was a ragged line of... men? No, not men, soldiers? Not just soldiers. *Monsters.* The word surged through her mind like a flash flood of madness washing away all reason. They stood shoulder to shoulder, wearing spiked and crested helmets, and dirty cloaks draped over leather and steel. They held square shields and bucklers, and clutched spears, swords, and double-headed axes. Beneath it all, sunk into dark recesses below boney green brows, were eyes that burned like tiny infernal fires. "Mother Mary and Joseph," Robyn breathed.

"Holy–," said Nelson.

The monster in the middle caught her gaze. On his head, he wore a horned helm decorated with tarnished green copper. That, along with a heavy crimson cape, marked him as their leader. Likewise, he seemed to instinctively recognize Robyn as the 'ranking officer'. *"Open up!"* he commanded. While muted by the thick glass, his accented words were still clearly audible.

Alex looked at Robyn, imploringly. The young guard's already pale complexion grew whiter still with terror.

"Don't. You. Dare," Robyn order him. As she spoke, she drew the pistol from her belt holster for the first time in her career. Robyn had threatened to draw it in the past. She'd unclipped it once when dealing with a bigoted drunk who kept calling her the 'n-word' and bragging about how his ancestors had owned slaves. Never, had she been forced to draw it. She had always been able to de-escalate the situation. It was a matter of pride. This was different. "Those doors are bullet proof and supposedly even bomb proof. You don't open it, they can't get in."

There was no way the creature outside could have heard her. Still, he seemed to infer her response. He smiled.

Robyn aimed her weapon at the monster and shouted. "Sir, step away from the door!"

The creature shrugged. Then, to her surprise, he stepped back. As he did so, more figures came into view behind. There were people. Was that billionaire Roland Griff? More of the creatures too. Now, they too stepped aside. They were parting to make way. Four more figures emerged from the darkness. These were different from the rest. They were taller, and straight backed. They were near-silhouettes, outlined by the lights of the building across the way and street lamps above. They wore armour, and bore shields marked with red insignias. One stepped forward. Only darkness could be seen within its ornately decorated black helmet. It raised a jagged sword, and brought it down in a blindingly fast stroke. Robyn had been there when they'd installed the new anti-terrorist doors in the Empire State Building Lobby. She'd seen the demonstration where they'd easily deflected bullets and sledge-hammer blows. Oh sure, they'd cracked and splintered, but always they'd held. She therefore had every reason to expect this strange knight's sword to bounce harmlessly off. Instead, the door shattered as if detonated from within. Alex and the other guards were showered with glittering glass particles. The red cloaked creature appeared once more. He smiled at the humans' look of dumbfounded terror. "Knock, knock," he growled. The obsidian armoured figure beside him said nothing.

All at once, the green skinned monsters spilled into the brightly lit lobby. The panicked guards opened fire. Marvin tried to make it to the stairwell, only to be struck down with three crossbow bolts. One orc was shot in the shoulder. A trio of orc soldiers paused briefly when the metal detector began beeping loudly as they passed. An automated voice instructed them to "Please try again." They began smashing the gate to bits with battle-axes and war-hammers. After that, it was a quick slaughter. Robyn, who had brought down one orc with a bullet through his banded breast plate, found herself pinned against the wall. The red cloaked commander had disarmed her himself, by chopping off her right hand as it still held her pistol. In a shocked daze, the security guard collapsed to the floor, clutching the stump as it pumped red blood down her neatly ironed uniform. Robyn gazed about in adrenaline-infused euphoria. The whole scene was so absurd, it could only be a dream, she reasoned. She thought of her baby girl, Christina, at home with Robyn's sister, Gloria. How would Chrisy manage without her? The rest of the security guards lay dead or dying. The polished marble floor was awash with red. Nelson lay on his back. His throat was cut. He was convulsing and glug-glugging as he drowned in his own blood. None of the orc soldiers seemed interested in ending his suffering. They busied themselves wiping their blades and scrounging for items of value. A group had found the Guard's 'Lost and Found' box where forgotten and contraband items from tourists were kept. One was trying on a Rolex watch, despite being unsure what its purpose was. The red cloaked monster nodded to another, who had a long nose like a hook. "*Grathka,*" he said.

The hook-nose one nodded and shouted an order in orcish. Two orcs brought forth a dirty cloak. They crouched down beside Robyn and wrapped

234

her bleeding stump. Robyn wanted to protest about the filthy cloth. "It'll become infected," she said. Then the absurdity of the concern struck her. "Whatever," she added. The seasoned orc soldiers, while not medics, knew how to staunch bleeding. They tightened belts around her arm as tourniquets, pulling until Robyn screamed at them to stop. She had been fading from consciousness from the blood loss—a soft wooly darkness pulling at her vision. Another orc brought a cup of water from the drinking fountain to her lips. He forced the cold water into her mouth. Realizing she was desperately thirsty, she swallowed. Finally satisfied, the red cloaked monster stepped forward. Robyn looked past him. "I am General Bragad'oc" she heard him say, "Commander of the orc forces." She felt as if she might float out of her body, as if she were just a detached observer. The lobby was now filled with green monsters carrying weapons. More were crowded outside, waiting to get in. The four black armoured knights stood as still as stone statues along the walls. Robyn also saw that she was right, there were humans among them, and one of them really was Roland Griff! In her shocked state, she wondered how that would fit into Marvin's conspiracy theory. Griff wasn't Jewish. Not that Marvin would ever know. There was also an old man, and two children—a young girl and an even younger boy clutching a blanket. Unlike Griff, they appeared to be prisoners. She met the girl's eyes and, for a moment, locked gazes. The girl's eyes were full of sorrow. It was at that moment, Robyn knew she was going to die. The girl had seen this scene before. The world had seen this scene before. It had played out again and again through the ages. The outcome was always the same. Something cold and hard touched Robyn's face. Standing above her, with his sword tip placed against her cheek, the lead monster tilted her head towards him. "So *Ro-ban*," he said, reading her name-tag, "We are going to take this tower. There's nothing you can do to stop that. Many of your people will die. You can make it easier on them, by telling them to surrender. You can do so over your ra-dee-o dee-vice."

Robyn stared it him, trying to force her brain to focus. She could see now that the commander's eyes did not truly glow. Like a wolf's, they caught and reflected the light. In truth, they were deep, dark, and full of cold intellect. "Then you'll let them live?"

The orc commander smiled. "I promise to make their deaths less painful."

"Screw you," she spat.

"If you prefer, you can simply tell us where they are located. What resistance to expect and so on."

"Then you'll let me live?"

"Then I'll chop your head off first," he said, "instead of last."

"Go to Hell."

General Bragad'oc chuckled, "You first." The orc commander nodded to Lieutenant Kragg, who waved four orcs soldiers forward, each with serrated daggers drawn. "Let me know when you change your mind."

Several minutes later, a troop of thirty orcs rose in a packed elevator towards the observation deck. Robyn had valiantly held out while three of her fingers had been sawn off. It was when the orcs began pulping them with hammers, that she finally relented. *What did it matter?* They were all going to die anyway. Eight guards on the Observation Deck would be little challenge for the orcs. One of the Grūshank Knights, holding a great axe, stood at the front, facing the doors. Despite the elevator being packed beyond legal capacity, the orc soldiers pressed themselves away from the darkly serene figure. It was said that even to touch a Grūshank Knight could bring death, disintegration, or worse. None wanted to try it. Over the elevator speakers, Mariah Carrey crooned *All I Want for Christmas is You.*

30

"Anger is the undoing of generals."
– General Pash Vaga

The guards on the Observation Deck had even less to do than their colleagues downstairs. The deck was closed but, until further notice, they were to remain here. As long as they continued to get paid to do nothing, that was all right with them. The TV monitors, usually there to show videos on the Empire State Building's construction on continuous loop, had all been switched to CNN. Five of the guards stood watching the scenes of battle caught on cellphone by residents, with commentary by Wolf Blitzer. The remaining three were outside on the wide balcony which surrounded the entire floor. They were peering down at the streets below. The amazing height of the tower, as well as the tightly packed buildings nearby made watching the action on the streets below difficult. Still, they could see the long columns of smoke that continued to rise for blocks. They could also see the surge of panicked crowds rushing down streets, and the police and army vehicles moving about. They could more easily follow the half-dozen army helicopters hovering above and below. "Here they come again!" yelled Roger, one of the younger guards. There was no need to yell. With a roar, three F/A-18 Hornet fighter jets arched across the sky, banked, and flew down Fifth Avenue. The jets had been scrambled hours earlier and passed by several times. With no clear aerial targets and a city full of innocents below, however, no actual strikes had occurred.

"They're God-damn useless!" shouted Laurie, "Ten million dollars worth-of-junk!"

"Seventy-million," said Clarke, who had wanted to be a pilot since he was five.

"That's worse."

Inside, CNN interrupted its own emergency broadcast with a news alert. "We've just received reports that the assailants, who some are calling either 'goblins' or 'orcs', have advanced successfully up Sixth Avenue to 33rd Street. There they have apparently joined up with others who had, again, used the sewers to reach the same point underground. This seems to a be rallying point for them."

"Sixth and 33rd!" gasped the guard Angela. "That's here!"

"I'm out of a here," said Brian, taking off his guard blazer. "Fifteen bucks an hour ain't worth dyin' for!"

As he said this, a chime sounded, indicating the arrival of the main tourist elevator. Suddenly fearful, the five guards turned and stared.

"I thought there weren't no more tours for the day," said José breathlessly.

"Maybe, it's Robyn come to check on us?"

The elevator began to open. A seven-foot tall, black armoured figure stepped out. It crossed the intervening dozen yards with a speed that seemed impossible and cleaved Brian in two at the waist. Behind it, a mob of orcs burst forth with weapons raised in roars of delight.

Moments later, whole bodies and dismembered limbs of the eight guards rained down on the city streets below. Angela, still alive, fell flailing onto an abandoned taxi cab, crushing the roof in. Despite being killed and having nearly every bone in her body broken, she appeared as perfect as a *Time Life* photograph. The rest of the guards fell in splats and bounces on asphalt and pavement. By this time, National Guard forces had completely surrounded the tower. Humvees and M1 Abrams tanks formed a ring of steel around the entire city block. Massive L7 cannons aimed at each doorway, along with hundreds of B&T APC9 Pro-K rifle barrels held by soldiers crouched behind and between the hulking vehicles for cover. These soldiers now stared in horror as bodies whole and in pieces landed on the street before them.

"Jesus Christ, those are people-parts!" screamed a young private.

"This ain't right!" said another.

Even with this latest horror, the soldiers made no attempt to advance. The orc resistance had vanished within the tower, though the lobby was clearly packed. The only guards facing the might of the US military, were the four Grūshank knights mounted on horseback, one at each entrance. Despite the seeming comical disparity between the two sides, the National Guard units now knew this was not the case. At first, their new commander, Colonel Douglas Irving, hadn't believed the intel from the survivors of the Time Square massacre. Tales of medieval knights shrugging off heavy artillery simply made no sense. "Shell-shocked," he said dismissively. He liked to use the archaic term because, as he told his men, "PTSD lacks a certain 'je ne sais quoi'." Then, the videos surfaced. Shaky cell phone shots from witnesses in hiding. There were too many to ignore, but still, it was hard to believe. So, when they had first advanced upon the tower and found the evil paladins standing guard, he had ordered his men to take them out. Their ebony armour sparked like welding as the bullets struck them. In the end, when the Colonel lowered his arm, the air reeked of gun smoke and the walls of the famous landmark were bullet riddled and crumbling. The Knights remained unscathed.

A NYPD SWAT marksman turned to the commanding officer, shaking his head. "We've shot 'em right through their visors," he said, tapping the bridge of his own nose. "Must've hit 'em square between the eyes... and *nothing!*"

"Do we use the tanks?" asked Major Tarmel.

Colonel Irving shook his head. Now, he knew the videos were real. "No," he said, "All we'll do is reduce the tower to rubble, and kill everyone inside. I'm damned if I'm gonna be the guy who destroyed an American icon fur nuthin'. Besides, I don't think it'd do more than get these guys suits dirty."

"Then, what do we do, sir?"

The Colonel hemmed and hawed, stroking his smoothly shaved chin and jaw. He then said something he knew a commanding officer should never admit, "Damned, if I know."

31

"Watch your children well, lest they stab you."
– Orcish proverb.

"We have to do something soon," said Diane. "God knows what they're going to do!"

Marc stole a sidelong glance at their children, still held tightly by the orc soldiers guarding them. At street level, despite its being winter, he had not felt cold. Even in the sewers it had been relatively warm. The constant fear, movement, and orc armour had no doubt helped with that. Here on the Empire State Building Observation deck, one thousand, two-hundred and ten feet above the street, the icy winds cut right through the primitive trappings and sliced through quivering flesh to shivering bone. Most of the orcs who had come up with them remained inside as a sort of garrison, where it was warm. General Bragad'oc, along with Griff, the old man, their children, and a contingent of two dozen guards, had come outside onto the observation deck that ringed the building. Why, Marc could not guess. Nor did he care to. The only question that concerned him was how to get their children back. "I know... I know..." he whispered, "but we have to wait until we have a chance. No point in grabbing them and we all die."

General Bragad'oc paced slowly back and forth along the wide brown tile walkway looking for something. A gentle snow had begun to fall. Big whirling flakes appeared in the night sky as if from another world. They landed on his crimson draped shoulders, dappling them with white. On one side of the walkway were the windows to the foyer. The glass was fogged with the collective breath of the nearly two hundred orcs packed within. Even through the misted panes, they could still be seen vandalizing and defacing the interior. Several had carved crude symbols on the walls with their weapons. One potbelly orc stood in the middle, urinating on the floor with a look of smug satisfaction. A group of five had a lit a fire in a trash can and were now warming their clawed hands. None seemed the least bit interested in what was going on outside. Along the exterior of the outdoor terrace was a row of antique-style coin-operated binoculars. These were arranged to look out at the city. The surrounding wall was topped with metal bars that turned inward like fish hooks, designed to stop anyone who might decide to jump. The snow gathered here as well. It formed a white line on the crossbars. Beyond these, lay the great sprawling city of New York, full of brightly lit towers soaring up from the canyon-like streets below. The iconic Chrysler Building stood directly across, with its silver art deco spire shining as if everything was all right. Lastly, held back by the haze of city light, lay night itself. Suddenly, to Marc, this seemed a gateway to strange universes beyond our own, just waiting for the chance to converge should the lights ever go out. The only occupants of that void where two Blackhawk helicopters. They hovered in the dark, gently bobbing in the updrafts. Their side doors were open. Gunners sat, legs dangling, with weapons trained on the assembled orcs. They were out of range for crossbows, and could decimate the entire orc contingent in seconds. They made no move to do so. Bragad'oc, upon exiting the building, had lifted the two children high in the air, one in each hand.

"Will they not attack with their Hell-o'copters, commander?" asked an Orc sergeant named Gruss.

"No. They see the little ones with their far-sight. Compassion for their young is another human weakness. That, and they cannot imagine what we are about to do. Failure of imagination is perhaps the greatest human weakness of all. It will be their undoing in the end. Even when the hour of doom is at hand, their incredulity ensnares them. They believe Armageddon cannot happen, simply because it has not happened before."

Bragad'oc stopped abruptly, as if he'd found just the spot he had been seeking. "*Erot,*" he growled to no one in particular. He drew a shiny black sphere the size of a bowling ball from within his cloak. Marc recognized it instantly as *the lodestone,* taken from the Arrivals Platform at Griff Plaza. The orc commander took the heavy orb and placed it carefully on the walkway tiles. The ball began to roll. The orc general frowned, caught it, and rolled it back. He released it again. Again, it began to roll. The General held the stone ball with one hand and reached up to unfasten his cloak from his shoulders. He then stopped, and stepped over instead to where Professor Pinchent, Naomi, and Jack were standing just a few feet away. He snatched the blue blanket from Jack's fingers and placed it under the lodestone. Jack cried out and went to retrieve it. General Bragad'oc struck him with the back of his gauntleted hand, sending the seven-year-old sprawling on the ground, where his head struck pavement.

"Jack!" shrieked Naomi.

"Ja–" Diane's cry was cut short as Marc's hand clamped over her mouth.

Jack lay stunned. For a moment, Diane struggled to break free. She then relented as she saw her son shake his head and sit up. Marc cast about, fearful that someone had heard Diane's cry.

"You need to keep your woman in check, Marc," hissed a familiar voice in his ear. Marc stared in surprise at Roland Griff, who stood beside him. The billionaire continued to gaze ahead, watching as General Bragad'oc formed a ring from the blanket to nestle the stone ball and keep it from rolling.

"Griff! I'll kill you if you —"

"Oh do shut up, Marc. I'm not going to give you away—provided you keep *still*. You can't stop the wheels in motion. All you can do now is be a witness to my ascension. Or die, of course."

"Your ascension? You mean, you're helping them?" spat Diane in disgust.

General Bragad'oc placed the lodestone within the blanket, and nodded with satisfaction when the sphere stayed put. He then snapped his fingers. A group of four orcs dressed in beige sackcloth robes, whom Marc and Diane had not seen before, stepped forth. These were plainly different from the orc soldiers. They were smaller, bent with age, and bore faces like wrinkled green grapes almost turned to raisin. Each carried rusted iron boxes fastened with locks. These were orc clerics—acolytes of *She Who Must be Obeyed*. They scurried forward now, and laid their boxes on the tile.

"I'm adaptable," said Griff with a shrug. "If you can't beat them, join them, etc. etc."

Diane glared it him through the eye-holes in her orc helmet. "Because allying with Bragad'oc worked out so well for you the first time!"

"That was then, this is now." Without turning, Griff smirked and gave a low chuckle.

Enraged, Marc threw a glance towards the orcs. The clerics had surrounded their commander and were handing him talismans, red chalk, and various carved bones, as part of some sort of ritual. Seeing they were all too engrossed to notice him, he turned, grabbed Griff by the labels of his coat and dragged him roughly behind a wall pillar. There, he threw the startled billionaire against the wall and snarled, "Listen here you tin-pot Napoleon! That's our little boy, and our little girl that monster's holding prisoner. If you don't help us save them, then you truly are the lowest of the low."

Recovering from his initial start, Griff sneered and shoved Marc away "You think you're so different from me? A tin-pot Napoleon am I? Bah! I despise your Augustinian remorse." The disheveled billionaire began to straighten his collar and pat down the rumpled labels of his black designer jacket.

"What do you mean?"

"I mean, until this... bump in the road, you were just fine with hopping on my bandwagon and conquering The Fourth World. Did you care about the consequences there? Did you care about the consequences anywhere you went? Africa? Iran? Venezuela? Drilling for oil, exploiting the locals is what *we* do, you and I. We're good at it. Oh sure, we don't call them 'empires' anymore. Our weapon is money. Our armies are their armies;

bought local militias; and private security firms. But make no mistake, just like the orcs, we leave ruin in our wake. We rape. We pillage. And by 'we', I mean *you*. If it makes you feel better, I also mean everyone who buys the gas made from the oil we drill, or enjoys the products shipped with it even as they protest against it. Methinks they doth protest too much. It's hypocrites all the way down, Marc. The only difference between you and me, is that I admit it. I'm just honest."

Diane, who had followed them behind the pillar, blocked Griff's path. "Doesn't it bother you, the great Roland Griff, to be playing second-fiddle to an orc soldier?" she challenged.

"A very temporary state, my dear, let me assure you. As I said, you're about to witness my ascension." With that, Roland Griff, pushed her aside and strode back to rejoin the roof top ceremony.

The orc clerics had completed their rites and retreated from the orb, wiping ruddy chalk from their hands. The orb was now surrounded by marks on the tile, piles of coloured powder, and tiny artifacts of bone, bronze, and iron. General Bragad'oc looked at Professor Pinchent. "Now," he snarled.

The old man tugged nervously on his ear, and adjusted his glasses, before looking straight into the grim warrior's glinting eyes. "If I do it, how do I know you'll let the children go?"

"You have my word of honour as a soldier."

"Orcs have no honour."

General Bragad'oc laughed. "Ah, professor! How do they say it in this world? ... it's funny because it's true! Of course you have no guarantee. Only the likelihood that I won't care enough to murder a couple of human whelps then."

Naomi who had been watching the proceedings in silence, suddenly grew alarmed. Neither child knew exactly what was about to happen, but both were overwhelmed with dread. "Professor don't do it!" she shouted.

"No, Professor, don't! Not for us!" Jack agreed. The young boy tugged on the old man's tweed jacket as if it were a bell pull.

Professor Pinchent put his hand on Jack's head and regarded them both with a sad smile. "You are very brave children. Braver than most adults I know."

"But it will help him in his evil plans!" said Jack desperately.

The old man looked at the orc commander and said, "Which begs the question General, what are your 'evil plans'?"

General Bragad'oc snorted. "Which in turn begs the question, why should I tell you, Professor? Now, are you going open the gate or do I start cutting off little hands?"

The professor hesitated, looking for other options, and finding none. "Fine." He then added with a nod to the clerics. "I'll need their chalk."

General Bragad'oc waved with his gauntleted hand. One of the clerics rushed forward to hand the old academic a stick of red chalk. As he did so, Jack saw, with a mixture of fascination and disgust, inside the priest's mouth. Behind the monster's ragged bric-a-brac of yellow teeth, was the stub of a long severed tongue. Peering about, he could see that none of the four clerics had tongues. This explained their mute behaviour throughout.

Professor Pinchent accepted the writing implement. He then crouched down, urging the children closer. He began to draw broad geometric strokes around the orb, outside of the primitive markings left by the clerics. "You see children, first you must mark where the gate will be opened. This, I expect, is where we get stories of pentagrams being used to summon demons. Although a pentagram, as you see, doesn't have enough points. One of several reasons it never worked for would-be occultists." The professor began to carefully inscribe runes at each juncture of the star.

"Those are like the symbols at the old gate!" said Jack. The boy was suddenly too fascinated to be afraid.

"Exactly, young master Jack, exactly."

"An ancient language. Written only, not spoken," said Roland Griff. The billionaire strode haughtily up to stand beside General Bragad'oc. He looked down at what the professor was doing and nodded, as if supervising. Marc and Diane, still in orc armour, drew closer as well—as close as they dared without drawing notice. Marc's fingers rested on the pommel of his sword. He was considering the best way to slay the commander.

"We could kill him," whispered Diane, echoing his thoughts. "That would end it."

"Would it?" said Marc. "Even if it did, the rest would never let us live."

"When then? When do we get a better chance?"

"I don't know."

Professor Pinchent rose creakily to his feet, grimacing at the pinch of arthritis in his knees. "And now... we begin the incantations."

The ensemble grew still. Even the normally restless orc soldiers stopped. Marc noted that evidently the orcs inside the building had been aware enough to cease their clamour. They too stood frozen behind the glass, all turned to watch whatever was about to happen. Marc wanted to say something to Diane, but realized that even a whisper would now be heard. The only sounds were of the night breeze, the distant clamour of the city, and the beat of the Blackhawk helicopters' blades as they hovered, watching. The professor raised his arms skyward. All at once, he no longer seemed a fragile old man, but the grand figure of a shaman or wizard. "Poolomas migrimbna, er doran cephla holm." he shouted. The air seemed to carry his words skyward, amplifying, rather than swallowing them as one might expect. "Oriskash ich naiem, danta!" The Professor knelt and made more marks with the chalk. He then stood and raised his arms once more. "Mitina, eros. Poolomas fedée thun. Kash hin er Kash vero. Fa-os." The surface of the orb began to shift, as if clouds were moving just below its surface. "Profeüs tre unum daga." He paused, then repeated, "Profeüs tre unum daga!"

A sudden gust of winter air rushed the lofty deck, piercing clothes and sending shivers down even the orcs' tough skins. The lodestone lit like a lightbulb, alive with swimming incandescence, before settling back into a cool ethereal, blue glow. The professor's face, illuminated from below, shone with pride. His wispy white hair blew in the wind. He smiled at Jack and Naomi. In that moment, he had forgotten their situation and was delighted only with his success. "Right then, you see children? The gate is now created."

"Where?" shouted Jack above the wind.

"I said it was created, not open," the old man replied.

"How do you open it?"

"Why, you just say the word!" The old man smiled kindly at Jack and gave him a wink, as if he were about to perform a clever card trick and the boy was in on it. He then raised his arms into the air and bellowed. *"Satamu!"*

A flash of white light, brighter than day, burst in the sky above New York City. The entire tower and surrounding city for blocks was bathed in brilliant, blinding illumination. None had been prepared for this. For a moment, no one could see. This included the Apache helicopter pilots. One of the pilots panicked and lost control. His chopper spiralled madly into the side of the Textile Building, where it exploded in a fireball, then plummeted as burning wreckage to the ground.

32

"Peace is the intermission of war." – Historian Dram

On the streets below, National Guard soldiers surrounded the iconic building. Police had set up lines to hold back the crowd of onlookers who would not be deterred despite obvious danger. All gasped when the night sky above lit up like a super nova. A disc of light formed and spread out around the Empire State Building observation deck high above. Even at this distance, onlookers were forced to squint at the dazzling display. Despite the apparent fireworks, there was no sound. This changed when the gunship helicopter hit the neighbouring Textile Building and exploded. A moment later, the crowd panicked and ran as the meteor of burning metal hurtled towards them. Shrieks and shouts filled the air. "Look out!" There came a second explosion as the flying machine impacted, killing three instantly. A fourth was stuck dead by a two-foot shard of rotary blade shrapnel. The victim was an online influencer who was taking a selfie video at the time. The result was a spectacular, if ghastly, clip that would later rack up millions of views on TikTok. Others fell to the ground with hunks of hot metal sticking from their bodies. After a moment of paralyzing shock, firemen and paramedics rushed to tend to the wounded. Some onlookers watched the fire and rescue. Most craned their necks to look skyward for what would come next. At each side of the great building, the Grūshank Knights continued their statuary vigil. They gazed impassively past the panicked throngs, roaring pyre, and suffering. Not once did their gaze shift upwards.

A frantic man wearing a black and orange Knicks jacket burst through the police lines and up to the nearest knight. Police moved to intercept, but stopped short as the man drew a pistol and aimed it at the armoured sentry from just feet away. "Go back to Hell!" the man screamed. He fired three shots directly into the knight's face. The bullets ricocheted, sparks flying. When the knight failed to react, the man moved closer. Police officers cautiously followed, their own weapons drawn. They yelled for the man to retreat. "Well?" the man shouted at the frozen figure. "What are you, a God damn statue? Aren't you going to do any—" At that moment, the man crossed an invisible line. The knight's hand moved faster than a human eye can track. In an instant, the vigilante had been bisected. The jagged edge sword had cleaved him in two, from left shoulder to right hip. The two halves slid apart and plopped wetly to the ground. Blood, bright red in the police flood-lights, swamped the street. The police officers and soldiers exchanged nervous looks. By unspoken concord, they retreated as one, leaving the corpse where it lay. The Grūshank Knight re-sheathed its sword and resumed its stance as if nothing of interest had occurred.

Everyone on the Observation Deck was blind. Everyone, that is, except Professor Pinchent, who had closed his eyes and covered them at the last moment. The old man had wanted to warn the children, to remind them of the flash that occurred when opening a gate, but doing so would also have alerted the orcs. He could only hope the effect was temporary. The old man grabbed Jack and Naomi by the shoulders and whispered, "Hush! Come!"

The orcs were in a state of confusion. None had donned their protective goggles. They groped about madly. They roared out curses and yells. The old academic struggled to weave his way between them with the children in toe. Without protective goggles, he too was impacted by the flash, but far less so for having closed his eyes. Spots danced in his vision, but he could see. The professor gripped Naomi's hand, who in turn gripped Jack's. Abruptly, the old man stopped short at the doors leading to the Observation Deck foyer. The two children plowed into him. Three orc soldiers, rubbing their eyes and blinking blindly, blocked their path. "We'll have to slide between them!" said the Professor. The two children nodded, although they didn't know exactly what this meant.

The Professor started to duck down to dive between the blinded soldiers, pulling Naomi behind him. She hesitated. "Hurry," said Professor Pinchent, "We don't know how long it will last!"

"I'm trying, Professor, it's Jack..."

Professor Pinchent looked back to see the young boy, trying desperately to follow, but held back by an iron gauntlet firmly gripping his shirt collar. "Not so fast, Professor," said General Bragad'oc, with a fang-tooth grin. "You forget we orcs can smell. We aren't nose-blind like you monkeys."

The Professor tried to pull Jack from the General's grasp. It was beyond hopeless.

"Seize them," ordered General Bragad'oc. Strong orc hands groped, then clenched Professor Pinchent and Naomi's arms.

"Let go of me!" Naomi yelled. She struggled frantically, and bit the green hand of one of the orcs, but could not escape.

"I'm blind!" shouted Griff from somewhere.

"Hold them while we wait," said the General.

"What do we do?" whispered Diane anxiously to Marc, whose arm she had instinctively clutched.

"We wait," said Marc, cursing himself for forgetting the flash. "We wait and see if it passes."

An eerie silence settled on the rooftop, broken only by Naomi's continued shrieks, and Jack's whimpering.

Minutes passed.

"I can see!" shouted one of the soldiers in orcish.

"Me too!"

"Yes," Bragad'oc agreed. Slowly his own eyesight had begun to clear, although still patched with black blotches. "The effects are temporary."

A murmur of orc voices confirmed this.

"I can see Professor!" said Jack. "Mostly."

"Me too," agreed Naomi, calming slightly.

"Good," said Professor Pinchent. "At least we didn't blind you for nothing."

"I can't!" said Roland Griff anxiously. "I can't see a thing!"

Marc and Diane exchanged glances, silently confirming their restored sight.

"I'm blind! Blind!" shouted Griff with growing panic.

The orc general snorted with amusement. "Well then, you really have no choice now, do you? Only *she* can heal the blind. Merger with her is your only hope."

"Yes... yes!" shouted Griff. "Quickly!"

Diane urgently squeezed Marc's arm. "Look," she gasped.

Marc squinted in the bright... daylight? He blinked. It wasn't the same bright flash which had marked the opening of the gate. It was bright nonetheless, compared to the night sky that had surrounded them before. "Dear God..." said Marc. Gazing about, he saw now that they were somehow standing both on the Observation Deck of the Empire State Building—*and in another world entirely.* An expansive landscape had unfolded about them.

A few yards away, Naomi and Jack were likewise astounded. "Where are we?" asked Naomi.

"We're inside the gate, children," said Professor Pinchent.

"Where's New York?" asked Jack.

"There," said the Professor. He pointed to the visible tops of towers and city lights, suspended as a double exposure in the air around them. "We're between worlds—the 'woods between worlds' as C.S. Lewis would say."

"There's no woods left, Professor," said Jack. "See?"

"What do you mean...?" The Professor now gazed more closely at the sprawling world below. His eyes went wide. It was a destitute and ruinous terrain. Scorched fields lay between entire forests reduced to smoking black stumps and ash. The smell of smoke and stench of death reached their nostrils, even at this great height. "No... no..." said the old man, aghast. "This isn't right! The other world has green hills and lush forests of ash, and beech, and..." Professor Pinchent frowned a moment. He then turned and fixed an accusing stare at Roland Griff. "You." The now blind billionaire had no idea he was the object of the Professor's wrath. "You, Roland Griff, you did this!"

"Who? Me?"

"Yes, you! You said you were only trading beads and useless gadgets with glowing lights to the orcs, but you weren't, were you? You gave them weapons! Real weapons!"

Despite his misery, Griff nodded and smiled. "Oh I see. Well, not really, but yes, I did give them some light munitions. Some guns, a few... rocket launchers, a bit of napalm perhaps. In trade for many thousands of miles of land. It was a very good deal. The best real estate deal in Manhattan since, well, Manhattan."

General Bragad'oc, who had been listening to the exchange, chuckled. "It was enough. Enough for us to turn the tide against the elves, humans, and dwarves. Even a dwarf fortress wall doesn't last long against C-4 plastic explosives!"

"But not enough to threaten us, old man," said Griff. "They'd run out you see?"

"Yes, clearly you had them right where you wanted them," grumbled the professor bitterly. "Wait... those pillars... the floor..." he gasped staring in horror at the remains of massive basalt columns rising blasted and broken from a plateau of black stone now juxtaposed about them. Slowly it dawned on him where they were precisely. The Empire State Building was occupying the same space as a mountain top. "Dear God, we're here. I didn't recognize it at first. She's sheared the whole top of the mountain off."

"Professor, what is that?" asked Jack. The boy was pointing

skyward. The professor saw then the strange anomaly that captured Jack's attention. For a moment, it looked like a swirling black cloud. Slowly, it began to take shape. All eyes were focused on it now. The orc soldiers gazed with a kind of eager anticipation. The humans felt an ineffable sense of dread. Naomi shuddered. Jack gripped her hand even more tightly.

"What? What is it?" said Roland Griff. "What's everyone looking at?"

The shape was now more of a black smear than a cloud. It began to change form symmetrically. Long tendrils extended, joined and became wings.

General Bragad'oc smiled with satisfaction. "*She* is here," he said.

"It's the black angel," whispered Jack, "from that tapestry on the wall in the museum!"

"Ich Nacht Däll," said the Professor.

Naomi, almost too terrified to speak, gasped, "What does that mean?"

"There is no direct translation," he said, "but she is evil made flesh."

"I... I can see her now!" said Griff, excitedly. "Nothing else, but I can see *her*!" The blackness, while a half-mile away, approached with long measured wing beats, gliding between each stroke like a giant bird. As it drew closer, it also grew in size. Its wingspan was now a hundred feet across."

"She's, um... bigger than I expected, bigger than before..." Griff admitted. The tycoon's voice quavered. His hands clenched nervously.

"The orcs' supreme mistress and creator," said Professor Pinchent in awe and horror. "She who rains pestilence and death upon the land—the quintessence of evil."

"We have to act soon," said Diane. Marc nodded.

At this moment, the orc clerics started to chant. They waved bones and rags in the air, and began to dance in slow circles.

"It all makes sense now," said Professor Pinchent. "That's why you had to come up here. The gate was not only a way between worlds for you, but a way out of her prison cell. By opening inside it, she can leave through this world and be free in both."

"Yes, wizard," said the orc commander.

"But, you need a shell. She is a magical being, too much of that world. If she wishes to exist in both she must take a form from this..." Professor Pinchent turned on the billionaire, who still stood transfixed by the only thing he could see. "Griff! Griff you fool!"

"It's a business deal really, a merger," said Griff, turning towards the Professor's voice. "Bragad'oc made me an offer I couldn't refuse. To become one with the Dark Lady and rule both worlds with her. I could help her with my influence and wealth here, and she could—"

"You're insane! You're getting set-up again! You don't do a deal with *her*! She doesn't *merge* with you—she takes you over."

The dark bird loomed above them. A shrieking wind rose with it, buffeting the rooftop in a miniature hurricane. "I don't... I..." Griff mumbled. A look of panic struck the businessman's face. In that instant, he knew that it was true. He knew she would devour him. He turned to flee. General Bragad'oc gestured. Two orc soldiers grabbed Griff's arms. The billionaire struggled but could not escape. Even if he had, he could not see where he was going. He could only see *her*.

Professor Pinchent confronted the orc commander. "This is madness. You'll not wreck devastation on this world as well!"

"Do nothing Wizard, or the little people die!" said the orc leader.

Professor Pinchent had seen enough. "If the Dark Lady enters this world, we'll all die," he said. He turned to Jack and Naomi. "Stand back, children—I'm going to close the gate!" The professor turned and raised his arms. General Bragad'oc who had been watching the old man closely, shot out his arm. The throwing knife struck Professor Pinchent between his shoulder blades. Jack stared in open-mouthed shock. Naomi screamed. Several feet away, Diane swallowed her own scream. Marc gasped. The old man, shaking with the effort, turned slowly. He locked eyes with Jack and spoke with trembling lips. "...so sorry... couldn't see... you were... *foretold...*" He doubled over in a spasm of agony, then collapsed, dead.

"Well, then let's begin," said the orc commander. "Prepare for the coming!"

Two orc soldiers took Griff by the arms and roughly dragged him to the center of the gate. They positioned him between the still roiling black orb and the Observation Deck's outer wall. Behind the steel fencing, the aurora of darkness and crackling green fire floated expectantly. Below and between the ruined black stumps of pillars, lay blackened hills and New York towers, day and night—two worlds interlocked as one.

"I'm scared," said Jack.

"Me too," said Naomi.

The orcs pulled back Griff's arms, availing him to the spectre. A storm now tore across the tower top with gale force winds, threatening to toss them all to their deaths.

A blast of green fire burst fourth from the center of the darkness as whirling cables of energy and plunged directly into Roland Griff's chest. The two were joined by an umbilical cord of spectral flame and black smoke. Griff flung his head back and screamed. Ghostly energy pumped into him in waves. The tycoon's eyes clenched shut in agony. "Make it stop! Make it stop!" he sobbed.

"Now's our chance," whispered Diane desperately.

Marc nodded. "I'll distract them, while you grab the kids."

"They'll kill you!"

Marc paused. He met his wife's gaze through the slit in her armour's visor. "You know I—even when I was a thousand miles away... the thing that kept me alive was knowing that there was a lifeline back to you. I was wrong, I wasn't there and I had my priorities all wrong. But I was never — ever confused about the fact that I love you."

Diane looked at him gravely, and said, "Seriously. We don't have time for this."

"Oh... right. Of course."

At that moment, Griff's expression changed. He ceased the struggle. Instead, a look of sublime satisfaction overtook him. "This... is... amazing. The power, coursing through my body... it's like... I'm becoming a god! Look on my works, ye mighty, and despair!" He raised hands that crackled with threads of green lightening.

Marc and Diane began edging closer. Marc drew his sword silently from its sheath. Diane did likewise.

"Wait..." said Griff, with dawning realization on his face. "I'm... I'm being *pushed*." Now, a new look of horror gripped him. His eyes shut tight. "Stop pushing! Stop pushing me out! No! It's me—*mine*—my body! Ahhh! You can't! There's nowhere for me to go... I... I..." Something changed in the billionaire's face. A new face, emerged from within, feminine and powerful. A cruel smile spread across his lips. His eyes opened. They now effused the same green fire that burned in the dark angel above. "*Yes,*" she said. The words came both from Roland Griff's lips and the ethereal being floating in the night sky above. The orc clerics threw their arms high in a dance of fanatical celebration.

With superhuman strength the body that had been Roland Griff tossed away the two orc soldiers restraining him. He threw back his head and beamed triumphantly. All the while, the coiling black and green energy from the black angel continued to flow into him. With each second, Griff seemed to grow larger, and stronger. His face stretched and smoothed, becoming *she*. The orc soldiers backed slowly away, heads bowed in supplication. The ceremony was almost complete.

Marc charged forward with sword raised.

Bragad'oc saw the attack, but was blocked by the clerics who gyrated madly before him. He drew his own sword and struck one dead to remove him from his path. So enflamed was their passion, the others failed to notice. "Stop him!" he bellowed.

The dark being saw Marc's approach. Still connected by the pouring magical torrent, it was vulnerable to attack. *The process is not yet done,* it seethed. At once, the distorted mask melted into the more human visage that was Roland Griff. With a voice that was Griff's, *they* spoke, "But Marc, I promised you a great future and a great job!"

Marc plunged his sword into Griff's chest where the dark energy poured. The weapon cleaved the billionaire's sternum and drove clear through to his spine. Both Griff and the Dark Lady screamed. The scream rose like the keening brakes of a freight-train. "I quit!"

At the same time, Diane put her hands on the shoulders of Jack and Naomi. For a moment, both thought it was another orc soldier grabbing them. They tried to pull away, then heard their mother's voice. "Jack, Naomi! Sweethearts!" The two children's eyes grew wide.

"Mummy!" shouted Jack, leaping into his mother's arms.

"Quickly now," she urged. Despite being impeded by the orc armour she wore, Diane rapidly moved away from the fray, pulling Naomi with her.

No one noticed them leaving. All eyes were on the figure of Griff, still standing despite the clearly mortal wound. The possessed tycoon crackled with viridescent energy and seemed to be pondering what exactly to do about sword struck through him. Marc made no effort to retrieve his weapon. Even General Bragad'oc was at a loss as to what would happen next. "I'm... *not*... finished," said both succubus and man, in stereo, "but this shell will no longer suffice." All at once, the course of energy that had been flowing into Griff, reversed. The darkness and green fire recoiled up and away, far more quickly than it had entered. No longer concerned with preserving the frame that had been Roland Griff, it rent and burned the flesh with its violent extraction. In a moment, the desiccated husk that had once been a world famous entrepreneur, collapsed to the ground like a marionette whose strings had been cut.

Bragad'oc pushed through the stunned clerics, and gestured to the two orc soldiers who had been previously tossed aside. They clambered back to their feet and drew their weapons on Marc. Crossbows were likewise trained on him. The orc commander approached with his own sword out. Marc resisted the urge to look to Diane or the children. In their hushed planning, neither could explain how they were to escape the floor, let alone the building, so crowded with orcs. Marc knew the first step, however, was for the children to be forgotten. General Bragad'oc drew close to Marc. He levelled his sword tip at the unarmed man's face. Instead of thrusting, he twisted the weapon, flinging off Marc's orc helmet. "Very good, Mr. Aaron. A surprise attack I didn't see coming. Of course, your own fate is now sealed."

"I expected that," said Marc grimly. "Go ahead. Do it!"

The orc general threw glance back at his mistress. The dark angel blotted out the stars and much of the city with her great wings. It seemed none-the-worse for the episode with Griff. General Bragad'oc returned his attention to Marc. "Oh, I'm not going to kill you, human. Griff was our first choice for a human shell for the Destroyer, but any human will do. You're not too old and..." he glanced down at Marc's figure, "...moderately fit. So it seems you have now volunteered for the honour." The commander then turned to the soldiers holding Marc. "Avail him."

"No, wait! I don't want..." The orcs jerked him sideways to face the outer wall of the deck and the shadow that rose beyond it. All at once, darkness flooded Marc's perception with a power that was somehow both repugnant and compelling. It blotted out his senses and stole his thoughts. He looked into the darkness and saw *her*. In the heart of it all, was a woman. She was easily ten feet tall, both strikingly beautiful and utterly terrible at the same time. Her skin was white marble. Her eyes shone with green fire that licked beneath spider-black lashes. Her long hair, ebony and billowing, joined with the darkness that enveloped her. "So... much... evil," he gasped.

The woman in the center of it reached out with long slender fingers that seemed to extend through the vortex that tunnelled around her. From the tips erupted a cyclone of green fire suffused with pitch. It struck Marc in the chest, like a javelin. He screamed. He thrashed about to escape the grip of the orc soldiers and the torrent of energy flooding into him. He saw again the burning oil fields of Kuwait, pouring through him instead of the sky. The torrent seemed more than his mortal frame could bear, and yet it continued. He now knew what Griff had felt, the strange sense of being forced from his own body with nowhere to go.

Diane heard her husband's tortured scream. She refused to look. Instead, she dragged Jack with one hand and Naomi with the other. She had spotted an emergency exit, unguarded by orcs. Reaching it quickly was their only hope. The children could not help but stare back at their father, and the magical force which impaled him. "Daddy!" shrieked Jack.

"Shhh! Jack, quiet," said his mother. There was little need to be silent. The whipping wind swallowed all sound. It was necessary to shout to be heard from inches away.

"We can't leave him!" cried Naomi, struggling to break free from her mother's grip.

Diane, realizing she hadn't the strength to force both, pulled her daughter's face to hers, meeting her gaze. Naomi's eyes brimmed with tears. "We have to honey. There's nothing we can do. Daddy *wants* us to go. That's why he did this."

"But we could close the gate!"

"What? No, only the professor could do that, and he's dead."

"No, we know, I mean, Jack knows. Remember Jack? Remember what the professor taught you?" Jack stared in surprise at his sister. Then a look of understanding dawned. He nodded.

"No, he doesn't," yelled Diane. "We have to go!"

Naomi struggled to break loose—and almost did. Diane caught her with both arms and held her tight. In doing so, she let go of Jack. Her son ducked down and ran between them. He ran directly towards the brilliant white-green beam of magic now lifting his father into the air like a claw of light. "Jack, come back! Jack*!"*

Bathed in incandescence, Marc struggled to reject the demonic force trying to possess him. "Get out... get out..." he moaned. His face contorted in a mask of iridescent evil. Green fire spat from his eyes. "You can't resist me! I'm so much greater than you, human!" Marc's mouth and the dark winged being above spoke in stereo. Abruptly, the mask melted and Marc's visage was his own again. "Can't hold on... much longer..." he gasped. General Bragad'oc watched with satisfaction, knowing his lady's triumph was a foregone conclusion. Still, he thought, the human puts up a surprisingly strong struggle.

Jack easily dodged between and under the legs of the orc soldiers. All were too awed to notice the small boy until he was already past.

"Jack!" cried Diane. She tried to follow, but could not. The orcs were confused by the disguise she still wore, but pushed back with irritation as she tried to plow through. One snarled and drew a dagger. "Get out of my way!" she yelled, and lopped his clawed hand off at the wrist.

Now, the orcs stared in surprise as Jack burst into the circle where Marc was held. Jack's father now floated six feet in the air above the orb, suspended by Tesla-coil spiderwebs of emerald fire. Still the power coursed through him. General Bragad'oc laughed heartily. "Well done child! See your father get a great promotion. See him ascend to greatness!"

Jack was terrified. He was dwarfed by the monsters with swords around him. He could see his friend, the professor splayed still on the tiles. His father now turned slowly in the blinding energy that threatened to consume him. The air was a crescendo of shrieks made of the keening wind, his father's screams, and the banshee's wails. Jack was seven years old. He had never known nightmares like this.

Marc's face fluctuated once more. Like a drowning man surfacing to gasp, it briefly became his own again. He saw the tiny figure of his son, strobed in light and dark. A horror greater than the evil itself filled him. "Run Jack! Run!" he implored.

Jack did not run. He stared up at the black angel that towered above them all. He too now saw the apparition within. He saw the beautiful face— and the terrible hideousness as she relished destroying the man who was his father. Jack turned toward the shimmering black orb and shouted *"Umatas! U-MA-TAS!"*

General Bragad'oc stared at the small boy with his fanged mouth agape. Hearing a dog speak would have surprised him less than hearing a human child utter ancient Elvish. At that moment, it seemed as if reality itself rippled like water in a pond. This was followed by an ear piercing shriek like the sound of rending steel.

General Bragad'oc, the orc soldiers and clerics, Diane and Naomi, all turned to stare at the shimmering light of the gate circle that formed a halo in the sky around them. Only Jack saw the look of fear that struck the face of the ghostly woman at the center of it all. She, who had only been interested in her quarry, now turned to stare at the tiny figure of Jack. She had not noticed him approach. She wore a look of shock and incomprehension. *A child? How... ?* Jack stared back at her. With a crash that shook the building and shattered windows, the gate snapped closed. The circle collapsed into the orb and was gone. The sphere ceased to glimmer, grew cold and black. The interwoven reality, with its shattered mountain top and hills of despair, vanished. The Angel of Darkness too was gone. The green and black rope of energy that joined Marc to it, was severed. For a moment it hung there, then folded up into itself and faded to nothing. Marc collapsed to the hard tile and lay still.

Diane wrested herself from the grip of the flabbergasted guards. She ran toward the orb. The General shook off his surprise. He moved to swiftly to stop her, swinging wildly. Diane blocked the blow, slid her blade across his, then cut low, slashing his leg above the greave. The orc commander stumbled and fell to one knee. Diane grasped the orb in both hands and heaved it as high as she could. The heavy ball of stone just cleared the fencing on the outer wall and plummeted down to the street below. The onlookers there were staring upwards, wondering what it all meant. Like a meteor, the orb struck the asphalt on 33rd Street and exploded into thousands of stone fragments. Police, National Guard soldiers, and onlookers stared at the sparkling haze of dust. The Grūshank Knight strode from his post at the lobby entrance to study the ruin. Flecks of magnetized rock attached to his metal armour.

Atop the great tower, orcs and humans watched as the last tendrils of the dark lady's evil magic dissipated like smoke in wind. "Re-open the gate! We must re-open the gate!" yelled Bragad'oc in orcish at no one in particular.

The three remaining clerics gazed at their palms as if looking for something. One turned to the General, with a look of horror. "Adush Ka!"

"What do you mean 'gone'?" roared General Bragad'oc with a tone of outrage. "She can't be gone! She is eternal! She is immortal! She is..." He then seemed to realize something, or feel something inside. *"...dead."* He turned to the assembled orcs with an apologetic look on his face. "Without her, there is no purpose. We are forsaken." As soon as he spoke he turned to face the orc clerics, his olive expression at once drawn and haggard. "Arikav, Adush ya." He then turned to the humans. Only then did Marc see the dagger hilt he clutched to his breast, its blade buried within. "You have won," he grunted. The orc general pitched forward to lie dead at their feet.

After an instant of stunned silence, total panic broke out among the orcs. At once, the previously tough and brutish warriors, turned into a confused and frightened rabble. They clawed, pulled, and pilled over one another in a race for the exits. Some were violently shoved aside, while others were trampled. In mere moments, the deck was deserted.

"Look, they're changing!" someone in the crowd shouted. At street level, police and soldiers still stood opposite the dread Grūshank Knights. There was a dry cracking sound. The lights in their visors dimmed and their black shiny armour dulled to basalt stone. For a moment, they stood as true statues. More cracking followed. Tiny fissures spidered across the petrified warriors. All at once, they crumbled to volcanic dust in heaps where once they'd stood. "No one move!" shouted one of the Captains. "We don't know what this means!" "Someone bring in hazmat!" yelled another officer. Suddenly, panicked orcs burst from the lobby doors. For a moment, it seemed an attack. The onlookers panicked and fled, while police opened fire. Quickly, it became a slaughter. The orcs were not even trying to fight. They dropped or dragged their sheilds. Weapons remained sheathed or slung. Most were cut down by National Guard and NYPD fire before they reached the police lines. Those that did, plunged into the crowd, not to attack, but to flee. More were slain by armed vigilantes and police as they were pushed and jostled. A handful made it to their instinctive objectives—the sewers and subway tunnels below ground.

Diane knelt at her husband's side. She saw immediately that he was still breathing. She lifted his head in her hands. She stroked his hair back from his eyes. All at once the Empire State Building observation deck was empty and exposed. Yellow floodlights on damp concrete. A cool night wind swept over them. Precipitation, the result of a low cloud passing, clung to skin and cloth. "Marc, can you hear me? Marc?" Marc's lashes fluttered. His eyes opened. He tried to blink away the spots that danced in them. "Marc!" shouted Diane with relief.

"I'm here," he said. He then groaned and put his hand to his forehead. "Not sure I want to be though." He managed a weak smile. With a wince, he met Diane's gaze. "I love you, you know?"

"I know," she said. Tears ran down her cheeks as she bent down to kiss him.

Marc's eyes went to his daughter who stood behind Diane. Naomi having seen her father was alive, gazed about at the devastated remains around them. "Hey kiddo," Marc said, "You okay?"

"I'm fine," said Naomi, "but, Mum, Dad...?"

"Yes, honey," said Diane, wiping her eyes.

"Where's Jack?"

33

"Endings are for authors." – Sage Elmok the Blind

Four blocks away, on 29th Street, a man lay on a gurney as a crew prepared to load him into an ambulance. The man gritted his teeth in obvious pain. "He's going to be all right, yes?" asked Tania anxiously. She could feel the tension and pain in Sam's hand as she held it.

"Should be," said the medic, as he readied a shot of morphine.

Tania, not satisfied with the white-coated man's seeming blasé attitude leaned into his line of vision. "You sure about that?"

The medic recoiled with a look of apprehension. "Jeez lady, yes!"

The driver called from inside the ambulance, "Look ma'am, if you want to ride with us, ya gotta lose the hedge-trimmer."

Tania looked down with surprise at the battle axe she still held in her other hand. She had been gripping it so long, she'd had forgotten she was holding it. Tania glanced once more at the crumpled remains of the orcs on the sidewalk. "Okay," she said. She then tossed the weapon aside, where it landed with a clatter. The ambulance crew loaded Sam into the rear. Tania followed. She sat beside him, out of the way as the medic went to work, but close enough to once more hold his hand. She gave it a reassuring squeeze. He weakly squeezed back.

The Aaron family wanted nothing to do with the news media. They had no choice with the government and police. All they cared about was the loss of their son. Just when they were ready to be a family again, they had been rent apart. It was Naomi who explained how Jack appeared to know ancient Elvish. "He didn't," she said. "but he heard the professor open the gate. The professor had taught him how to deduce the word to close it." Jack had a gift for that kind of thing. As for what happened to the child, that was a mystery. No body had been found. No drop of blood. No fragment of clothes. There had been news cameras on every exit. Had an orc snatched him, it would have been seen. Jack had simply vanished. The police detective assigned to the case said he would be presumed dead. Marc and Diane were tortured by not knowing. Naomi was not. She was convinced he was alive. "He vanished at the same time the gate closed," she said with certainty. "We know where he is. We just don't know how to get there."

EPILOGUE

"To know life, know death." - Orc natal chant *(trad.)*

Rain fell across the muddy flats, quickly forming streams and puddles that, in turn, joined into pools. Dark rain clouds formed a heavy ceiling above a land that was bleak and still. Slowly, the rain subsided into a steady, but light drizzle. Nearby, a blasted tree stuck out of the ground like a gnarled limb. In the middle of a field, lay the ruins of peasant farm house, burned black, roof fallen in, soaking wet interior. A dropped round shield lay upside down in the mud, brimming with rain water. From the ditch emerged a small fox-like creature, nose down, sniffing its way along. Nearly hairless, with large dinner-plate eyes, this was a 'squim'. It was forced from its usual cave tunnel habitat by the need that drives all desperate acts in nature, hunger. Smelling something interesting, it darted forward over a low rise.

There it froze. A piece of meat simply lying on the ground. Small, yes, but delightfully putrid. The squim lifted one careful paw, ready to dart forward, snatch and retreat. *Thwip!* A long arrow shaft appeared in the fox's middle, throwing it to the dirt, dead. A green cloaked figure rose from the grass and strode forward to retrieve the arrow and toss the limp body into a rucksack.

Above this scene, rose the great rock known as Narth G'tor, the Widow's Peak. Some called it a mountain, but it was a strange and improbable one for sure. It was made of black, volcanic stone, that soared abruptly from the otherwise low surrounding landscape. Most recently, it had lost it top. Millions of tonnes of rock had exploded and rained down upon the surrounding fields and hills. Great chunks had sunk feet into the black soil. This was not the result of an eruption or seismic event. The top had been flung off by its lone inhabitant, or rather inmate, in anticipation of being set free. Now, the sullen black stone glistened with the cold disappointment of rain water. Far above, its flat top was crowned with the broken bases of basalt pillars standing evenly spaced upon a grid of obsidian floor tiles. There was no sign of the erstwhile prisoner. Her body had vanished somewhere between here and there. The spell of confinement had been released by her demise. Now the tiles, sheltered for centuries, shone with pooling rain. There was, however, one diminutive figure amid the great plateau. It was that of a seven-year-old human child. He lay sprawled, unmoving, in the center of the black grid. His skin was pale and clammy with damp. His brown hair lay plastered to his forehead, wet with rain and his own red blood. To all appearances, he was dead. Until he moved.

Jack blinked. He scrunched his brow in puzzlement. Where was he? Aches at once filled his every limb. He knew then that he'd fallen hard on a hard stone surface. He had, in fact, fallen over twelve feet. It could have been worse. The Empire State Building Observation deck was a near, but not exact match for the mountaintop's height. With painful slowness, he touched the part that hurt the most. A spot on his forehead just above the hair line. Squishy. *Ow.* He pulled his fingers away and saw blood on them. Normally, he'd burst into tears and call out for Mummy. Jack, however, was in shock. He simply pulled himself to his knees and rose to his feet.

He knew then where he was. He recognized it as the other world seen superimposed upon their own. Where was Mum and Dad? Where was Naomi? Terrifying reality rushed in upon him. Still, he felt nothing. "Mummy? Daddy? Someone?" He looked down at his hand. In it was his blue blanket. It was soaked dark blue like when Mum put it in the wash. He lifted it, and thrust his thumb reassuringly into his mouth. He sucked.

The grid of tile stretched hundreds of yards in every direction, where it disappeared into the haze of a low hanging cloud. The effect was to make the space seem covered and even more dreamlike, as if this were the entire world unto itself, floating adrift in a void. There was only one feature of interest. There between a pair of pillars, on a slightly raised dais, was a large stone box. Seeing nothing else, Jack walked slowly towards it.

As he approached he could see it better. There was an inscription on the side. Strange characters carved into the stone. Jack had no idea what they meant, but they reminded him of runes he'd seen in Professor Pinchent's study. He walked closer until, at last, he stepped up on the raised platform. There he was able to see that the box's lid had been removed. It lay just on the other side. Despite weighing over three hundred pounds, it had been flung, and now lay shattered. Jack did not notice the lack of water inside the coffin. It was only damp, with the drizzle that now fell. Jack did notice the sound of horse's hoofs on tile. He turned to look. Out of the grey oppressive mist, a figure on horseback emerged. It was draped with a heavy hooded cloak, the colour of pine. A short bow was slung from its back. Despite the rain, the rider had not removed the bow string. The rider approached cautiously but quickly, before reigning up just a dozen yards away. Able to see the removed lid of the coffin, the rider drew back her hood. She looked past the small boy at the sarcophagus. Her narrow, angular features grimaced. "Ish tafas ul."

"What does that mean?" asked Jack, pulling his thumb from his mouth. He then observed the pointed ears poking through the rivulets of her long blond hair. She regarded him with surprise. Her primary objective gone, she now regarded the boy with interest. He should not be here. No one should. "You're an off-worlder?"

Jack wasn't sure what that meant, but nodded.

"I'm too late then," she said. She shook her head. "No, matter, I'd have had no chance of stopping it."

"Too late for what?" asked Jack, suddenly shivering with the cold.

"Who are you and how came you here?"

"I'm lost. After I closed the gate—"

"You? You closed it? You did this? Karas tif!"

"Are you an elf?" he asked.

"Of course, I'm an elf. Are you a human?"

"Yes." For the first time, Jack felt tears welling up on his eyes. He could feel the dam of emotions preparing the burst. "I... I just want to go home."

"Well, you should have thought of that before you closed the gate. In saving your world, you've doomed ours." Jack began to cry. The elf sighed and urged her grey mare forward with a gentle press of her heels. She drew up alongside the boy and looked down at him from what seemed a great height. "Well, I supposed you'd better come with me." She reached down and scooped Jack up by the scruff of his collar like a cat lifting a kitten. She planted him neatly on the saddle behind her. "I'll take you to the council and they can decided how much you are truly responsible for this disaster."

"Then what?" whimpered Jack between sobs.

"Then? I supposed you'd better learn to speak Elvish. I, for one, have no desire to keep groaning in these guttural grunts you call a language. What should I call you?"

"Um..."

"Your name?"

"Oh... Jack."

"Very well Jack, you may call me Holwyn. I am the Valpier of Rä." With that, Holwyn pulled her hood back over her head and wheeled her horse about. Her mount cantered forward, hooves clacking across wet tiles, into the enveloping fog, guided by instinct to the exit she sensed was there. With one hand, Jack clutched her cloak with the grip of child who has nothing else in the world to hold on to. His other instinctively went to the cold, round pendant that hung from his neck.

Also by Colin Robertson

Chaos Theory
A Feel Good Book About the End of the World

Fifty-years-ago, the United States created the most powerful weapon of all time, capable of destroying not just the Earth, but the entire Universe - then managed to lose it. Now, it's been found, by a thirteen-year-old boy, named Alex Graham, who decides to sell it on eBay.

"Who knew the end of the world could be so much fun? ... When the news all seems bad in the world, Colin Robertson's raucous farce, Chaos Theory, a "feel good story about the end of the world," puts an amusingly absurd spin on heavy affairs. His variety pack of eccentric characters--terrorists, politicians, and scientists--are sketched out in witheringly funny detail alongside a fast-moving plot. Despite the daunting premise, there's no fear in seeing this book through to the end (of the world). — Kirkus Reviews

Spyware
It's Not What You Think

Someone has just released a virus capable of infecting the most advanced computer of all — the human brain. Fortunately, it has been discovered by a brilliant computer programmer. Unfortunately, that programmer is Eddy Pending.

"Spyware is a timely satire that is entertaining and thought-provoking in equal measure ... its satirical edge is on point, raising the question of whether this novel has figured out what might be causing current troubles in politics and media." — Forward Reviews

The Siege of Walter Parks

Walter Parks's life has fallen apart. Until a few days ago, he had it all — a beautiful wife, baby girl, home in the suburbs and a not-so-beautiful, but reasonably well paid job as a pencil pusher at a pen company. Then Walter learned how quickly "having it all" can turn into "losing it all".

So, when the bank decided to foreclose on his home, Walter Parks decided to simply say "no". Well, say "no" and turn his home into a fortified castle not seen since the days codpieces were considered sensible outerwear. Thus begins the ever escalating war that is, The Siege of Walter Parks. In this post-modern comedy of errors, some grammatical, one man shows that an act of shortsighted idiocy may be the only reasonable response to an irrational world.

Links and more at
GinTonicPress.com

About the Author

Colin Robertson is originally from Toronto, Canada. Determined not to be ruined by success, he decided to become an indie author in 2012 with the publication of his debut novel, *The Siege of Walter Parks*. Since then, he has published two more novels, including his award-winning bestseller, *Chaos Theory*. He is also the author of several short stories and currently lives with his wife, son, daughter and loving, if somewhat neurotic dog, Zero, in Culver City, California.